CONFESSIONS OF A PTA MAFIA MOM
Copyright © 2010 by ELSIE LOVE

Published in Australia

Dare Empire eMedia Productions

ISBN: 978-1463563615

dare empire
e m e d i a p r o d u c t i o n s

This book is dedicated to my mother, who never wavers in her belief that I am destined for greatness. And to my dear friend Cheryl, who appreciates running away and eye candy, not necessarily in that order.

CHAPTER ONE
MONDAY, AUGUST 21ST

The last day of summer vacation hit Glen Ellyn, Illinois like it did most summers—with intense heat and misery. Elaine Elizabeth Jackerson, or Lanie, as her friends liked to call her, had mistakenly chosen this day for her annual checkup. She'd made the appointment the prior year. "How's August twenty-first for you?" the perky desk clerk had chirped. "We have a nine a.m. slot open."

How was she supposed to know what August twenty-first was going to look like for her an entire year in advance? "Sure, sounds great."

The year ticked by, and the calendar filled to maximum capacity. Being only half organized in every area of her life, she never thought to double check the calendar for any conflicts. If she had, she would have realized that it was not just the last day of freedom for her children, but also the day her husband, Bob, was leaving for California, yet again. Bulldog's Fine Rides, the dealership he'd opened and named after himself, required his attention. Car expo. Necessary for growth at the dealership. Blah, blah, blah. She wasn't included, so she tuned it out.

The alarm rang at seven sharp, sending her into a momentary panic attack. Remembering the dreaded nine a.m. appointment, Lanie hit the OFF button and rolled over. Empty. Bob was gone. The cab had arrived while it was still dark to take him to the airport. He had kissed her goodbye—at least she thought he had—somewhere around five. She could have driven him. The kids were old enough to be alone for a few hours.

But he never asked and she never offered. They'd been married long enough for him to realize that asking Lanie to get up even one second earlier than required on the last day of summer break was a suicide mission.

The coffee pot sat empty in the kitchen sink. It was a passive-aggressive move on Bob's part. A swipe at her for not driving him to the airport. She wrote it down on her mental score card right underneath making only half the bed in the morning. What the hell was that about anyway? Who made half the bed? Every time she saw the rumpled covers on her side next to his military corners, she wanted to laugh. She ignored it, continued picking up his dirty socks, and went on her way. Making half the bed didn't hurt her. Leaving her without hot coffee did.

The trip to the refrigerator to grab fresh beans was another disappointment. Before she could open the door, the note scrawled on her to-do list caught her limited, caffeine-deprived attention.

Buy more coffee.

She silently cursed Starbucks for not being able to keep their drive- through in business. McDonald's coffee might be free on Mondays, but that did not make it suitable for human consumption. She glanced at the clock on the microwave; 7:35. Not enough time left to shower, dress, and wait in line at the local Caribou. She'd have to face her morning sans java.

An hour later, she was dressed and out the door. Dr. Woo was one of the busiest physicians at the Roosevelt Road clinic. If Lanie wasn't there at nine on the dot, she risked an overzealous booking agent marking her as a no show and filling her slot with the next patient. She didn't drag her saggy, middle-aged butt out of bed early for nothing.

Lanie was struggling. She knew it. Bob continually harping on her to *do something* was not helping. She tried to explain it to him—make him see that saying and doing only worked if you knew what the problem was—but it never sank in. Even starting the SUV and pulling out of the driveway to make the quick trip across town felt like a monumental task. Every part of her felt fake. She got up, stepped onstage, and acted out her day the way a good wife of nearly two decades was supposed to. But, she was slipping inside, losing herself to the character more and more each day. There was a time when she relished her role of mother, wife, and community activist. Now she simply got up and put on a "Lanie suit." The suit felt too tight, scratchy and restrictive, but she did it anyway. What other choice did she have?

The DuPage Medical complex parking lot was full, forcing her to park in the empty church lot across the street and navigate her way across four lanes of speeding traffic. *Just make it to the median, Lanie. That's all you have to do.* A short gap appeared and she bolted, clutching her purse to keep it from bouncing while she ran. Five steps into the road a horn blared at her from the lane closest to the median. She stopped and the blue minivan blew past her.

"Fat bitch," the balding male driver cursed as he sped by. "Watch where you're going!"

The woman trailing the swearing minivan stopped to let her cross. She was older, and heavy. She shot Lanie a smile that said: *Been there honey. Don't let that asshole ruin your day.* Lanie waved in appreciation and took the last few steps to the safety of the median. The last two lanes she had to cross were eastbound heading into Chicago. They were full of commuters who skipped the expressway, taking their chances that a side road would be less congested than the 290. A losing bet any day of the week. They crammed their cars together pretending not to see her waiting to cross. That was fine. It gave her time to settle her nerves and nurse her wounds over being called *fat* and *bitch* in the same sentence. Yes, she was fat by the impossible standards of American men. A fact that she faced every day when she looked at herself in the mirror. A fact that she was at peace with. As for being a bitch, who wasn't from time to time? It still didn't give him the right to scream at her through an open window for the entire world to hear.

The cars were forced to stop at the red light two blocks down. Begrudgingly, two of the sardine packed vehicles left a small, tight space for her to squeeze through. If either car moved forward a half inch, she'd be stuck. Lanie wiggled through the front and rear bumpers praying the light would stay red until she landed on the sidewalk. No luck. A few cars back, another horn bleated sending her anxiety back into high gear.

In her hurry to avoid any more fat comments, she yanked her leg from between the last pair of cars and came away with a long red scratch. Safe and sound on the sidewalk, she did a quick check for blood. Nothing. Just flesh-searing pain. She brushed the loose skin from the site of the injury. Hopefully the nurse would have some Bacitracin for her wound.

If the start to her Monday was any indication, this was going to be a rough week.

*   *   *

Dr. Woo wanted Lanie on medication. Something to lift her spirits. Help her navigate her way through what she deemed "second puberty." At forty-five, Lanie knew that was code for menopause.

"Do you have a good support system at home? Do you take time for yourself?"

Resisting the urge to punch her in the face or come back with a sarcastic remark, Lanie nodded. "My husband is very helpful." It was a measured response spoken through gritted teeth.

Dr. Woo raised an eyebrow. It was her challenge to Lanie. She wanted her to dig deep, come up with a life-changing confession, but Lanie refused to play the game. She would not numb herself any further. Wanting more out of life was not a mental illness as far as she was concerned. Plenty of Stepford wives on her block were sent to physicians by their husbands for pills to make them behave. Lanie had no intention of joining their ranks. Bob may have wanted her to consider it, but Bob wasn't there. Bulldog only got to vote if he was a present and willing participant.

"I'm worried about you, Elaine. You seem very flat."

Flat. A word that described her mood perfectly. If only it described her body. "I'll be fine. I always struggle with the transition from summer to fall." Liar, liar, pants on fire.

Dr. Woo flipped back through the sheets in Lanie's thick file. "I don't see any evidence of that here."

Damn her doctor and her record keeping. "It's true. It happens every year. This year I just happened to schedule my appointment in the middle of it."

"You come every year at the same time."

She did. Without coffee her brain couldn't stay a step ahead of her lies. Damnit again. Why hadn't she used coffee as her excuse?

"Lots of women find antidepressants to be helpful during life transitions. It isn't permanent and it doesn't mean you are crazy."

Tell that to the overpaid psychiatrists who discussed their crazy patients over dinner with their spouses. "What are the side effects?"

"If we decided to go with Prozac, you could rest assured that it is very safe. It has been widely studied and the generic form is inexpensive. Only five dollars a bottle on average. The most common side effect is weight gain."

Next. "I'm okay. Really, I am. This is just a transition."

Dr .Woo tapped her pen impatiently on the desk in front of her. "Okay. But, I'm making a note of this conversation in your chart. I want you back for a recheck in one month. If you don't look one hundred percent better than you do today, we will be revisiting this issue. Don't think I'm above calling in your husband on this one. Depression is a serious issue."

"I know."

Time to find a new doctor.

*   *   *

On the drive home, Lanie found herself rehashing her fight with Bob from the previous night. That's how it went. They fought, he left, and she felt bad. He went on to an expo in sunny California and she was left to stew, the argument replaying in her mind until the sharp edges were blunt and she could move forward. He sipped drinks by a hotel pool and she shuttled people to and from their daily activities. It hardly seemed fair.

"Christ, Lanie, what do you want from me?" He'd practically spit the words at her across the bed. "I have to attend the business expos. They are essential to keeping the money coming in. I don't see you complaining about the checks."

It wasn't that he left, she was used to that part. It was that he pretended that leaving was a *chore*. Like being in a hotel for a week or two at a time was a punishment.

"It's work. Don't you think I'd rather be here?"

No. She didn't think anyone with a rational, working brain would rather be there picking up dirty laundry and vacuuming. "I know it's work, but when you are finished with your seminars you get to go back to a quiet room where someone else makes the bed. You get to have meals that you don't have to cook or clean up after."

"I work so you don't have to. Do I complain when you spend a day reading? What about the last twelve weeks? You've slept in every single day. Did I say one word to you about that?"

No. But it sure cast a new light on making just half the bed.

He didn't get it—he never would. It was a man's world in so many ways. Sure, everyone talked a good game when it came to equal rights, but the reality was far from the speeches.

"If I came to you and told you I had to leave for a few weeks, what would you do?" She challenged.

He shrugged. "We'd manage. One way or another, we'd work things out."

Bullshit, she thought. She almost said it out loud. She wanted to so, very badly. The words bubbled up from her belly tickling the back of her throat. *Bullshit, bullshit, bullshit.*

Bob was not known for his ability to communicate. If she said it, put those words out into the atmosphere, he would shut her out immediately. The Great Wall of China would go up blocking her out of his line of vision and every other part of his existence until she couldn't take it anymore. She would go back, undo any good she might have done for her own self esteem, and ask him to open up. She'd done it a hundred times. Make that a hundred times a hundred. She would not do it this time. Clamping down on her bottom lip, she ground her teeth together willing herself to silence. They'd gone to bed not speaking. The space between their bodies on the mattress a Grand Canyon of unspoken hostilities.

Her head throbbed. The Dominicks at Baker's Hill Mall was coming up. If she wanted to salvage what was left of her last day of vacation, she was going to need coffee and aspirin. Maybe she'd splurge and pick up a nice bottle of wine. She had some white left at home, but red seemed more appropriate. It didn't matter how hot it was outside—fall called for red. Wine and a long soak in the tub, to celebrate being a fat bitch. That, and to forget the very same thing.

*   *   *

TUESDAY, AUGUST 22ND

"Mom! Seriously—get up. I don't want to be late for the first day."

Lexi yanked the covers back. Lanie's head throbbed. The wine glass sat empty on the nightstand beside her. "Poodle awake yet?" She asked pushing herself up into a seated position. Charlie, Lanie and Bob's eight-year-old son, was starting his first day of third grade and he was not happy about it.

"He's up."

Satisfied that Lanie wouldn't crawl back under the covers to cocoon, Lexi turned and fluffed her hair in the mirror over the dresser. Alexis Marie Jackerson was a typical seventeen-year-old girl. Beautiful and completely selfish. She had inherited the best genes of both parents. Her skin had a hint of olive; unusual for a blonde, and mesmerizing. She was long legs, long hair, and attitude.

Lanie got out of bed and pulled on her robe. "Have you eaten anything?"

Lexi eyed her mother in the mirror. Her green eyes raked the wide frame covered in pink cotton. "No. I'm good, thanks."

Lexi was disgusted by her mother's middle-aged frame. She'd tried to hide it, but Lanie saw it. The way she ran her eyes up and down checking out every inch with disdain. Lexi skipped breakfast for a very specific reason. She didn't want to end up like Lanie.

Lanie hadn't wanted to end up like Lanie.

Feeling self conscious, she chided herself. *She's a teenager. You were the exact same way when you were her age.* "You have practice after school. It's not good to starve yourself, Lexi."

"I'll grab something later in the cafeteria. I'm not hungry in the morning. You know that."

Lanie pushed her leggy daughter toward the door. "Go get your stuff together. Tell Poodle his lunch is in the fridge."

"We have to leave in twenty minutes."

"I know that, Lexi. My God, I've been getting you to and from school for the last twelve years without any problems. I'm not likely to drop the ball now."

Lexi shot a look over her shoulder to the wine glass on the nightstand. It was her silent slam against her mother's capabilities. Lanie puffed her chest. She was an adult. A glass of wine was permitted whenever, wherever she felt it was acceptable. She got enough lectures from Bob about how she should live her life. She wasn't going to start taking advice from an exploding estrogen factory. "Lexi Marie, I need to get dressed."

Lexi flipped her hair back over her shoulder and left.

*　　*　　*

"You alright back there Poo—Charlie?"

He had forbidden her to call him Poodle. Charlie had been born Poodle. A full head of bright orange curls trimmed out skin the color of half and half. His green eyes turned a shade of grey whenever he was upset. Today was one of those days.

"I thought dad would be home to take me today."

Lanie cursed Bob's inability to plan in her head. "He wanted to, buddy, he really did. He called me late last night to tell me to write everything down so you guys can talk when he gets home."

"Really?" A hint of emerald popped behind the grey.

No. Bob would never be that creative. "Yep, he sure did. Pretty awesome, don't you think?"

He smiled. She breathed a sigh of relief. She'd fixed things, for now.

Pulling in front of Herschel Grammar School, she threw the SUV into park. Lexi's early drop off meant that they were some of the first people there. Lanie glanced down at her clothes. Her tee shirt had a small stain on the front from her dinner last night. "Poodle, can you throw me the sweatshirt that's back there?" It would be blazing hot outside, but the gym was air conditioned.

He scowled. "Mom, please don't call me that. The kids will make fun of me!"

"I'm sorry. I'm trying—it's just hard. You've been Poodle since the day you were born."

"I know, I know. I've heard this story a million times."

He tossed the ratty, blue sweatshirt up to the front seat. She threw it on. Checking her reflection in the rearview mirror, she slapped on a coat of caramel colored lipstick.

"You're coming in?" He sounded horrified.

"It's the first day of school—coffee for the moms. I'll be tucked away in the gym." Lanie saw the relief pass across his face. He would have wanted Bob to walk up with him. But Bob would have known what to wear. He never would have slipped and called him Poodle.

"Can you wait a few minutes before you go in?"

Her mouth opened. She was torn between laughing at his ridiculous request and feeling sorry for herself. She was the person who helped with the homework, did his laundry, threw his birthday parties— and she was also an embarrassment to him. "Sure, Charlie, I'll wait until the bell rings."

"Thanks, mom." He hopped out of the car. Throwing on his heavy backpack loaded with school supplies, he gave her a quick wave and took off for the playground.

"Little shit." She muttered under her breath. A smile crept across her freshly glossed lips.

Her little Poodle was growing up.

CHAPTER TWO

The grammar school gym was a nightmare to navigate. Never in a million years would Lanie choose to attend a PTA morning coffee. In her opinion, it was all a ruse. The promise of fresh, hot coffee and pastries lured in the young, less experienced moms. Once everyone got comfortable and started to chat, wham! They strong-armed you into volunteering. She learned when Lexi was little. The PTA never gives anything for free. They want your name signed on the dotted line. Bob had been the one who suggested she go.

"Don't you think it'd be a nice way to make some friends in the neighborhood?"

Not if it meant she had to type up school rosters and try to plan parties with a one dollar per kid budget.

"Think of it as a compromise." He'd continued. "If you try it and you honestly don't like it, you can quit—and I'll stop bugging you about getting out more."

So she'd agreed. She showed up, but that didn't mean she had to stay. She grabbed a fresh, hot, Styrofoam cup of coffee and headed for the exit.

A voice boomed across the gym. "Excuse me…can I have everyone's attention? I know we all have busy lives. I'd like to get this meeting going so we can get back to what we need to do."

Don't turn around, Lanie. Just keep walking. They can't get you if you don't make eye contact. The exit sign loomed overhead less than ten feet away. She picked up the pace. If she was going to get out, it had to be before the last person was seated. Milling people provided camouflage—sitting people put a bulls-eye on her back.

She was so close to freedom that she could smell the freshly laid woodchips on the playground. Almost home. Just a few more steps—

Two women with sticky name tags stepped in front of the door blocking the exit. One was a tall blonde; the other was a short, plump, suburban version of Reba McEntire. Sticky paper nametags identified the pair as Yvette and Babette. They rhymed—how cute. Lanie smiled politely. "Excuse me. I need to use the bathroom."

"Wrong way." The blond—Yvette—pointed back in the direction she'd come. "The bathroom is that way."

I have to use the bathroom? She really needed to work on her lies. Taking a deep breath she tried again. "I'm pretty sure I left my car running. I really need to go."

Babette piped in. "Which one is yours, Sugar? I'll send someone out."

"I think it would be better if I just ran out and checked myself."

The two women shook their heads in a resounding no. Babette smiled at her patronizingly. "It's okay, Sugar. The meeting won't take long."

These women were not going to budge without a fight. Lanie turned around, scanning the gym for another escape route. All the doors were flanked by veteran PTA members. She'd know them anywhere. Each reeked of suburban perfection. Their hair professionally highlighted, lowlighted, curled and sprayed.

Defeated, she took a seat in the back row. The meeting was scheduled to run for an hour at most. After that, the gym had to be opened up for regular PE classes. She would rather have her body waxed than sit through an hour of heated debates about whether Campbell soup labels offered a good return on their investment, but she had no choice. There was no escape from the henchmen of the PTA.

* * *

The meeting felt like a never ending event. All of the women in the room hung on every word that came from the podium. Lanie was far enough back that she couldn't see the speaker, although she doubted very much that her appearance would make topics like collecting box tops and soup labels any more appealing. She looked at the women seated on either side of her—both were taking notes.

Notes. Like there was a test at the end.

Lanie pulled her sleeves down over her hands to hide her chewed fingernails and slunk lower in her seat. It was just like a high school popularity contest—she was bound to fail.

"Excuse me." Podium speaker called to the crowd. "Isn't there anyone out there who wants to take the position of coordinator for the Founder's Day celebration?"

There was a general murmur from the crowd, but no one raised their hand.

"Come on, ladies. The Founder's Day celebration is the best part of being in the PTA. It's the annual celebration of Glen Ellyn's *existence*."

Maybe it was the way the speaker emphasized the word existence that struck a chord with her. Or maybe it was Bob's promise that if she gave the PTA a whirl, he would leave her alone for a bit. Before she could talk herself out of it, Lanie raised her hand. The women on either side of her gave her a once over and scooted their chairs a few inches in the opposite direction.

"Wonderful! Well ladies—that was the last position we had to fill this morning. The rest of you got off easy."

There was a polite chuckle from the crowd. Lanie wanted to kick herself. She had been moments from another year of unnamed bliss in the DuPage County school district—and then she'd stuck her hand in the air. Now she was one of them. They had her under their control until the bell rang on the last day of school in June. She turned and looked wistfully at the double doors in the back. If she ran now she might be able to escape. Nobody knew her name. It was worth a shot.

As soon as people began to stand, Lanie grabbed her purse off the gymnasium floor and made a run for it. Dodging her way through the crowd, she tried not to look to anxious or suspicious. *You can do this. Just keep your eyes on the exit sign and keep moving.* She could do this; she knew she could. At one point in her life she had been damn near a hippie, following the Grateful Dead around the country. Of course she'd never touched a drug. Illegal things that might land her in jail were a tad too scary to be messed with. But she had packed up her two-man pup tent and kept Leroy—her then boyfriend—from getting his ass thrown in jail for attempting to sell a security officer some acid. If she came out of that summer unscathed, she could handle Herschel Grammar School PTA.

Lanie was feeling successful and rather smug as she set her Styrofoam cup down on the cookie hospitality table next to the back door. She was going to escape this sprinkle-covered sugar cookie mess without a scratch. She had learned her lesson. Next year she would skip the morning coffee. This morning had been a near miss. She wouldn't dare to repeat it. The hand on her shoulder was a shock. It took a minute for her to register that someone from the crowd knew who she was and where she was going.

"Excuse me—didn't you volunteer for the position of coordinator for the Founder's Day celebration?"

Lanie heard her, and tried to pretend that she didn't. She got one step closer to the door before the woman stepped in front of her, effectively ruining her escape.

"You are Charlie Jackerson's mom, aren't you? I'm Suni Calverson. Ajay's mom?"

Suni Calverson, a petite firecracker with black hair down past her shoulders and a gigantic diamond ring on her finger, was the current president of the PTA. Lanie cursed under her breath, both for forgetting that Suni was the reigning queen of the Glen Ellyn PTA court and for not realizing that was why she couldn't see her behind the podium. She was too tiny.

Suni was also impeccably dressed. Her dark denim and stilettos capped off with a crisp white blouse and black blazer made her look like she was about to close a multimillion dollar real estate deal instead of drag Lanie back to the annual signup sheet. Lanie looked down at her sweatshirt and gym shoes. Suni Calverson had her number. She was dead in the water.

"I'm so glad that you decided to take over the Founder's Day celebration. Last year was a total dud." She gently turned Lanie back in the direction of the mob of women clamoring to put their signatures on the dotted line. "We could really use some fresh talent."

Lanie cringed. If Suni wanted someone talented, she had come to the wrong person. The only thing Lanie had a talent for these days was drinking just enough wine before bed to put her to sleep, without waking up a few hours later in a hot flash. That was something she had taken to an art form—otherwise she was a flop. In desperation she made a decision. She would try the raw truth.

"I think I made a terrible mistake." She spit out in desperation.

Suni smiled at her. "No Lanie, you didn't. You just think you did."

Lanie bristled. She knew she looked a mess to the outside world, but who the hell was Suni Calverson to talk to her like that? She was going to give her a piece of her mind—really let her have it—and then she could be done with this mess and move on. But before she could open her mouth and get started on her verbal thrashing, Suni took her by the arm and led her out the side door and into the hallway.

"Listen, I know that we don't know each other very well, but I can tell you need the PTA. I mean, for Pete's sake, look at the way you're dressed. You look like you've been shopping at the Goodwill and living at the PADS shelter."

Lanie felt the air being smacked out of her lungs. The last time she'd been this shocked was when her father told her he was leaving her mother to go live in a pop-up camper with his girlfriend, whose aspirations included becoming a famous mime on the streets in Paris. Last she'd heard, they hadn't made it past Romeoville.

"Don't get upset, I'm not trying to insult you. I just know what is going on with you. I can see that you are struggling. I can help you."

Lanie stammered. "I'm fine, thank you." But she was struggling. Even if she wasn't, there was no way she could come off as convincing in her soiled bedclothes.

"We've all been there. Do you think I always looked this good?"

Yes. Yes, I do. I think you probably came out of the womb that way.

Suni's raised eyebrow spoke volumes. Lanie tried to hide her emotions as they passed through her. First, rage at being called out in the hallway of Herschel Grammar School. Then, sadness as she realized that she wasn't anonymous. People noticed that she didn't care about herself anymore. Even her own son had been embarrassed at the very thought of her entering the double doors of his school. He didn't want people to see Lanie and connect that they were related.

Suni flipped a shiny, black strand over her shoulder. "A few years ago I was just like you. My husband, Mike, was traveling all the time for business, my son was growing up, and I was left to my own devices for the first time since he was born. I'd given up my career as a consultant years ago. I didn't really know where I fit in the world anymore. Sound familiar?"

Lanie swallowed. It did. It sounded like Suni Calverson had been inside her head spying on her life and taking notes. Tears sprang up behind her eyelids. *Damnit, Lanie, do not cry.* She bit her lower lip and swallowed again. She was mad at Suni. Mad that she thought she had the right to make such horrible assumptions about her, but even more mad that she was right—about everything.

Suni reached out and patted Lanie on the shoulder. "There is a reason you came here today. It's the very same reason that I ended up here for the morning coffee when Ajay had just started school. I needed something. Something bigger than planning what type of wine goes best with salmon. I found it right here at school."

Lanie blinked hard. Suni's voice, whether the kindness was patronizing or genuine, made her want to crumple to the ground. She was searching. She was lost. Just like the super glamorous Suni, she ended up at the Herschel Grammar School PTA morning coffee. Could it be that this little mundane group of volunteers that seemed so pathetic on the surface was exactly what she needed?

Suni must have read the indecision on her face. Like a shark dressed as Mother Theresa meets Wall Street, she moved in for the kill. Guiding Lanie gently back to the volunteer sign up table she whispered, "I promise you, Lanie, you will not regret this. Today is the first day of the new you."

In an emotionally induced hypnotic state, Lanie allowed Suni to guide her back into the gym. Before she could come to her senses, the paper was pushed up in her face and the pen was in her hand. She took one last look around the school gymnasium at all the other women. They seemed happy. They were gathered in small groups, talking, laughing, and enjoying each other's company. Could she be one of those women? Did she have it somewhere inside her empty being to find fulfillment planning classroom parties and strong arming donations from her neighbors to fund a new playground?

Suni squeezed her arm impatiently. She took a deep breath and signed.

*　*　*

"Mom....MOM!"

Lexi's voice forced Lanie back to reality. She slammed on the brakes just in time to avoid hitting the car in front of her. The Explorer stopped on a dime. She silently thanked God that the SUV was in such good condition. One of the many perks of having a car dealer as a husband was never worrying that her brakes would go out. Before she could even put twenty thousand miles on her current car, Bob would show up with a new something for her to drive.

"God, mom! What is wrong with you?" Lexi asked, shaking her head and pulling her long hair up into a high ponytail.

"Watch your mouth, Lexi Marie." She wanted to tell her daughter to shut up. Shut her big, fat, pouty lips and have a little respect for once. But the truth was that she had been lost in her own thoughts. If Lexi hadn't hollered at her at that very moment, she would have barreled into the car in front of her at full speed.

Lexi rolled her eyes and kept her mouth shut. Lanie maneuvered the large SUV out of the tight traffic and into the turn lane leading to their subdivision. She was in a hurry to get home. She'd left Charlie at home, alone, while she picked up Lexi from her afterschool activities. She didn't like to do it, but he pitched such a fit about having to come with her that she gave up. The door was locked and the neighborhood was safe, but you could never be too careful. Lexi sprawled out in the seat next to her, texting and listening to her iPod. Cheerleading practice and a round of cross country left the girl too winded and spoiled to take the late bus. Lanie knew it was her fault for agreeing to drive the kids from day one. A bad habit, once started, was too hard to break.

She had just pulled into the drive when her cell phone rang. She checked the screen. It was Bob. Most likely calling to check in on how the kids did on their first day of school. She waved Lexi out of the front seat. "It's your dad, go in and check on Poodle while I fill him in."

Lexi rolled her eyes again and gave Lanie a heavy sigh while she loaded her gear bag onto her shoulder. Lanie resisted the urge to give her daughter a good hard shove and answered the phone. "Hello?"

"Oh. Oh God. Oh Bob..."

Lanie pressed the phone to her ear. Who the hell was on Bob's phone? The voice she heard was female. She tried to make out who it was, and what they were doing. Heavy static and a drumming dance beat made it difficult to decipher what was going on.

"Oh, God, yes. Just like that."

Was he watching porn? Lanie sat completely still in the front seat of her Ford Explorer, parked in the driveway of her brick, custom-built, two-story piece of perfect suburbia, and listened. The voice that she heard on the line was one that she had heard before, she was sure of it. A long time ago, she'd feigned interest in Bob's porn collection. It was possible he had taken some of his stash with him to occupy his time in the hotel.

But the voice had called out directly to Bob, and that really bothered her. Could it be that her husband of roughly twenty years, the man who had promised to love and cherish her forsaking all others, was right now in the arms of someone else?

The phone line went dead. Lanie pulled the receiver away from her ear and stared at the screen. Call ended. That was all it said. The words left a lot to be desired. She kept her eyes glued to the screen. Waiting for the phone to ring. Wishing that Bob would call and tell her that he missed her. Tell her that his desire for her was so great that he had ordered a skin flick to masturbate to—and wouldn't you know it? The guy in the movie was named Bob. Then they would laugh and she would tell him that she missed him. Loved him. Loved the life they shared.

The phone just sat there. Call ended. Did she dare to call back?

A hand pressed on the glass of the driver's side window. Lanie turned, startled by the sound and the size of the palm. Milky white, attached to an arm with loads of freckles. Charlie. She rolled down the glass. "Hey Poo—hey Charlie."

"Are you coming in? What's for dinner?"

Lanie took in his face. He was so innocent. Still just a baby in so many ways. He had Bob's skin. His hair was a mystery to everyone. She was a brunette, always wishing to be a red head. Bob was a dirty blond. Not a drop of real red between them. When Charlie was born it had been a joke between them. Charlie had been the mailman's child. Not really, of course, but still…

"Pizza?" She offered weakly.

Satisfied, Charlie ran back into the house. That left Lanie sitting alone in the quiet, late afternoon light on the very perfect driveway, of her very perfect house. Questioning what was left of her once very perfect life.

CHAPTER THREE
WEDNESDAY, AUGUST 23RD

Through the red wine haze, Lanie heard the alarm clock. It was the second day of school. Not nearly as important as the first, yet she knew better than to turn over and shut off the alarm. Last night, she had sat for a long time in the dark, sipping wine with her phone in hand.

Call, damnit. Tell me this is all just a misunderstanding.

She had dialed Bob's cell a dozen times only to hang up before it rang. She would not be a desperate woman. The first day of school was the perfect excuse to call. It really irked her that he hadn't bothered to call to see how it went. If she called under the guise of good parent, maybe she could ease her way into the mystery call? No. She would not be that person. She had watched her mother chase after her father desperately over the years and it sickened her. The day she chased Bob like that would be the day she was laid to rest somewhere in the green ground.

She sat up, hit the OFF button, found her glasses, and pulled her body out of bed. Her head pounded from the Cabernet. An entire bottle was not her norm, but the orgasm on the phone had drilled into her brain until she gave up sanity and polished off the bottle. Her sips long and deep until the green glass was transparent and the wine filled the gaping wound in her heart.

Oh, Bob...yes...just like that.

The coffee was stale. Lanie forgot to put fresh grounds in the basket the night before, and in her hurry to get to the PTA morning coffee, she hadn't even emptied the pot. She filled her ceramic mug and threw it in the microwave. This morning, anything would do.

Charlie came into the kitchen. His curls were a mop of copper on his head and his blue-grey eyes were slits in his puffy, cream-colored skin.

"Morning." Leaning down she planted a kiss in the copper halo.

"Hrmph," he grumbled taking a seat at the kitchen table. She pulled out the Pop Tarts from the cabinet and waved the box under his nose. He opened his eyes just wide enough to take in the chocolate and marshmallow scent. He nodded his approval and Lanie threw two in the toaster. Lexi burst into the kitchen, took one look at Lanie still in the clothes she worn the day before, and shook her head in what Lanie could only assume was disgust.

"I have to be at school early today for track practice."

It was a statement meant to throw Lanie into action. The microwave beeped and she opened the door, ignoring her daughter.

"I have to leave in fifteen minutes or I'm going to be late."

Lanie took the cream out of the fridge and emptied the last of the thick white liquid into her coffee. It hit the bottom of the cup and sprang back to the top making pillows of caramel in the black brew. She was aware of Lexi watching her. Waiting for her to react. Slipping her finger inside the cup she swirled the mixture, purposely ignoring her daughter's death stare.

"Are you going to drive me or not?"

Not. She took a long sip allowing the java to work its magic on her foggy brain. Even if she wanted to drag herself out the door to get Lexi to school early today—which she did not—that would leave Charlie to fend for himself. "No. I'm sorry Lexi, but on this short notice, I will not be jumping in the car to get you to school in the next fifteen minutes."

"What am I supposed to do? I can't miss track practice. Tryouts for long jump will be in a few weeks. If I miss a practice now I won't make varsity. Not to mention that Mrs. Blanchard talks to Ms. Sigmond all the time..."

Ah, yes, Ms. Sigmond. The High school cheer squad coach and, in Lanie's opinion, a royal bitch. Still, Lexi was going to have to figure this one out on her own. Right now, she was probably deeply regretting her decision to speed until she landed her third ticket; thereby losing her car and license until she completed ten weeks of traffic school. Even then, her driving privileges would remain restricted until her twenty-first birthday. Illinois traffic laws were tough for a reason: kids do stupid, life-threatening things. Lanie needed the time to take a hot shower and try to sort out what to do about the mysterious call from Bob last night. She put up her hand. "Not my problem. It is your senior year. Next year you will be off on your own at college. It's time you started figuring this stuff out for yourself."

Lexi flared her nostrils. Her heavy breathing reminded Lanie a cartoon bull with steam coming out of its gold-ringed snout, ready to charge. The only thing missing was the paw striking the ground in anticipation.

"Fine." She stormed out of the room. The front door slammed. Through the kitchen window, Lanie watched her daughter open her cell phone and dial. Within two minutes, a car came to a screeching halt at the end of the drive. Lexi flipped her hair over her shoulder before jumping in the passenger side. Lanie didn't recognize the young, male driver who was now carting her daughter around, and frankly, she didn't care. Lexi had solved her own problem, leaving Lanie to focus on Charlie, and eventually herself.

The Pop Tarts sat forgotten in the toaster. She pulled a napkin out of the drawer, grabbed the gooey pastries, and presented them to Charlie. He picked his head up from the table and gave her a smile. "Nice one, mom."

"What do you mean?" She asked sucking down the last of her coffee.

"You really gave it to Lexi. She was m-a-d mad."

Lanie smiled and rumpled his hair. "Eat your breakfast. I don't want you to be late."

* * *

Lanie was looking to do the quick drop and run. The one she'd missed out on yesterday. In all of the drama that had ensued after Bob's mystery call she had almost forgotten that she had signed her life away to Suni Calverson and her roving gang. The sight of Herschel Grammar School, with all its happy, stay-at-home parents was a harsh reminder. She put the car in park and slunk down in the front seat of the Explorer. Better safe than sorry.

Charlie grabbed his lunch from the front passenger seat and opened his door. "Bye, mom."

"Bye, Charlie."

He smiled. "You remembered!"

She wrinkled her nose at him. "I'm not happy about you growing up, but I guess it has to happen sooner or later."

He was halfway out of the SUV when he stopped and turned back to her. "Hey mom...maybe you could take a shower today? You know, in case you have to come into school or something?"

Lanie nodded. Her third grader could see that she had slacked on her personal hygiene. How embarrassing. "You got it, kiddo."

She watched him run off to join his friends before pulling herself back up to her full height. Throwing the Explorer into reverse, she turned to make a visual sweep of the parked cars before backing out. There was no car; but standing there looking like a million bucks was none other than Suni Calverson.

"Damnit." Lanie cursed through the fake smile plastered on her face. Suni came around the side of the car, stopped next to the driver's side window, and motioned for Lanie to roll it down. Lanie glanced in her rearview mirror. She had a clear shot to the road. What if she played dumb and pretended not to see Suni? She was only inches away. It would never work. Resigned, Lanie hit the button. "Hey, Suni!"

Oh, God. Her greeting sounded so pitiful. Forced cheer had never been one of her strong suits. Her voice came out thin and whiny.

Suni gave her a quick once over. "We have a meeting this morning. It starts in fifteen minutes."

Fifteen minutes. That magic number of the day that kept popping up was now biting her directly on the ass. Perhaps she'd been hasty in giving Lexi the boot this morning. If she had caved and driven her, then Charlie would have walked to school and she wouldn't be stuck in this personal hell right now. "I haven't showered yet. There's no way I can go into the school like this."

Suni pulled her sunglasses up to rest on top of her head. Reaching into her purse she pulled out a small card and handed it to Lanie. "We never meet at school. Today is your initiation. You have to be there."

Lanie took in the business card. Instead of listing an occupation under Suni's name it had a corny catch phrase in raised gold letters. *Your Time Has Come.* Suni's phone number sat in the lower right corner. Lanie was reminded of the cards the carnival fortune tellers passed out when she was child. The promises and suspense of those ostentatious ladies never matched the hype. The mysterious PTA initiation would most likely fall short of even those low standards. She bit the inside of her cheek to keep from laughing.

Suni waved her arm in the air. Clearly a signal to someone Lanie couldn't see in her rear view mirror. Out of nowhere, a silver Jeep roared up and stopped on a dime. One of its tinted windows rolled down. "Hey, Sugar. Glad you decided to join us."

It was one of the door blockers from the morning coffee. Lanie flashed back to her blundered escape attempt trying to remember the lady's name. Slightly plump with short spiky hair in a multitude of colored stripes that never coexisted in nature, she wore flawless makeup. It was a look that took hours in front of a dressing table to achieve. Her body sparkled whenever she moved from all the jewels she was sporting.

Suni nodded at the Jeep. "Babette, you remember Lanie? Today is her initiation. She'll need to follow you to my place."

Lanie never would have remembered the French moniker on her own. She'd blocked it, along with every other nasty detail, from her mind as soon as she escaped the gym.

Babette nodded and smiled at Lanie. "Okay, Sugar, looks like today is your lucky day. Now follow me...and please...try to keep up!" Without waiting for a response, she threw the Jeep into drive and took off. Lanie watched the silver bullet roar down the road. She turned back to throw out a final plea for mercy but stopped short. Suni was gone. Twisting into a pretzel, Lanie scanned her surroundings for long, dark tresses and a matching blazer. Nothing. In an instant, Suni Calverson had evaporated.

A gold Lexus turned the corner. It came to rest in the middle of the road a few feet behind the Explorer. Lanie recognized the platinum blond behind the wheel as the tall counterpart to Babette. They had names that rhymed. Both were French in origin. Could it be Nanette? Suzette? Neither sounded quite right; but once Lanie buried something, it was gone for good. She told herself it was a useful skill that saved her from reliving painful experiences. Or, it could just be early signs of dementia. Either way, the name of the Lexus-driving leopard wouldn't come to her. She'd have to wait for another Suni introduction.

The engine of the luxury vehicle purred patiently. The driver inside was waiting for Lanie to move. She must be the tail end of the motorcade. Through the glass, Lanie saw her painted pout part, revealing perfect pearly whites. A long manicured nail pointed at the road and she hit the horn impatiently. Through the blast, Lanie read her lips. *Let's go.*

The blond woman with the French name she couldn't remember made Lanie uneasy. Suni was crisp. The woman had everything in order. She gave the air of authority and smarts. Babette had the southern, holier-than-thou, rich image working for her, complete with snooty charm. But the blond was different. There was no sweet coating over her words. No cajoling into compromise. She gave an order—*Let's go*—and expected it to be followed. No questions asked. Lanie threw the Explorer into drive and stomped on the gas. Ahead, she saw Babette's Jeep idling at the stop sign. With one escort in front and one in back, they'd turned her into a PTA initiation sandwich.

There was a cop on the corner running an early morning speed trap. Lanie checked her speedometer as she blew past him. Forty in a school zone. Momentary panic over getting a ticket with a hefty fine was fast replaced with hope. A speeding ticket might be just the excuse she needed to get out of this stupid meeting. Twenty miles over in a school zone was big for the local cops. They could probably arrest her if they really wanted to make an impression. If they played their cards right, the story might even make the front page of the Glen Ellyn Gazette. She covered the brake in anticipation.

A full five seconds later, he hadn't budged. In fact, she could have sworn she saw him wave at blond Frenchie as she zipped past, right on Lanie's bumper. At the stop sign, she took her time. If he wanted a double arrest, that was fine by her. Checking her rearview mirror for movement, she was quickly defeated. He sat at the corner looking in the opposite direction of her vehicle. He had no intention of stopping her car, not even to issue a warning. Up ahead, Babette accelerated around the corner leaving her in the dust. If she didn't pick up the pace, she risked getting lost. That would put her under the direction of the platinum panther in the Lexus. Lanie took one last look in her mirror to be sure the lawman hadn't changed his mind before stepping on the gas.

*   *   *

Suni called out as they walked in through her front door. "Ladies—come join me in the kitchen for a drink."

If Lanie had felt out of place in the Herschel Grammar School gym, Suni's house made her want to shrink down until she was small enough to fit under a crack in the door and run away. It was enormous. The entryway was as big as her kitchen—maybe even her kitchen and dining room combined. The floors were marble. Each piece was a large square that gleamed reflecting the light from the amber pendants that hung from the ceiling. Off to the right was a large sweeping staircase and to the left was a sitting room decorated with plush carpeting and chairs that looked like they belonged on an episode of *Masterpiece Theater*.

Babette threw her Channel purse on one of the velvet chairs. "You got it, Sugar." Turning to Lanie, she smiled. "Come on now, darlin', don't be afraid. We don't bite." Checking her reflection, she wiped the corners of her lined lips. Satisfied with the image in the gold, oval frame, she strutted down the long hallway lined with Greek columns. The echo of heels on stone was eerie. In a blink, the southern belle disappeared from view.

A sharp poke in the lower back jolted her. "Let's go." The poke and command were followed by a firm push in the same direction Babette had gone. Feeling like a kidnapping victim, Lanie stumbled forward. She didn't want to tangle with the tall blond.

It felt like a death march. Each step led her further into the unknown cavern. The clip of heels from her guardian following closely behind made her queasy. *Don't stop or the Warden will get you.* Keeping her gaze straight ahead, she focused on the light in the distance. The closer she got to the source, the more sounds she could identify. The clinking of glass and china filled her ears. Laughter and chatter swirled in the air. It sounded too cheery to be a prison. More like a party in the kitchen. The entrance was a few feet in front of her when another shove from the Lexus driving Lolita sent her into the wall. "God, you are so slow," she hissed as she passed.

Regaining her composure, Lanie crossed the threshold. The room was yellow. A bold choice in the mansion filled with shades of chocolate and cream. Morning sun poured in from the back wall which was floor to ceiling glass. Under her feet the floor had changed from marble to slate. The contrast between the light of the kitchen and crypt-like atmosphere of the entrance was blinding. Squinting at the group, she tried to identify a familiar face in the crowd. Right now, any friend, no matter how casual, would be a welcome sight. She didn't recognize anyone. These were women that lived in her neighborhood. She'd seen them for years. They milled about the playground chatting before the bell every day. They ran Market Day. They sat together in the stands at tee ball games. They all knew each other intimately and she couldn't address a single one by name. Bob was right. She really needed to get out more.

A hand cupped the small of her back. "I'm glad you made it," Suni purred in her ear. "Good thing Yvette was bringing up the rear on your motorcade. Betts drives like a bat out of hell. Before I introduce you to the group, we have some business to attend to. I'll get you a drink. Try to blend in until I call you up before the girls."

Yvette. That was the name of the other half of the French monikered dynamic duo. How could she forget a name like that?

Lanie smoothed the front of her stained tee shirt. *Try to blend in. Sure.*

There were six women who stood out from the rest of the crowd. Their designer clothes and bags spoke of big money. They stuck together like glue, leaving the other more "typical" moms on the outskirts of the room. Lanie guessed they were key players in the PTA. Chairs of committees to do important things around the school. None of them gave Lanie a second glance.

Even Babette and Yvette had forgotten their lowly prisoner and were sipping cocktails out of fancy glassware.

"I got you a Mojito. I hope that's okay?"

Lanie greedily grabbed the glass from Suni and swallowed the contents in three gulps. The warmth ran down the back of her throat and spread into her belly coating her nerves.

"Nothing like a little hair of the dog to smooth things over." Suni observed haughtily.

Lanie sucked in air. How did this woman seem to know so much about her personal life? Did she have spies watching through the windows while Lanie poured until the bottle was drained?

"It doesn't take a mind reader to realize you're a heavy drinker," Suni hissed, snatching the empty glass from her hand. "I can smell it on you. I would offer you another, but I need you sober for the meeting. What you choose to do tonight behind closed doors is your own business."

Her words stung. Lanie was acutely aware that she was out of place in this gathering. But she hadn't asked to be a part of it. On the contrary, she had been dragged here to this freak show of women who never had a hair out of place. She stuck out her chin in defiance. "I'm leaving." Too late. Suni was gone again and her words hit the air with no more force than a feather in the wind.

"Alright, ladies, let's get down to business, shall we?"

Lanie had lost sight of Suni in the group; but her voice was unmistakable. She was somewhere in the middle of the flock calling out the gathering cry. The women all responded by finding a seat somewhere in the enormous kitchen. That left Suni standing alone in the middle of the room. Lanie scanned the space looking for a place to become invisible. The hall she'd entered from was blocked by Yvette and Babette. Yvette locked eyes with her and shook her head. Her red lips moved. *Sit down.* Lanie swallowed. This was worse than the morning coffee. Much, much worse.

"What do we have on tap for this morning?" Suni asked the group. Her broad smile made the already impossibly bright room ten kilowatts brighter. Lanie cringed.

One woman, a brassy redhead in a leopard-print sheath dress, raised her hand.

"Yes, Amalia?"

The woman moved to the center of the room. "My boy, Jack Junior, is about to be cut from the high school football team for poor grades."

There was an audible gasp from the observers.

"It isn't his fault." Amalia insisted. "How was he supposed to know that they would be counting his summer school grades?"

Suni snapped her fingers. "Betts...who do we know that has something on Coach Ryland?"

On cue, Babette clicked to the center of the circle. Now all eyes were on her. Enjoying being the center of attention, she took a calculated moment to fluff her multicolored flip. "Well, let's see now, Sugar. If my memory serves me right Coach Ryland was sleeping with the coach of the cheer squad this summer. Oh drat—what is her name again?"

"Ms. Sigmond?" The words fell out of Lanie's mouth before she could remind herself to shut up and stay inconspicuous. Everyone turned at the same time. In a protective move, Lanie crossed her arms across her chest. She'd forgotten to slip on a bra before leaving the house. Yet another thing about her that would live in infamy. Hell, she might even have it put on her tombstone. Here lies Elaine Elizabeth Jackerson. An embarrassment to all that knew her for her lack of self respect, poor hygiene, and inability to remember to do the simple things, like wear the proper undergarments.

"Yes! That is her name." Babette drawled. The heads of the crowd snapped back to the southern tart. Their movements choreographed by some prehistoric muscle memory requiring mob conformity.

"Now, that Ms. Sigmond, she isn't married...but good, old, coach Ryland is!" Babette finished triumphantly.

Suni tapped her manicured index finger on her front tooth. "You have proof?"

Babette smiled. "Sure do, Sugar. My sweet little Sonja walked in on the two of them in Coach Ryland's office. Got pictures on her cell phone and everything."

"Duplicates in print?"

Babette nodded.

"Dated?"

"Yes ma'am."

Suni turned to Yvette. "Betts is too close to this one. We don't want it coming back to her and Sonja. We'll need you to make the call."

Yvette nodded. "Get me the photos."

Babette nodded. "Will do."

Suni turned her attention back to Amalia. The awestruck woman was gazing with adoration at the three conspirators as if they were the holy family in a Christmas manger. "This one is a slam dunk. Go home and tell Jack Junior to keep up those grades. His football career is safe—for now."

Lanie was stunned. These women were talking about bribing the high school football coach to keep a kid with failing grades on the team. Sure, the guy was a cheating sleazebag, and Ms. Sigmond was a bitch, but blackmail was illegal. She wished she'd kept her mouth shut. When they got caught, she didn't want to be in the middle of their mess. Bob would kill her if they had to hire a lawyer because she was accused of being part of a blackmail scheme. It would destroy his reputation as a business man.

Amalia smoothed her dress and blew both Babette and Yvette a kiss. "I love you ladies."

"That's one item tackled. Anybody else have any business we need to attend to today?"

There was a general murmur among the crowd, but nobody stepped up.

"Good. Then let's move on. Today we have a new member that I would like to put before you for initiation."

Lanie felt sick. Yvette was still blocking the door and she didn't see any other means of escape. *Just get through this, Lanie. Let these insane women have their little initiation and then get the hell out.*

"Lanie Jackerson..." Suni held her arm out in a sweeping motion, like the announcer at a beauty pageant. Lanie tried to force out a smile, but her lips tightened across her teeth, refusing to open. She was sure it looked like a nasty smirk. She stood.

Everyone was watching her with interest. Was there a hint of pity? She couldn't be sure. Somehow she managed to make it to the center of the circle where she found a spot between Suni and Babette.

"Ladies of the Herschel Grammar School PTA, I present Lanie Jackerson for your consideration. I'm requesting that you vote her in as a full-fledged member of our group, with the same rights and privileges as the rest."

"Who here takes responsibility for Lanie?" Babette asked loudly.

"I do." Suni puffed her chest and took Lanie's arm.

"Will you teach her? Guide her? Make her wise to our ways?"

"I will."

Babette turned to the seated women. "Does anyone here have any reservations about Lanie Jackerson that would prevent her from becoming a full-fledged member of the Herschel Grammar School PTA?"

The room fell silent. Babette took a deep breath ready to conclude the ceremony. *You're almost finished with this ridiculousness. Just grit your teeth and get through it.*

Yvette stepped forward. "I do."

The school of fish mentality was holding strong. PTA women turned in unison, their mouths agape. Suni's frustration came out in an audible exhale. Her grasp on Lanie's arm tightened, and pain shot through her skin from squared off acrylic tips digging in. She was pissed. Apparently this part of the initiation was not planned.

Babette waved her closer. "Step up, wise one, and tell us your reasons."

Yvette squared her shoulders. "I don't think she can be trusted."

"She can be trusted. You have my word," Suni hissed through clenched teeth.

Babette moved in between the two women. Her physical presence created a solid divider. If they wanted to come to blows, they would have to go through her. Suni released her and Lanie took a giant step backwards. With the two women facing off, she had a clean shot to the hallway. The attention was on the combatants. All she had to do was slip away quietly before they noticed.

"Why do you feel she can't be trusted?" Babette pressed.

"Last year, her husband, Bob, *sold me my Lexus.*" It was an accusation so profound that some of the women seated looked as if they might swoon.

The bizarre statement left her confused. Yvette seemed to like her Lexus. Bob's dealership was local and he offered discounts to neighborhood residents. Half the women in the room were scooting around town in rides from Bulldog's. "My husband sells cars for a living." Lanie offered. There was a general murmur and a good round of head shaking in the room. *I've fallen down a rabbit hole into the lair of the Queen of Hearts. Next they'll offer me a mushroom and I'll grow until I pop out of the top of this suburban castle.*

Suni put up her hand. "She needs us, ladies. She has no idea how much she needs us."

Lanie thought she heard someone in the group whisper 'pathetic' to the woman next to her. Yvette shrugged. "Fine, Suni. If you want to take on this charity case, go ahead. But please, for the love of God, take it slow with her. If you overload her brain too quickly, she'll blow for sure."

Babette clapped her hands at her breast. "All in favor?"

"Aye." The group responded in unison. Lanie watched Yvette. She was fairly certain she mouthed *nay.*

CHAPTER FOUR

After Lanie's acceptance into the elite group had been voted on, they spent a good amount of time discussing who owed the group favors. And who, of those that owed them, would be useful in transforming their newest member from the disastrous creature that she currently was into something divine and worthy of the PTA. Lanie had been poked, prodded, had her hair pulled and her nails checked. Just like cattle to market. Once a plan of action had been agreed upon, the crowd dispersed leaving her alone with Suni in the massive kitchen.

Suni passed her another Mojito and a plate with some crackers and cheese. "Good job today."

Lanie gratefully accepted the nourishment and the compliment. "Was that for real?"

Suni cocked her head to the side. "What do you mean?"

Lanie didn't know where to start, so she chose a deep slow sip of the sugared lime concoction before continuing. "I mean the whole thing. Bribing coach Ryland, getting me all that free stuff from people 'that owe you favors'..."

Suni stirred her drink. "Some of it was real and some of it was show. I can assure you, Lanie, *all* of it was necessary."

"What kind of favors do you guys do for people that they give you all that free stuff?" Lanie wasn't sure she wanted to know. Knowledge without follow through could still make her an accomplice.

"Don't worry so much. Most women would kill to be you right now. You were hand selected to become part of one of the most elite and powerful groups of women in the western suburbs. Why not relax and enjoy the ride?"

Lanie had no intention of enjoying the ride. Her plans included getting out of Suni's kitchen, picking up her children from school and going into hiding until the PTA forgot about her and fixated on someone else. If that wasn't possible, then she would sell the house and move.

Suni checked her watch. "Kids will be out soon. You might have enough time to get home and take a quick shower if you leave right now."

That was her cue to leave. Queen Suni had relinquished her hold over her pet project. Lanie didn't need to be told twice. Standing, she pushed her plate toward the pile of dirties. "Why did Yvette make such a big deal about the car Bob sold her?"

Suni rubbed the spot between her brows. "She hates that car. It has been nothing but trouble since she bought it."

* * *

The hot water was heaven. Lanie closed her eyes and let the soap run off her skin and down the drain, feeling the insanity of the morning's events go with it. After a few minutes in the steam, her muscles relaxed and the adrenaline that made her heart drum in her ears disappeared back into its hiding spot deep within her belly.

She shut off the spray, grabbed a towel and twisted it around her hair. Stepping out of the tub, she slipped on her terrycloth robe. She wiped fog from the mirror and paused to take stock of the person in the reflection. When had the last of her youthful appearance slipped away? It wasn't all that long ago that the signs of age were small and insignificant. Now age had flip-flopped with its counterpart, youth, leaving her squinting in the mirror trying to catch a glimpse of who she'd been.

The bedside phone rang, ending her game of count-the-crow's feet. It was Bob, she was sure of it. The hoopla of the PTA indoctrination had extinguished her anger and worry about the misdialed phone call from the previous evening. Bob was her husband of more than twenty years.

She trusted him. Whatever she heard had been a mistake on her part. Or porn—it could have been porn.

By the time she recovered the handset from its hiding spot in the tangled sheets, it had stopped ringing. Turning it over, her thumb pressed the call log button. Just as she suspected, the number on the lighted display was none other than the Bulldog's cell. He'd made the first move by calling. That meant he was ready to talk, possibly even apologize for leaving the house in a huff on the first day of school. She hit the call button and pressed redial.

"Bob Jackerson's phone. How may I help you?"

The voice on the line was female and all too fresh in her brain. She hadn't been able to place it last night through all the moaning and static, but now she knew. The Mojito and cheddar spread from her time at Suni's threatened to come back up on her. "Let me talk to Bob."

"Oh, hi, Mrs. Jackerson. Bob—Mr. Jackerson is in a meeting. He gave me his phone to make appointments for him. Do you want me to have him call you back?"

It was Brittney Baylor, Bob's Barbie doll secretary. That was who she heard moaning and grinding against her husband last night. "Get him out of the meeting. It's urgent."

"Yes ma'am, right away."

Lanie thought she heard the sound of gum cracking and then everything was muffled. *She's covering the mouthpiece.* She held out her hand and watched the tremors that were rolling through her body take over. It was Bob and Brittney. They had been having sex and she heard the whole thing. From the noises she had been making last night—the things she was saying—it sounded like he was...

"Hello? Lanie—what the hell is wrong? Are the kids okay?" He was panting. Like a dog. An old, out-of-shape, yellow lab that spent its days sleeping under a sunny window.

"Why is she there, Bob?" Her voice sounded so calm. It was hard to believe that it came from her shaking body.

"What? Who?"

He was confused. Lanie didn't know if she should laugh, cry, throw up, or all of the above. She was the one who got a random butt dial and heard her husband pleasuring a girl that was only a few years older than Lexi, and he was the one confused? "Brittney. Why is your secretary answering your cell phone?"

"Christ, Lanie, tell me you didn't have me dragged out of a meeting to have a jealous fit. Tell me that something happened to warrant this call. Something real and serious..."

"I heard you. Last night when the two of you were in bed together—I heard you."

There, take that. The silence on the line was deafening. Every second that ticked by gave him time to think. Time to assess if what she swore she heard was possible or a desperate attempt to wrangle a confession out of him with no evidence.

"I don't know what you're talking about—

"Goddamnit Bob—I HEARD YOU. Your phone, the one that 'Little Miss Barbie sleeps with her boss' is running around with dialed the house last night. I heard everything."

"You're nuts, you know that, Lanie? I've tried to ignore all your mood swings, your lack of desire to do anything except pound the Chardonnay, but you've gone too far this time..."

"Check your call log." She spit into the receiver. And then she hung up.

* * *

Somehow, Lanie picked up Charlie and Lexi from school without losing it. Her sanity was being held together by Scotch tape. One good yank would unravel the façade. Lexi wouldn't have noticed if she showed up bleeding out of her eyeballs and missing an appendage, but Charlie could be pretty sensitive. She didn't want to upset him.

Lexi threw her bag in the back of the Explorer and surveyed her brother's dirty clothes. "God poo-pile, do you always have to be so disgusting?"

"Mooom," Charlie wailed. "Lexi is calling me names."

"Lexi Marie, get your ass in this car without another word or so help me God I will ground you until prom."

Lexi rolled her eyes and snorted. "Keep your knickers on. I was talking about his clothes. They're filthy."

Lanie squinted in the rearview mirror at her son. His shirt was covered with mud stains. Way more than just the usual playground dirt. "What happened to your shirt, Charlie?"

He shrugged. "I got into a fight with Elijah."

Great, Bob was sleeping around and their son was turning into a troublemaker.

Lexi flipped around in her seat. "You got in a fight?"

"It wasn't a big deal. It was over in less than two minutes."

"Who won?" Lexi demanded.

Lanie slapped her daughter's thigh. "Charlie, are you alright?"

"I'm fine."

"Are you sure? Do you need me to call his mom, or talk to the teacher? I could..."

"I said I'm fine," he snapped.

Lexi reached over the backseat and ruffled his head. "Of course you are champ. But if he bothers you again, you let me know. I'll have him taken care of for you."

Lexi's threat against those that would do harm to her baby brother must have worked. Through the rearview mirror, Lanie caught him smiling gratefully at his older sister. Maybe when Lexi grew up she could be in the running for president of the Herschel Grammar School PTA.

*   *   *

By nine o'clock, the kids were in bed. Bob made a big point out of calling to say goodnight to Charlie. Lanie passed him the phone without even saying hello. Whatever bullshit Bob was selling tonight, she didn't want to hear it. She needed time to think. Time to sort things out and come up with a plan of action. She knew that the minute she talked to Bob he would do one of two things: he would either call her crazy and make her feel small, or he would take the complete opposite approach and try to convince her that what she heard wasn't what she thought it was because he loved her way too much to destroy what they had. Either way, she felt like she was on a sinking ship. Life without Bob was something she couldn't picture in her head, not yet anyway.

God she wanted a glass of wine. In her desperate state, she'd be sure to throw down too much, so she fought the urge and went into Bob's office to look for something that would give her peace of mind. Or, on the other end of the spectrum, send her straight to the loony bin. Bob had been telling her she was slipping for years. Maybe perimenopause was making her certifiable.

She flipped on his computer and sank into the soft, brown leather of his desk chair. It was so damn comfortable that she could sleep there. No skimping on creature comforts for the Bulldog. Even his primal desires for flesh had developed high standards. She knew she'd passed the expiration date of hotness. She just never realized that meant he'd go elsewhere to keep it spicy. Her delusions of being an old couple holding hands, smiling sweetly at young couples in love were shattered. She might find the image sweet, but Bob would be dreaming of getting in the young girl's panties.

Stop making assumptions, Lanie. You don't have any proof.

If there was proof, it was sure to be somewhere in the home office/ man cave. The private space had been his fortieth birthday surprise, courtesy of Lanie's years of scrimping and saving. Over the years, she sold sketches and put the money aside. It couldn't have been a more perfect surprise. The best part was telling him that the renovations were accomplished without tapping into a dime of their joint finances. To date, it was the best feat she'd ever pulled off. If Bob had been hiding a secret life behind the door, it would be a real shame.

The contents of the desk drawers were typical. There wasn't one scrap that proved she was right about Bob and Britney. Sliding the cursor to the Quicken logo she opened the financial statements for the dealership and their home. When Bob had first opened Bulldog's New and Used Rides ten years ago, Lanie had been his personal secretary. She gave it up when Charlie came along. If she'd stayed, it might have kept her marriage on track.

Everything was in perfect order. Their personal and business records looked exactly the way they should. No red flags jumped out at her. If he was spending large amounts of time and money on Brittney, he'd

ELSIE LOVE

buried it elsewhere. Even the cell phone bills were clean. The online call log showed the call to the house. Nothing new there. The home phone caller ID had told her as much. Not proof of anything other than an incoming call. But she heard what she heard. That voice was Brittney's, she was sure of it.

Without anything concrete, the doubt that nagged at the back of her conscious was sure to linger. There had been static and other noise in the background. Could she have heard the lyrics to some raunchy song in a nightclub? She'd been to enough car expo's to know that the minute the workday ended, there was drinking and carousing until the wee hours of the morning. It was just part of the game. Maybe what she had heard was nothing more than people gyrating to the pulsing beat at a bar. Or porn. All guys liked porn. Neither felt true, but she would cling to them until proven wrong. The alternative was still too painful.

She shut off the computer and left the office. The longer she sat mulling over the events of the last few days, the more likely she was to go running for the wine cabinet. Bob would be home in a few days. Whatever he did or didn't do would have to be sorted out then.

* * *

THURSDAY, AUGUST 24TH

It was Thursday. The worst day of the week—every week. Not quite the weekend and infinitely longer than the other days of the week. Lanie was sure that if scientists did a study of time, they would find extra minutes or hours that snuck in undetected making Thursday long and insufferable in every way.

This Thursday was no different. Her phone conversation with Bob had thrown her for a loop. In her current state of disarray, she had forgotten all about her plans to call Suni and tell her that she would not be able to join the PTA after all. Babette showed up in her silver bullet Jeep right at nine on the button to escort her through her first day of being transformed. Lanie smelled the fresh, roasted coffee through the front door and squashed her desire to run and hide under the covers. She might as well temporarily give in. If she didn't go willingly, Suni would unleash Yvette to hunt her down and take her by force. She had to convince Suni to release her free and clear. She opened the door.

"Morning, Sugar. Brought you a little treat."

She put her thoughts of freedom on her ever growing mental to-do list and sucked down the large Mocha Latte.

* * *

Lanie sat in a chair at the Shear Madness salon being poked and prodded by Ginger, the salon owner. Watching her expression as she picked through her brunette locks was a quick reminder that these people found her to be a poor excuse for a person in her current state. Babette sat in a nearby chair having her nails painted a bright shade of orange. Lanie heard the manicurist tell Babette that it was *coral*, and all the rage this fall, but Lanie thought it couldn't be more orange if she had picked it off a tree in a Florida grove.

Ginger plucked a gray hair from Lanie's scalp. "She's gonna be rough. The hardest one yet."

Babette nodded sympathetically. "I know. But you can do it, Sugar. I have faith in you."

"She needs everything. Cut, color, maybe even some highlights with the color..."

Lanie glanced at the clock on the wall. It was already noon. Charlie needed to be picked up in three hours. "How long will this take?"

"Coupl'a hours."

"My son gets out of school at three."

Ginger checked the clock and made a sour face. "You want to bring her back another day Betts? She says she has to get her son."

"No, Sugar. You can get her finished in time. I know you can."

Ginger tapped on Lanie's back and pointed to the sink in the back of the room. "We better get started. We don't want to rush it so much that your hair gets all fried up and nasty."

* * *

"Sugar, you look like a whole new woman!"

Lanie blinked. She did look like a whole new woman. One that had time and money to sit in a salon and let others make her into a Goddess. Her hair was smooth and shiny. The shade of chestnut gleamed with hints of gold when she turned her head. Ginger beamed.

"You did good, Sugar—real good. Suni is gonna love it!" Babette leaned in and gave the tan, blond woman a kiss on her cheek.

"Are we good?" Ginger asked.

Babette slapped her playfully on the arm. "Girl we are always good—you know that!"

"I meant with...you know..." she looked at Lanie warily.

"Oh, that! Yes, Sugar, we are all good. Suni has Molly and Lila taking care of Mister Bad News for you. When they get done with him, he won't dare set foot in the same state as you!"

Relief passed over Ginger's face. Lanie pulled herself away from the mirror. No matter how good she looked right now, she needed to remember that these women were not her friends. The sooner she got away from them, the better. She checked the clock. Two forty-five. Charlie would be out of school in fifteen minutes. He was slow, normally the last child to pass through the double doors. That gave her an extra fifteen minutes, which helped a little. If she didn't leave now she'd still have to speed. Would the cop recognize her as one of Suni's crowd? *Stop*, she commanded. *You are not one of them.* "Babette, we'd better go. I have to get home in enough time to get Charlie."

Babette smiled warmly. "Sure thing, Sugar."

* * *

Charlie had passed the Explorer right by. He slowed down, took a good look, and kept on walking. Lanie rolled down the window and yelled to him. "Poo—Charlie...over here!"

He ran back. "Wow, mom, you look so different!"

"Do you like it?"

He nodded enthusiastically. "You look like one of those ladies on T.V."

"Thanks, kiddo."

"I bet dad will really like it."

She turned so he wouldn't catch the anger on her face. "Maybe."

Lexi's reaction was even bigger.

"MOM. Oh my God—I can't believe it's you!"

Lanie cupped her hand under the ends of her silky strands and preened. "So I guess you like it?"

"Who did it?"

"A woman named Ginger. She owns the salon in town. Shear Madness?"

Lexi's jaw dropped. "Wow, that place is f-a-n-c-y. How'd you afford it?"

"It wasn't that much." It had been free thanks to whatever unscrupulous deal Babette had worked out with Ginger.

"Can I go there?"

"Absolutely not. You are too young."

Lexi's face fell.

Lanie relented. It wasn't fair to wave all her new luxuries in Lexi's face and deny her a small slice. "Maybe for prom you can go there for an updo." She would have to find out what the going rate was. There was no way she was going to be able to get the free deal. She'd be long removed from the PTA by next May.

"Really? Thanks mom. You are the best."

* * *

FRIDAY, AUGUST 25TH

The excitement of the hair excursion had made Thursday whip by. It was the first fast break into the weekend that Lanie could remember since her kids started school thirteen years ago. Friday morning dawned bright and early. This time she was ready. It was her day to shop with Yvette at LaFemme Fatale Boutique. The name of the store fit the dragon queen. She made the coffee extra strong to keep her on her A-game. If she let her guard down, Yvette was sure to chew her up and spit her out like a bad baguette.

Lanie drove herself to the boutique. Spending time alone in a car with Yvette, even for a quick jaunt across town, was too terrifying to consider. There had to be at least one witness left alive to recount the horror of her head being ripped off by nothing more than a full set of acrylic nails. She made it two blocks before the gold Lexus pulled out behind her and rode her ass the rest of the way to the shop. It was still scary, but better than being seated next to her.

The agony of the fashion fitting made a car trip with Yvette sound like a day at the beach. Nothing fit her full, middle-aged figure. Everything was impossibly tight across her hips and thighs. Her breasts exploded out of the tops in every direction—up, down, sideways—you name it. Zipper after zipper caught and stuck miles from the hooks at the top. *Doesn't anyone have curves anymore?*

Charlize, the ultra-thin sales clerk, swiped at a bead of sweat that formed on her brow. The intense workout of pulling armloads of clothing and yanking zippers that came with fitting a size never imagined in Europe was getting to her.

Yvette made it no secret that she deplored fat anywhere—on anyone. Each outfit that Lanie tried on drew gags and coughing fits. "No. That won't do. There must be *something* here that will work! She has to be ready for our next meeting on Monday."

Lanie waited in the dressing room for the next truckload of clothes to be delivered. Every tag she'd seen so far had a six or an eight on it. If they didn't jump into the double digits this round she would scream. The clothes were beautiful. The clothes were amazing. The clothes were too darn small. The only way she could make them fit would be to start cutting off random body parts. No thanks. Her body was the vessel that carried her through life. She wanted it whole.

Finally, Charlize dug out some pants suits that Yvette deemed passable. It took so long for her to return from the back room that Lanie suspected she made a run to the Dress Barn next door. Yvette spun her in a circle, clucking and pulling at the fabric. Lanie complied with the mandatory grooming. She turned slowly, trying not to topple out of the Coach Wedge sandals that had mysteriously fallen into the back of the Explorer with a note that simply said 'wear these to the meeting on Monday.'

Satisfied, Yvette snapped. Charlize ran to her side. "We'll take these. Nice work, Char."

The sales clerk looked as if she might piss her pants. "Very good. So glad I could be of service."

"She'll wear this one home. Bag the rest."

"Of course."

Lanie frowned. "What about my clothes?"

"You won't be needing them. Go wait in your car. I'll have Charlize bring out the rest of the clothes when they are wrapped."

"But..." She liked her clothes. They were comfortable.

Yvette crossed her arms and tapped her toe. Her ice blue gaze pierced through Lanie's flesh at the jugular. She did as she was told.

CHAPTER FIVE
MONDAY, AUGUST 28TH

The Monday meeting in Suni's kitchen was far less shocking than the first. With her new hair and clothes, Lanie wondered if anyone realized that she was the same woman that had shown up there five days earlier unshowered in soiled bedclothes. Introductions were the first order of business. Suni paraded her around the room like a prize hen at the county fair.

"Lila, Molly, you remember Lanie?"

The two women stopped mid sentence to take in the new and improved Lanie Jackerson. They nodded their approval. After a minute of small talk, she was ushered along to the next group.

"Kelsey, Brie, Donna, Trisha—you remember Lanie, don't you? She is our newest member in training."

Brie brushed blond fringe out of her eyes. "I love the new color. Isn't Ginger marvelous?"

Before Lanie could answer, Kelsey jumped in. "And those clothes! Charlize can make anyone look good. Not that you weren't wonderful before, Lanie."

Trisha laughed. "Nice, Kelsey. Very nice."

Lanie marveled at the group. Each one of them was a unique individual. Just like snowflakes, no two PTA moms were the same. They had unique DNA. They came from different backgrounds, from different places, and yet—they were all the same. Sure, Kelsey was obviously Irish, with her creamy skin and long black hair. Brie was as short and blond as Trisha was tall and brunette, but they were the same. They laughed the same, they dressed the same, and they even turned to look at the same thing at the same time. Lanie didn't care that it fit her like a glove. She despised her new cream colored pantsuit and heels. It was the uniform of the suburban mob. She had become one of them.

With the introductions behind them, Suni guided her out of the kitchen and into the sitting room off the foyer. "Wait here until we finish going over the business agenda. I will call you back to the kitchen for the closing."

"I was there on Tuesday when you went through your agenda." Why did she bring that up? She didn't want to be there when they went through the list of crimes they were about to commit. The less she knew, the better. What she really wanted was for the meeting to end so she could resign her position with the PTA and go home to deal with Bob.

Suni picked an invisible piece of lint off her shirt. "That was small potatoes compared to what we have on our plate today."

What could be worse than bribery and getting rid of unscrupulous men that bothered women in hair salons?

Suni changed the subject. "Do you like to read? You can help yourself to anything from the bookshelves. I'll be back soon."

She turned on her heel and took off toward the kitchen at a fast clip. Lanie sank down in the wingback chair and put her feet up on the ottoman. Any other day, the mention of a good book would be tempting. Today, she would use her time in the sitting room to think about her 'I quit' speech.

* * *

Brittney Baylor was gyrating to the song *Maniac* from the movie Flashdance.

Her fuchsia-colored bodysuit and striped legwarmers complimented her high side ponytail in a way that only a person old enough to catch the rated R flick on its first run could understand. She wrapped her leg around the stripper pole and swung herself gracefully through the air.

Watching her spin made Lanie want to grab her by the pony tail and swing her over her head, letting go to launch her into deep space. Feeling her anger about to bubble over, she crossed the room, stopping just shy of getting slapped by blond tresses. "Get out of my life you home-wrecking whore."

Brittney slid down the pole and came to rest on the floor. "Sorry, Lanie, you can't wreck something that doesn't exist."

Lanie wasn't sure if the nasty comment was directed to her disgrace of a marriage or lack of a life in general. "Listen up, sister," she growled. "If I catch you near my husband again, I will call your mother and tell her you're sleeping with a married man." Lanie prayed the blond bimbo was young enough to care what her mother thought. If Lexi's lack of consideration for her were an indication of when girls stopped caring, she was a few years too late. Her next threat would have to pack a harder punch.

Brittney rolled her eyes. Without a word, she blew a Hubba Bubba bubble the size of a dinner plate. In a flash, she was nose to bubble with Lanie. Sucking in sharply, she pulled the bubble back with a loud *Pop!* "You don't scare me. I steal men from women like you all the time. Face it, Lanie, you're nothing but a washed up housewife. The last time you looked good, Bill Clinton was serving his first term in the Oval Office." Sticking the heel of her stiletto in Lanie's belly, she gave a push, sending her in the direction of the floor.

Lanie knew she wouldn't be able to catch herself. Flailing in front of Bob's Barbie doll didn't create the strong protective momma grizzly image she was going for. She thrust her arms behind her and braced herself for the pain.

But the pain never came. Instead she found herself in free fall, surrounded by darkness.

*   *   *

"Lanie...wake up."

Lanie opened her eyes. If someone told her she'd be glad—

thrilled, even—to find Yvette standing over her like a cross child ready to tantrum, she would have declared them insane. But here she was, so relieved to find out that the bubblicious version of Brittney was a nightmare, that she gladly would have planted a smooch on her pout. The fear of getting a solid smack that would knock her into next week kept her in the blue wingback. "Is it time for the closing?"

"You missed the closing. The meeting is over. Go home."

Suni had promised she would come and get her before the meeting ended. Her plan was to slip in, listen to the end, wait for the crowd to leave, and hit Suni with the sad news of her resignation. Perhaps this turn of events benefitted her more than the original plan? If everyone had already skedaddled, she was guaranteed a private audience with president Suni. If she could get past Yvette. "I need to speak with Suni before I leave."

Yvette pulled her to her feet. "You need to go home. Suni isn't here."

Confusion tugged at the corners of her mind. Leaving Yvette to skulk around unsupervised seemed unwise. "Where did she go?"

Yvette snorted. "She had some business to attend to. Now, if you'll excuse me, I have some loose ends to tie up as well. I trust you can show yourself out?" Without waiting for an answer, she turned and stalked down the hall.

Not much of an explanation. She was tempted to push her luck. If she followed Yvette and continued to harass her, she might get sick and tired enough to let something slip about Suni's whereabouts. The hallway was dark. Not even a slit of light as far as the eye could see. It had swallowed Yvette instantly. Better to wait and schedule a meeting with Suni—just Suni.

Reaching for her purse, she kept the dark hallway in sight. The clip of Yvette's heels was no longer audible. The hench-lady was either far enough away that Lanie was safe, or she had stopped and was peering out at her from the cloak of black. The second possibility sent gooseflesh crawling up her neck. Finding the strap, she hoisted the bag. Cream-colored leather caused her to stop short. That wasn't her purse. Her purse was a vinyl Wal-Mart special. A bright yellow sticky note on the side of the bag caught her attention.

Lanie—
Saw this at the store & thought it would suit you.
S.

The leather was butter in her hands. It was a perfect match for the wedge heels that had shown up in her trunk. Gingerly, she ran her finger around the trademark C. Clearly this was an expensive accessory. It contained the magic found in upscale boutiques that could turn grungy streetwalkers into classy ladies; Julia Roberts' looks not included. Undoing the gold snap, she peered inside. All her personal items had made the switch from pumpkin to coach. The smell of new leather filled her nostrils. It was divine. Simply the best bag she'd ever put her mitts on.

But it wasn't hers. No matter how badly she wanted it, Lanie knew that keeping it was out of the question. Her purse was in a trash incinerator by now. Suni had probably used grill tongs to move it. It was doubtful that Suni Calverson allowed anything other than animal skin branded by a designer to taint her flesh. The clock on the shelf read 2:45. Fifteen minutes until Charlie had to be picked up. By the time they got back home and he settled in for the afternoon, it would leave her with three hours to decide how to handle Bob. Time to get a move on. Giving back the delicious bag would have to wait. All the black market goods would be turned in with her resignation.

*   *   *

Bob arrived after eight. A full hour later than Lanie had anticipated. The extra time should have helped in the planning department, but sadly had left her more anxiety-filled. Her plan for dealing with Bob was the same as her plan for dealing with all life's major events—there was no plan. She would just have to wing it and hope for a good outcome. His disheveled blond hair, raccoon eyes, and absence of a tan raised her guilt meter. If he'd been frolicking with Brittney, wouldn't she have requested a trip to the beach? Or at least some strolls in the California sunshine? Forcing the guilt to take a back seat, she set her lips in a tight line.

Bob dropped his small, rolling travel bag in the front hall and stopped at the kitchen table to kiss Charlie on the head. "Hey, big man, how was your first week of third grade?"

"Great." It was an automatic reply that slipped out from behind the screen of their son's Gameboy.

Bob rumpled the halo of curls before moving to the fridge for a beer. Twisting off the cap, he brought the bottle up for a sip. His gaze came to rest on the new and improved Lanie. "Holy cow."

His words were so unexpected, so out of character considering the silent fight they'd been having, that it broke her resolve. "Thanks." She answered running a hand through her hair and smoothing her new suit.

His eyes pierced through her. Her cheeks burned hot under his gaze. She knew that look. He thought she looked good. Not just good, but totally, completely fuckable. It was a look she hadn't seen in at least ten years—not from him—and not directed at her. Her heart hammered against her ribs as he took in her body, a small smile forming on his lips. Charlie kept right on playing his game unaware of the new sexual tension in the room. The raw heat was making her sweat in the now uncomfortable suit coat. She unbuttoned the jacket and placed it over the back of one of the kitchen chairs before she remembered that her shirt underneath was a bronze strapless number, something she would never have picked out for herself, but let Yvette talk her into at the boutique. She knew it outlined her every curve, just skimming her less-than-favorite midsection and highlighting the fact that her nipples were now rock hard.

Shit. She crossed her arms covering her chest. Too late. She could tell by the way he stopped the top of the amber-colored beer bottle just in front of his lips that he'd seen it. Her desire so easily roused by the slightest bit of attention, surprised and sickened her at the same time. Like an abused dog that wags its tail and forgives the minute the master holds out his hand. She tried to conjure up an image of Bob with Brittney. The lame attempt to counteract her growing desire was futile. Her long dormant pleasure centers were fully charged and ready to rumble. She took a deep breath and held it in, trying to force herself to regain composure.

Bob set the beer down next to Charlie. "Hey, bud, why don't you go see if there's a new episode of Clone Wars on?"

Charlie looked up from his game and checked the time on the

microwave. "It's eight-fifteen—I already missed some!"

And just like that he was gone. Leaving Lanie only inches from her sexed-up, possibly cheating, husband.

* * *

Lanie cursed under her breath. She'd caved. The minute he put his hands in her hair, running his fingers through the freshly caramel colored strands, she'd attacked him. The force of her slamming him into the table, wrapping her legs around his waist and tugging at the button on the front of his pants, had startled him.

"Easy...easy." He chuckled, picking her up and carrying her to the bedroom.

Lanie was drained. The sex had sapped every ounce of strength from her body. She had been like a starved animal, pushing any concerns about his infidelity to the back of her mind and letting her carnal instincts take over. Now, he snored, asleep in the way only a fully satisfied man sleeps. And she was wide awake. The body craved sleep, the mind was unwilling. Another curse of middle age. She rolled out of bed and threw on her bathrobe.

The T.V. was still on the cartoon channel and Charlie was fast asleep on the couch. His body twisted into a ball with his Nintendo clutched in his hand, the game still on. Picking up the remote, she aimed it at the set, and with the push of a button, the screen went black. Leaning down, she pulled the game system from him and switched it off. Brushing damp curls from his forehead, she planted a quick kiss on his freckled skin. He stirred slightly and settled right back into sleep. She decided to leave him there. He was getting too big to move. Standing, the top of his head came to just under her breasts. Secretly, she missed the days when she could swing his limp body up over her shoulder and carry him to his room. It was such a special moment—tucking the covers under the chin of her sleeping angel. Now she'd have to bring the blankets to him, or ask Bob to move him.

Bob. Her husband. The man she had just spent the last hour and a half pleasuring in ways that she had forgotten over the last few years.

Oh Bob...yes...just like that.

The thought of him sleeping with Brittney wasn't nearly as threatening to her as it had been before the sex. Why? She had no idea. The thought occurred to her that maybe she was still stuck in the childhood delusion that if a man had sex with her, then he couldn't possibly be fucking someone else. How could he? She couldn't bed another and return home to her husband—but she was a woman. Men operated differently. She knew it, learned it many times over as a young girl, but she didn't want to. She sensed it could be true, but pushed the thoughts of infidelity away.

She made her way to the kitchen and checked the clock. Midnight. Lexi should have been home an hour ago. Eleven on a school night had been Bob's idea. She was a senior, so close to leaving home. Why not give her more freedom? Give her a chance to practice being a grown up before she left the safety of the nest. Lanie thought it was ridiculous. Give a kid enough rope and they'd be sure to hang themselves—especially during their senior year. Here it was the first week of school and already she'd blown it. Now Lanie was stuck with the aftermath. She'd have to decide if it was worth the fight; maybe even try to ground her. Any other night it would have been a no brainer. You break curfew—you get grounded. Relaxing the rules, even once, would undermine her authority. Erode it beyond repair for the rest of the school year. Still, the energy it would take to ground her at this point was more than what was left in her reserves. She'd had enough drama for one week. She would let Lexi see her waiting, but say nothing. Let her worry silently that Bob might ground her in the morning. That would be punishment enough for Miss Lexi Marie. Turning on the light above the stove, she took a seat at the table.

Bob's suitcase sat in the entry hall beckoning her. *Open me. Come on...you know you want to.* Would he be so callous as to leave a bag full of evidence in the entry hall? Normally, no. But tonight she had blown him away with her sudden transformation. For an encore, she'd blown him away in the bedroom. Hiding incriminating evidence would be the last thing on his mind.

Except for the rhythmic ticking of the grandfather clock, the house was silent. Looking over her shoulder to make sure Bob hadn't stirred from his slumber, Lanie made her way into the hall. The porch light cast a glow through the oval glass on the front door, surrounding the bag with a golden halo. Her hands shook as she put her fingers on the zipper. A lock, small enough to fit through the holes on both zipper pulls, stopped her. Flipping it up, she saw the tiny keyhole. It looked new. There was no way he got the bag on the plane that way. Security after the World Trade Center wouldn't allow it. This lock had been put on somewhere between the airport and home, after it was pulled from the luggage carousel.

Where would he hide the key? Bob kept his house and car keys on a key ring at home when he traveled, so there was no way it was on there. It had to be somewhere else—somewhere close where he could keep an eye on it. She remembered something rattling in the front pocket of his chinos when she ripped them off of his body and threw them against the bedroom wall. That had to be it. He hadn't been wearing a jacket. The weather was still much, too warm for that. The pants were still on the floor. As long as Bob was snoring she could rummage through his pockets with no fear of being caught. It should be easy. Even in the dark, a luggage key would stand out among the receipts and loose change.

A shadow passed in front of the glass temporarily blocking out the light in the entry hall. Lanie shrank back, frightened, until she heard the voice on the other side.

"I know—she's so lame." It was Lexi, talking on her cell phone. "Oh God, are you fucking kidding me? There is no way he would take her. She's on crack if she thinks she has a chance. Come on— he's Jake Caldwell—he could take anybody."

The key fumbling inside the keyhole forced her into action. Lexi was astute. If she caught her mother crouching over a locked bag in the dark, there were sure to be unwanted questions. Abandoning her plans to send the fear of an impending grounding, Lanie scooted back against the far wall and stood. There. Now Lexi would think she was just waiting, like any other good mother, to say goodnight to her daughter. She crossed her fingers hoping that Lexi would buy that excuse. It was a long shot. Lexi was suspicious of most things Lanie did. It didn't help that she was always fast asleep long before Lexi came home. This new and sudden appearance was sure to bring questions that she wasn't prepared to answer. Second guessing her plan, Lanie toyed with the idea of making a run for it. She wasn't very fast, but in the dark she might be able to zip past the glass without being caught. Before she could make a move, the door flew open. She pressed her body flat against the wall as her daughter swept past. Chatting away to whomever was on the other end of her call, she closed her bedroom door. Lanie let out a sigh of relief. Lexi hadn't given her a passing glance. Her suitcase follies were safe, for now.

She was free and clear. Safe to commit her criminal act. Lexi wouldn't come back out. Once she was tucked into the safety of her bedroom, she only came out to eat or leave. She wouldn't be caught dead eating late at night—it might ruin her already perfect body. Lanie could retrieve the key and open the suitcase right there in the hallway. She was two steps closer to the master bedroom when she heard Lexi's voice float out from behind the door as clear as a bell.

"Oh my God. He moaned so loud I thought we'd get caught for sure. His parents sleep with their bedroom window open. Can you imagine the look on their faces if they came out and found us in the back of their brand new Caddy?"

Her stomach dropped. Her daughter was talking about a sexual act with a boy. Lexi didn't have a boyfriend—at least not that Lanie was aware of. Did that mean she was sleeping with someone that she wasn't even dating? She turned in the direction of her daughter's room and tiptoed closer to the closed door.

"Oh God—I know! I swear, sometimes it still smells like pee. So *disgusting.*"

She had to be talking about blow jobs—but who had she been doing this with? Maybe it was Mark Henry? He and Lexi spent a lot of time together over the summer. Maybe they had developed a relationship and she had failed to notice?

"I'm not interested. I just want to screw around, ya' know? It's my senior year. I don't want a *relationship*. I just want to have fun."

Well, that answered that question. Lexi was not dating anyone. She was just screwing around. Fabulous. Lanie put her hand on the doorknob. This was one of those moments when she had to make a choice. She could either go in like a tornado screaming and threatening the way her mother would have, or she could be better than that and go in with wisdom and sincerity. Or, she could turn around and go bury herself under the covers—

pretend she never heard any of this.

Burying her head was tempting. It wasn't that she was afraid of having the sex talk with her daughter. That part was easy. It was the advanced knowledge that anything and everything she said would be seen as an assault, no matter how she phrased it, that made her uneasy. She wasn't sure how or why she had become the enemy, but she had.

"My mom? Still a drunk. Good for nothing. She wouldn't even drive me to school the other morning. I had to hitch a ride with Steve and Mari. I know. I can't wait to be out of here, either."

The insult hit home. Lanie yanked her hand off the knob. There was no way she could go in and talk calmly to her daughter now. She would go in like a fire breathing dragon, screaming and spitting. That would only leave Lexi even more secure in her smug, but false, teenage beliefs. She would deal with the sexual stuff another day. Lexi was practically an adult. In eleven short months she would be on her own at college. Lanie had done far worse than give a guy a blow job by the time she was Lexi's age. She cringed remembering the sadness of her pathetic attempts at early adulthood. She was a disaster at seventeen. If Lexi wanted to blow some guy in the back of a Cadillac and risk sinking her reputation, there wasn't much Lanie could do about it. Not tonight, anyway.

She tiptoed back across the hall and into her bedroom where Bob was still snoring. He had the luxury of being oblivious. A luxury that mothers of teenage daughters never had. In Bob's mind, Lexi was a superstar, above reproach in every way. She crawled into bed next to him, her head throbbing. She was almost asleep when she remembered the suitcase and the key in Bob's pocket. *Tomorrow* she decided. It would have to wait until then. Right now she needed to sleep.

CHAPTER SIX
TUESDAY, AUGUST 29TH

Lanie woke up after eight. She shot up in a momentary panic attack. It was Tuesday. Summer was over. Why hadn't she set an alarm? Then she remembered it was the first in service day. No school. The kids had only been back a week. Somehow, the district managed to sneak in one or two days off every month. It was one of the many reasons that she had refrained from returning to work after Lexi was born. Sporadic childcare throughout the year was expensive and practically impossible to find. Why go back to work when she could freelance from home when the kids were in school? Having the house to herself nine months out of the year would give her more time to devote to her art. The theory made sense—putting it into practice was the issue. Between caring for the house and running the kids where they needed to be, she found a mere hour or two a week to draw. Just enough to frustrate her to the breaking point. By the time Lexi was in third grade, she'd stuffed all her supplies away. They were an eyesore. A painful reminder of her failure.

There was no school to rush off to. No pressing meetings or orthodontist appointments. She rolled over and took in the empty side of the bed where Bob had been asleep so soundly the night before. His pants were still in the spot against the corner of the baseboard and the carpet where she had thrown them. The rolling suitcase, now unpacked, sat in front of the closet door. Now she would never know what secrets Bob had been hiding.

She was irritated. She allowed herself to become distracted from what was important to her—again. She did it all the time. Her art, her friends, herself. She was a transparency. A paper doll that got laid across each member of her family. Whatever they needed, that was her need. Whatever they wanted, it was up to her to find. She let Lexi's teenage meanderings distract her. Because of that, she would never know what Bob had thought important enough to put under lock and key before he came home to his family.

Lexi's promiscuity was a serious parenting issue. It would have to be addressed. How much good it would do this late in the game was debatable. Lexi was a strong willed girl that had grown into an even more willful young adult. She was leaving next fall. If things panned out the way Lexi planned, there would be a track scholarship that would land her a spot at the University of Illinois. It wasn't the biggest party school in the state, but it was big. Lexi had already spent a lot of time researching which sorority she would pledge. She'd get in—the parties and boys wouldn't be too far behind. The best Lanie could hope for was that her daughter would be safe, both mentally and physically.

Bob's infidelity, if it wasn't a figment of her imagination, threatened their entire comfortable existence. She should have chosen to file Lexi's late night call away and stayed on track. Then she might have found something to put an end to the constant questions and misgivings that filled her every waking thought. She'd blown it. In the light of the morning she realized how foolish that was. Like everything else in her life, it was a day late and a dollar short.

The kitchen was empty. Fresh coffee told her that Bob had enjoyed their romp. He only made fresh as a gift to her. He could drink week old brew that had sat on the counter the entire time. She picked up his empty mug. Cold. The auto shut off light on the base of the machine blinked its five minute warning. Finding the biggest cup in the cabinet, she emptied the rest of the brew from the pot.

He was gone for at least an hour, at the dealership no doubt. She thought about calling him—telling him that they needed to have a sit down about the new adventures of their half grown hormone queen—but decided against it. Lanie hadn't been a teen in many moons, but she could still recall the horror of having to talk about sex with her mother. If she'd been forced to talk about it with her father, she might never have had sex again. A talk with mom, some time to shape up, and then, if all else failed, a talk with both parents. That would be her plan of action.

The silence of the house settled on her shoulders, sending her into a reflective state. The kids' days off were free from scheduled activities by design. Originally, it had been part of her plan to get back to her art. She quickly learned the hard lesson that even without play-dates, ballet lessons, and soccer games, the kids would eat up her free time. Nine minute snippets were not long enough for her to even come up with ideas for her sketchbook. Disgusted and disappointed, she put her work on the back burner until she forgot about it completely and dove head first into being a stay at home mom. It was just easier that way. Bob was happy. The kids were happy. Without really being aware of what she was doing, she gave away the first piece of herself. Now the kids were older. It was time to go back and revisit her artistic side. If she could find it under the layers she'd piled on.

Thinking about her young ambitions gone awry made her anxious and she was glad to see Charlie pad out onto the kitchen, fully dressed. "Morning, Poodle," she said, ignoring his frown. "Why are you up so early on a day off?"

"I'm going to the skate park with Ajay. His mom is picking me up at ten."

Lanie was immediately suspicious. Ajay was Suni's son. Charlie and Ajay had never been close. In fact, they'd never hung out together in all their nine years of life. Elijah was Charlie's best bud—had been since Kindergarten—but he was also Ajay's arch nemesis. "Ajay, huh? Is that why you and Elijah had that fight the other day?"

She watched Charlie's face cloud over. His bottom lip stuck out in a mini-pout. "Ajay is my friend. If Elijah doesn't like it, then that's too bad."

"Elijah has been a good friend of yours since you started school, Charlie, I don't see why you can't all be friends."

"He was *mean* to me mom. He said that Ajay didn't want to be my friend. He said the only reason he was being nice to me was because he had to."

"He was just hurt. It's hard sometimes when friends grow apart."

Charlie sat at the kitchen table and buried his head in his arms. Lanie felt bad for him. He was only nine years old, too young to have to start all this social crap. She sat next to him and ran her hands over his copper curls. He shook his head like a dog trying to shake off fleas.

"Charlie, come on, it can't be that bad..."

He lifted his head. "You don't get it. Elijah was right. Ajay doesn't want to be my friend, not for real. He's doing it because he *has* to. His mom is making him."

Lanie knew he was right. Ajay was a bully, a ringleader that picked who would be popular that year. As great as Charlie was, Ajay never would have picked him. He wasn't a super jock and he respected his teachers. In Ajay Calverson's book, Charlie Jackerson was a butt-kissing wussy, not someone to be friends with. Suni had put him up to it. Lanie was seething. It was one thing for Suni to walk all over her, but she would not hurt her kids. "Do you really want to go to the skate park? I can call Mrs. Calverson and tell her you're sick."

His eyes doubled in size and his face turned red. "No! Don't do that. I want to go. Maybe if I hang out with Ajay today—then maybe—

Oh, God, Poodle, please don't say it.

"Maybe he'll like me for real."

She felt sick. The raw emotion on her son's face, the power that he'd given to another child to decide whether or not he was worthy of friendship, the unfairness of how youth graded what mattered—all of it made her want to wrap him in her arms and take him back to a stage of growth where she controlled the input and outgo of information. "Charlie..."

He set his jaw in a line. "Mom, I want to go. Please—don't ruin this for me."

She nodded. "Okay, bud, if you're sure."

"I'm sure."

* * *

The doorbell rang promptly at ten. Lanie stood back in the shadows long enough to make sure that Suni hadn't come to the door. There was no way she could keep her cool around her. Not after Charlie's revelation at the kitchen table. Ajay was alone. His hat perched backwards on his head. Dark sunglasses, probably Oakley's, hid his eyes from view. He smiled showing off two rows of perfect teeth.

"Dude, you ready?" He asked tipping the glasses down and looking over the top.

Lanie looked at her son and tried to see him from the eyes of another third grader. His hair needed to be cut, the curls were getting taller in a pseudo afro, and his clothes looked like Geranimals compared to the teen wear on Ajay. She would have to take him shopping. Get him clothes that would help him fit in.

"I have to get my board. It's in the garage."

"Cool. See ya', Mrs. J."

She gave him a curt nod. "What time will you be back?"

"Don't worry, Mrs. J—I'll take good care of him."

They disappeared out the door. Charlie was practically jumping out of his skin with gratitude. Ajay sauntered like the kids Lexi hung out with, demonstrating his superior knowledge of how to be popular. Staying hidden behind the window sheers, she watched the pair climb into the depths of Suni's black Cadillac Escalade. Lanie fought the urge to run after him and smother him with kisses, her secret mom protection against pain. He was out there, growing up and joining the world. Unfortunately, he had to share with people like smart ass Ajay Calverson.

* * *

Lanie had managed to shower and dress in record time. With Charlie gone for the morning, she decided to have her talk with Lexi, which would be painful but brief, then spend the rest of her free time looking through some of her old sketches that were hidden in the back of the closet. Pain first, more pain later.

The bedroom was a tomb of darkness. Lexi was still asleep, her body tangled in the sheets. Lanie walked to the far window and threw open the dark suede curtains. "Wake up, sunshine—you and me need to have a heart to heart."

"MOM! God—I'm sleeping—can't this wait?" She pulled a pillow off the floor and threw it over her face to block the sun.

"No, it cannot. You need to get up or you will be spending the rest of the weekend at home."

"Look, if this is about curfew, I'm sorry. I lost track of time. I won't let it happen again."

Lanie sat on the edge of the bed and pulled the pillow away. "It isn't about curfew. I want to talk about sex."

Lexi groaned in protest, but she sat up. "We already had this talk—three times. I know about sex."

"What I want to talk about today is a little bit different, Lex. I want to talk about relationships. More specifically, I want to talk about what *kind* of relationship you should have with someone that you are going to have sex with."

Eye rolling. The universal sign for boredom. She pressed on. "I want you to understand how important you are. Don't give yourself away just to do it."

"I know, mom."

"Then why are you giving blow jobs for fun?"

Lanie wanted that statement to be shocking. She wanted to see an upheaval of emotions: horror at being caught, worry, denial. Anything that would lead her to believe her daughter was not blowing guys for fun.

"You listened to my phone call?" The anger in her voice was unmistakable.

The shock was hers, not her daughter's. "Yes, Lexi—I listened. I stood outside your door and I listened. How can you do these things? Don't you understand? You could get hurt."

"We use condoms."

Condoms. Of course, that made everything better. "Is that all you have to say? You use condoms? Where did I go wrong with you, Lexi? How do you not see what you are doing is wrong?"

"Mom, you're making too big of a deal about this. It isn't sex—it's just oral sex. I'm being safe."

She couldn't listen anymore. She kept picturing Lexi as a little girl. Her twin pigtails tied in blue satin ribbons. She was missing her front teeth and saying with a Cindy Brady lisp, *It's okay, mommy, I use condoms.* She stood. "You are grounded until further notice."

Lexi's mouth dropped open. "You can't do that. It's not fair!"

"I can and I did. This discussion is not over, not by a long shot. Now, if you're smart, you'll keep your mouth shut before I decide to share the details of your private life with your father."

Lanie watched Lexi flare her nostrils, but her mouth stayed shut. She turned to leave the room.

"What do I have to do to be ungrounded?" Lexi cried out in desperation.

Lanie's mind spun. What was her goal in all this? Besides having Lexi go back to a pre-blow job stage and having her mouth wired shut until she was twenty-one, she couldn't think of anything. "I don't know yet, but you could start by cleaning up this pigsty."

* * *

The nightmare conversation had sapped Lanie's energy. Her morning aspirations to dig out her old work faded back into the file folder of 'should do's.' Tackling dreams from a seventeen year hiatus would depress her beyond words. She cast her vision outside. The sun was out and the air was sure to be warm. She decided to take a ride to see Bob at work.

It was a short ride down I-355 to the dealership. Skipping the air, she rolled down the windows to catch the breeze. Chicago winters lasted an eternity; better to catch the light and warmth now. Something she could hold in her memory bank and recall on the long, dark days. Cranking the volume on the radio, she sang at the top of her lungs. It always made her feel better to belt out a few tunes. Gawkers be damned. The wind whipped her hair across her face, and she marveled at what a good dye job could do for the quality of her tresses. Instead of a harsh sting, the locks were a soft tickle. Not to mention the looks she was getting from those around her. If she kept her eyes on the road and avoided glancing at her reflection in the mirror, she could almost believe she was in her twenties again, or at least in her early thirties.

By the time the Explorer rolled into the dealership lot, she was feeling like a new woman. It had been so long since she cut loose, she had forgotten how the little things could make the biggest difference. Who needed fur coats or big diamonds when some Jefferson Airplane and the sun on your skin was a choice? She pulled into the empty employee of the month parking space and ran up to the door.

It was locked. She looked back at the lot—there was nobody there. Not a single customer browsing, not one sales person watching traffic, and the lights were out. She pressed her nose to the glass, but it was no use. The blinds were closed. She couldn't see a thing. Bob had to be in the back, tucked away in his office. The lot wasn't open for sales, which was admittedly odd. He must have closed an extra day to run numbers. When she was the head secretary, everything was finished promptly. They never closed. But then again, she was a secretary, not arm candy. Pulling the key ring from her purse, she found one that opened the front door and let herself in.

It was dark. The bell that sat on top of the frame rang, its dainty jingle lost in the cavern of quiet black. She put out her hand to feel for the desk that she knew would be right in front of her waiting to catch her shin and send pain shooting up her leg. She found the back of the chair and worked her way around the heavy wooden furniture.

A slice of light at the back of the showroom caught her attention. The bluish glow seeped under the door giving her direction without illumination. It was Bob's office. He'd switched all the desk lamps over to CFL bulbs to save money. Her vision adjusted and she was able to move without fear of being maimed. Crossing the room, she covered the distance and climbed the two steps to his door in less than ten seconds. Papers rustled on the other side of the Walnut wood. He'd be sitting at his desk, a pencil tucked between his teeth, going over last month's numbers. She knew each crease of his forehead by touch. How many times had she come across him doing the monthly numbers and run her fingers along those folds, straddled his lap, and ground her hips against his to take his mind off the stress? Too many to count. The memory wakened the beast inside her. Heat radiated from her groin. The day he opened the dealership, they had christened the desk that he was sitting at right now. Today felt like the perfect time for a repeat.

"Oh, Bob—oh, God!"

She froze with her hand on the knob. He moaned. Such a familiar sound. How many times had he made that very same sound when she was the one sending spine tingling pleasure through his limbs? And how many, she wondered, when it was someone else? *Open the door. See it for yourself.*

She pulled her hand away as if she'd been burned. She didn't need to see. She already knew. The voice in the office was the same as the voice from the mystery call. The voice that answered the phones here every day for the last two years with a very perky, *'Bob the Bulldog's, how may I direct your call?'* The voice that went with the long, tan legs and the very blond extensions. The voice that was only a few years older than their daughter.

The heat that she had felt seconds ago turned to ice. Lanie began to shiver. Her teeth chattered uncontrollably. The sound of clattering porcelain was so loud in her head that she feared being caught. Then what? Would they open the door, naked or half clothed—oh, God, which was worse? She took a step back. She had to get out of there, go home, think...

She missed the first step. Her foot twisted underneath her. A sharp crack rang in her ears as she went down. Pain, worse than what she remembered of being in labor, shot through her leg. *Don't pass out—they'll find you!* She begged as she lost sight of the light and her brain threatened to go dark.

From there, it became a scene from a bad movie. The B-rated kind, where there are no famous players and everyone tries to make up for it by overacting. She yelped. She couldn't help it. Her ankle was broken. No way a sprain could hurt that much. Her body crumpled in a heap on the floor. The size of her frame, combined with lack of reaction due to the shock of hearing her husband fucking his secretary, made it a rather obnoxious fall.

"What the hell was that?"

It was Brittney, stopped somewhere in mid coitus.

"Shut up. Put your clothes on."

Bob. Panicking, no doubt.

She should have been pissed, flaming beyond words, but all she could think about was getting the hell out of there before they came out and saw her. Miss Manners never wrote a book that covered how to catch your spouse cheating and walk away looking good. Being the person that was cheated on gave her the upper hand; but she was a mess. Her ankle throbbed. She had started crying, and she was dirty from landing on the floor. If they found her in this state, she would look a fool. Putting her weight on her hands and knees she crawled back toward the front door. Behind her, she heard the office door fly open and slam into the wall. Lanie dove under the nearest desk to avoid being seen. Through the legs of the rolling desk chair she could make out Bob's shape. He stood in a Superman pose. His fists balled and pressed into his hips, just above his boxer shorts. Next to him stood tiny Brittney. Other than the long button down men's shirt she had thrown on to cover her breasts, she was naked. Her hands encompassed Bob's bicep. He turned and grabbed something from inside the door frame. Lanie squinted trying to figure out what he was holding. He wrapped both hands around the tip. Long, like a cylinder. It had to be a baseball bat.

She bit her lip to keep from emitting an audible sob. She wasn't sure what hurt more, the fact that her ankle would need to be in a cast for the next six weeks, or the fact that her husband was so goddamn cocky that it never occurred to him that she might catch him. Oh no, not Bob the Bulldog Jackerson. He was way, too smooth. It had to be a robbery in progress. Bastard.

He flipped the switch next to the door flooding the room in a yellow, fluorescent glow. She scooted back, trying to fold her limbs into the minute cave under the desk. Her body was twice the size of the space—she was sunk. He was sure to see her, half in and half out. Would he have the guts to call her out? What on earth could he possibly say? He'd find something snarky. Then she'd be forced to say something in retaliation. Something that would allow her to keep the tiny shreds that were left of her dignity. It would end in a dramatic scene that rivaled anything the daytime soaps could produce. Too bad it was real. There was no golden

Emmy waiting for her next spring. She took a deep breath. Maybe she should just give up. She could pop up from behind the desk and scare the shit out of both of them—

Bob's gaze stopped on something on the floor. His expression went from concern to surprise. He pushed Brittney back into the office. "Go back in and get your stuff. We're done for today."

"Okay." She sounded deflated, pouty even, but she went.

He closed the door shutting Brittney in the office. "I know you are here, Lanie. Go home. I'll meet you there and we can talk this out." Without another word he went back into the office, latching the door behind him.

Fuck. How did he know it was me? She scanned the floor for a telltale sign. And there it was. Sitting just off to the side of the door, open with all its contents strewn about on the floor. The brand new Coach purse.

CHAPTER SEVEN

After crawling back to her car, Lanie realized that she was stuck. Her broken ankle was on her right foot. She wouldn't risk driving with her left. A car accident was something she didn't want to add to the day's list of events. Afraid that Bob and Brittney would come out and see her in the lot, she pulled out her cell phone and dialed.

Suni picked up on the first ring. Lanie could tell that she was at the skate park with the boys. The sounds of screaming and laughing were so loud that she had to plug her other ear to try and make out what Suni was saying. The throbbing in her ankle was unbearable. She put her leg up on the passenger seat of the Explorer. Bruises were already forming a purple ring where her foot met her calf, the swelling making it impossible to determine where one ended and the other began.

"What's wrong, Lanie? You sound like hell."

"I think I broke my ankle. I need a ride to the hospital."

"Where are you?"

She paused. Logic told her that once Suni knew where she was she would start to ask the obvious questions. The ones that Lanie didn't want to answer. But she had no choice. The longer she waited in the lot, the more likely a run in with Brittney became.

"I'm at the dealership." She bit her lip praying that Suni wouldn't ask.

"North and Main, right?"

"Yes. Can you drop Charlie off at home first?" If Suni brought him, he would ask about Bob. With her luck, he would see his car—or him. She couldn't deal with that.

"Not a problem. Sit tight, I'll be right there."

Lanie hung up and sank down in her seat hiding herself from any prying eyes that might peek through the blinds. She'd been hiding so much lately that she wondered if she should become a spy in her spare time. She was the invisible woman in the room. People passed her every day, but no one ever saw her. It was so unfair. She gave up everything to become a part of something bigger, and now, in one harsh slap across the face, she discovered that what she had really done was lose herself for a gigantic loser. A cradle robber that would go on to live a comfortable life while she was stuck in an empty shell with a broken ankle to boot.

She reached up over her shoulder and hit the lock button—just in case.

* * *

Suni didn't ask. She stayed silent during the drive to Good Samaritan hospital. Patted her on the shoulder when she got the news that it wasn't a break after all—just a sprain. According to the doctor, it wasn't even a bad sprain. Just a run-of-the-mill, take-a-few-days-off variety. And, like any good friend, Suni retrieved her Escalade so Lanie could be returned home to rest.

Once Lanie had been hoisted up by the strong, male orderly and the door was shut, Suni broke her silence. "Do you want to go home?"

Lanie took a deep breath. She did not want to go home. By now Bob had returned and discovered—from talking to Lexi—that she was in the emergency room having her ankle x-rayed. The fact that he hadn't shown up at the hospital to check on her led her to believe that he thought it was a ploy for sympathy. Coming home without a cast would only strengthen his delusions.

"No." She did not want to go home. The sad reality was, she had nowhere else to go.

Suni maneuvered out of the circular drive and onto the road.

"You're coming home with me. After a day like today, you need a drink."

Lanie leaned back resting her head on the cushioned headrest and closed her eyes. She did, in fact, need a drink.

* * *

"Take a sip. It will calm your nerves."

Lanie was propped up on a chocolate-colored, suede couch in what appeared to be Suni's private hideaway. She knew it couldn't be her master bedroom—that was on the second story of her house. This was some sort of guest bedroom on steroids. It was set off the main living area, or media room, as Suni liked to call it. In one corner, there was a round bed adorned in what Lanie could swear was mink. The rest of the room was filled with luxurious furniture, the kind that she had only seen in episodes of *Lifestyles of the Rich and Famous*. The walls were papered in cream satin. The room was bathed in a soft glow from an ornate overhead chandelier. There was a marble bathroom and a walk in closet along one wall. And no windows. Not even a slit of natural daylight. The bat cave wasn't as secretive as this room. Even the entrance was hidden by a carefully placed tropical plant that was taller than Lanie.

Bubbles gathered around the sprig of crushed mint. Her nose caught the scent of the Gin before her lips touched the rim. A Mojito. Good and strong, just the way she liked. The first sip burned her throat. It always did. The sweetness of the sugar chased the burn. If only there was a salve that could do the same for her life. How nice it would be to have something sweet follow the pain of this day. She ran her tongue over her lips pulling the last of the granules into her mouth.

Warmth spread through her outer limbs pulling her back from the brink of a full-blown panic attack. She downed the rest of the drink without stopping for air. "Thanks."

Suni pried the empty glass out of her hand. Setting it on top of the large, matching, chocolate ottoman, she curled up on the leopard print chaise directly across from Lanie. "You ready to talk yet?"

"I fell down a step inside the store..." There was so much more there. Suni knew it. Lanie could tell she was just waiting for her to spill the rest. She wanted to get it out, share it with somebody, but she just couldn't do it.

"Lanie, what is it that you want?"

What did she want? She wanted her life back. She wanted herself back. She wanted her husband to keep his dick in his pants. "I don't know."

Suni tapped her front tooth. Pulling out her cell phone she dialed. "Yvette, get Betts and get over here. We have an emergency."

* * *

The two-lady wrecking crew arrived before Lanie had a chance to finish her second drink. She was planning on getting good and sauced before the day was out. There was nothing to stop her. The kids didn't need her to drive them anywhere. She couldn't even walk. Might as well drink.

Yvette eyed her with the same scornful look that she always had when Lanie came into her sightline. Babette's face seemed to be full of pity as she watched Lanie throw back more gin. She didn't care. They could think whatever they wanted. Her life was a joke. The opinions of the PTA moms were the least of her concerns.

Suni came back with a large mug of coffee and set it on the ottoman, gently pulling the glass away from Lanie's lips. "Easy, lady. I think we need to move on to coffee time."

Lanie didn't want coffee. She wanted to blur everything with gin and worry about coffee tomorrow morning. She looked with longing at the empty glass that Suni had passed to Babette for safe keeping. Yvette caught her lusting after the empty glass and mouthed the words 'no way.' Damn Yvette, always acting as Suni's henchman. She begrudgingly took the coffee.

Suni smiled approvingly and patted her on the arm. "Good choice, Lanie." She threw herself back on the spotted chaise. "Ladies, as I told you over the phone, we have a problem. A pretty serious problem if you ask me."

"What's that, Sugar?" Babette asked, climbing up to perch on the edge of the chocolate loveseat. Yvette kept her distance, choosing to sit on on the bed. Lanie didn't like it that Yvette was now behind her. She could feel her eyes drilling into the back of her skull.

"Lanie doesn't know what she wants."

Babette nodded. "That is serious."

Yvette said nothing, but Lanie guessed she was mouthing something to Suni. Probably *'pathetic.'*

Babette ran her manicured nail along the inside of Lanie's coveted gin glass. Popping it in her mouth, she slurped off the syrup. "How'd you hurt your ankle, Sugar?"

"I fell off a step."

"She was at Bulldog's when she fell. Called me to come get her."

Babette raised her eyebrow, but said nothing. Lanie didn't get it. What was all this concern about her falling down? They weren't there. They didn't hear Bob fucking his secretary. What possible concern could they have? So what if she told them she didn't know what she wanted?

Yvette had gotten up off the bed at some point in her usual stealthy, quiet way. She stood in front of Lanie. Her svelte figure a ramrod for Suni's pet projects. "You are not that stupid, Lanie. Nobody is that stupid. Now, what do you want?"

Lanie felt the rage. It started deep inside her belly, just below her navel in the same spot that she had felt lust just the night before. It tore up her gut, climbing into her throat before spilling out of her lips. "I want her dead. I want that little fucking whore that destroyed my marriage put in a box and set in the ground. And as for Bob—I want him castrated!"

Babette's eyes went wide. She knew she sounded crazy, like a lunatic that had been released before her meds kicked in, but she couldn't stop. "I want his balls cut off. I want my daughter to stop blowing every guy that looks at her twice. And I want myself back. I want every part of me that I gave up for a big pile of lies back—intact." She stopped. She was out of breath. Tears streamed down her cheeks. She felt something she hadn't felt in years—relief. She'd shared her most private sufferings and the world had not ended. Nobody came in with a straight jacket to take her away.

Yvette crouched down in front of her and smacked her bright, red lacquered lips together. "Now we are getting somewhere."

WEDNESDAY, AUGUST 30TH

It had been a long night. After her first outburst things had unraveled fast. Under Suni's watchful eye and Yvette's coaching, she had called Bob and calmly explained that after her surprise discovery at the dealership that morning she had decided it would be best if she took some time to think things over—alone. She would not give him a time or day that she would return, only the promise that she would. At that time of her choosing, they would talk about what had happened—or not—she hadn't decided. Somehow she managed to remain flat during her monologue. Yvette had been insistent that she show zero emotion. If she acted like she cared, he got the upper hand. If she acted like she was in charge, she was. It worked. She could hear the frustration and what she thought might have been a note of fear in his voice. It should not have been such a shock. He'd been doing it to her for years.

Then Suni had really laid it on her. "He's done it before, Lanie. Many times over the years. You need to come to grips with the truth. The PTA couldn't stand by and watch him humiliate you. That's why I cornered you after the morning coffee. "

"Cheating?" How could that be? How many years?

Suni nodded. "I've known for the last four years. Might even have been longer."

Brittney had only been working there for two years. That meant there had been someone else before her, and maybe someone before that. Four years ago, Charlie had just turned five and was starting kindergarten. Lexi was beginning her high school career. What had she been doing back then? The dealership was doing well and the kids were in school. That's when it hit her. She'd been drinking.

That's when it had started. Her nightly glass of wine that soon turned into two and then later a whole bottle. But why? *Because Bob wasn't there.* That was when he stopped coming home. He stopped paying attention to her as a person and started treating her like a paid employee. One without the sexual benefits that Brittney seemed to be enjoying on a regular basis. That had happened before her drinking got bad. It wasn't an excuse—but it was an explanation.

"Bob was the one who suggested I come to the coffee that day."

Suni shrugged. "Sure, after we sent Yvette over to get some maintenance on her Lexus. She was there awhile. It gave her plenty of time to chat with Bob about what a great group of ladies we are."

Babette raised her glass. "We sure are, Sugar."

"Why me?" There had to be plenty of women in the western suburbs who had shitty husbands.

"Why not you? My God, Lanie—you really are lost! Don't you see how great you are? You are a beautiful, strong woman. You let yourself go. And for what? A cheating spouse and an ungrateful teenager? A house in the suburbs and all the wine you can drink? I researched you. You graduated from The Art Institute at the top of your class. What happened to your passion?"

She was still passionate, wasn't she? Why just that morning she had been considering pulling out her sketch book. But then Lexi had dropped her bomb about hooking up and—oh God. Suni was right. She had lost her passion. "I don't know." She confessed.

Yvette snorted from the bed. "It went right out the window with your dignity."

Suni waved her hand at Yvette to shut her up. "When I took over the job as president of the PTA, I had been through the ringer and come out the other side. I wanted to take what I had learned and use it to help other women. Why should we be held hostage as wives and mothers while the men have all the power and fun? So I started looking at what skills we had. I figured out ways we could take our knowledge and create something big. More powerful than the corporate world. Now, I spend my time seeking out women who want to be part of our mission. Everybody has some skill they can contribute to our cause."

Cause and mission were kind words to describe the blackmail she had heard them discussing at their first meeting in Suni's bright, yellow kitchen. "What cause? Blackmailing the football coach to keep a kid that is flunking summer school on the team doesn't qualify as a mission. If they turned you in to the cops, you could go to jail."

From behind, Yvette laughed. "Yes, Suni," she drawled from the fur bedspread. "How do you plan to keep us from going to jail?"

Babette smoothed the front of her pleated capri's and waved her finger at Yvette. "Don't be mean. Poor thing—she's been through enough."

Suni pointed at her. "Lanie Jackerson, when you signed on to become one of us, you joined more than a ladies' social club. You raised your hand before God and country and joined the PTA mafia. We are women, we are powerful, and we are not fucking around."

*   *   *

If a sprain hurt this much, Lanie never wanted to experience a break. Twelve hours in bed with an ice pack did nothing to alleviate the pain. She had to crawl to get to the door. Crutches would have been a good idea. If her brain hadn't gone into hibernation, she would have asked for them at the hospital. She'd have to get somebody to drive her to the medical supply store on Main to rent some. Using the door handle for leverage, she pulled her weight up.

It was locked. Lanie rattled the knob, twisting and turning it forcefully, but it only moved a fraction of an inch in either direction. She was a prisoner. Granted, the cell that she was being kept in was palatial, but it was still a cell. No windows, no phone, no alternate means of escape. She pounded on the door. The echo of her fist hitting the wood bounced off the shiny marble in the bathroom and drummed in her ears.

Shit. It was no use. She was stuck until Suni came back to let her out. She had been given her strict instructions about what types of interaction were allowed between her and Bob. Clearly, Suni was worried she wouldn't follow directions, hence the locked door. It was Wednesday afternoon. The kids had school and Bob would have to reopen the dealership, eventually. If she didn't go home soon, he might decide that she was gone for good and move his floozy in. Standing made her ankle scream in pain. She gave up and went back to her perch on the round, fur covered, porn star bed.

She hadn't had this much time to herself in seventeen years. Stretched out on the mink bedspread, she replayed the events of the previous night.

PTA Mafia. Those had been Suni's exact words to describe the Herschel Grammar School group. It sounded so absurd. Lanie had laughed when she heard it. She was the only one. Yvette went on the attack. She launched herself at Lanie, casually wrapping her arms around her from behind. Her hands came to rest on either side of her collarbone. Lanie felt the dagger nails dig into the base of her throat. It was just enough to cause panic and a small amount of physical discomfort.

"I told you she wasn't a good choice."

Suni stared over Lanie to Yvette. "She is new. Give her time."

Yvette dug her nails in deeper, releasing her grasp just as Lanie was about to cry out and grab at the hands around her neck.

Rubbing the spot where she had been clawed, Lanie looked behind her. Yvette had moved back to the bed, where she laid as cozy as a Cheshire cat. *How the hell does she do that?*

Suni drew her attention away from Yvette. "You told us what you want, Lanie. We have the power to make those things happen. All you have to do is say the word and we will set things in motion."

"Are you talking about killing people?" Was she nuts? Bob was a world class asshole, but she didn't really want him dead.

"Isn't that what you want, Sugar?" Babette interjected. "You said you wanted him castrated and 'that little whore put in a box in the ground'..."

"*Fucking whore.*" Yvette clucked. "You forgot the 'fucking' part."

Babette winked. "Right, Sugar, how could I forget?"

They all sat there, staring intensely at Lanie, like she was a science experiment ready to explode or a trained monkey ready to dance. Lanie blinked. She was afraid to laugh. She was also afraid to speak. If this wasn't a joke, then she was in real trouble. Because that would mean that this absurd discussion, the one about killing her husband's love toy and cutting off his balls was the real deal. If that were the case, then these women were more than just oversexed housewives that liked to bully people into doing what they wanted for kicks—they were murderers.

"What if I made a mistake?" She choked out.

Yvette sighed. "That would be a shame."

"What kind of shame?" She continued nervously. "The kind of shame like, 'oh shoot I was looking forward to that,' or the kind of shame where I don't walk out of here alive?"

Suni laughed. "Lanie, we aren't animals. We don't turn on each other!"

"So you don't want her dead? You don't want him castrated?" Babette asked looking confused.

"No. I don't want anyone in a box in the ground. As much as castration sounds fitting for Bob, I don't really want that, either."

"Then, Sugar...we are right back where we started. We have to figure out what it is that you do want."

"Can we come up with some kind of punishment—something humiliating and awful that won't put me behind bars for life if I get caught?"

Babette smiled. "I think we could arrange that. What do you think, Suni—a wakeup call, or total annihilation?"

"I vote for total annihilation." Suni said matter-of-factly.

"But no one dies, and no one commits any felonies, right?" Lanie needed to know that whatever happened, she wouldn't end up on the six o'clock news in an orange jumpsuit.

"Don't worry, you'll be safe. No one will die, or be maimed. But when we are finished with them, death will look like a walk in the park compared to what they are left with."

Babette turned to Lanie. "What do you think, Sugar? Total, wipe-the-floor-with-your–sorry-ass annihilation sound good to you?"

Lanie chewed her lip. The effects of the gin were long out of her system, making the decision to mop the floor with Bob just slightly harder than it would have been with a nice, fuzzy buzz. On cue, her ankle sent a shooting pain up her leg. "Total annihilation."

"Hot dog! Suni, we have got ourselves a plan!"

"I still think it's a shame," Yvette purred from the bed. "I wanted to be the one to do the castrating."

CHAPTER EIGHT

"**Wake up, sunshine. You have a plane to catch.**"

Lanie opened her eyes. Going over the events of the night before, she must have fallen back asleep. Suni hunched over her, plane tickets in her hand. "Plane? Suni, I can't leave. Who will take care of Charlie?"

Suni reached out and pulled her up. "I will. He's staying here while you're gone."

Lanie swung her legs over the side of the bed. The throbbing picked up right where it had left off a few hours earlier. "No. Seriously, that's a nice offer, but I can't."

"Staying isn't an option for you, not now, Lanie. You have to be gone for awhile. Keep the heat off."

She opened her mouth to protest when Charlie burst through the door. "Mom! Is it true? Do I get to stay with Ajay? That's so cool!" He threw his body into her arms giving her a quick hug. "What happened to your foot?"

She kissed his curls. "I fell. It's just a sprain. Didn't your dad tell you?"

He shook his head, pulling away from her. "He said you would come home today, but he didn't say you were hurt."

Of course not, why would he? Wouldn't want to risk too many questions. "Where is he now?" She asked trying to sound casual.

"He went to work early."

"Charlie, why don't you go on up to Ajay's room and unpack your stuff?" Suni suggested. "We have a trampoline in the backyard, a pool table in the basement, a Wii in the media room…"

He ran off without waiting for her to finish. Suni held her hand out in front of her admiring her perfect manicure. "He's with her right now. He doesn't care where his son is. He doesn't care that you caught them. All he cares about is getting laid."

"What if he thinks I kidnapped Charlie? Or files paperwork with an attorney claiming that I abandoned the kids?"

"He won't. Yvette has been assigned to handling Bob. After today, he wouldn't even consider it." She threw the tickets down on the bed. "Don't you want to see where you're going?"

Lanie was afraid to look. Looking meant seeing, and seeing meant wanting. She was sure that Suni only picked good travel destinations—being on the lam included.

"Don't be a baby, Lanie—look."

She picked up the tickets. Chicago O'Hare to McCarran International Airport. "Las Vegas?"

"You sound disappointed. Don't be. I have a very close friend that has a custom Platinum level suite at the Venetian. You will *love* it."

Lanie had never been to Vegas. In her mind it ranked the same as going to Disney World. Something she knew she should do, but had very little desire to make happen. It just didn't call to her. "I don't know, maybe I should rethink this. Lexi is in a teen crisis. I need to get a game plan together to keep her from becoming a statistic for teen pregnancy."

Suni rolled her eyes and shook her head. "No time for that now. We are past the point of no return. Betts is on the Lexi issue. She'll keep her in line."

No return. Her life had reached past the point of no return in just about every aspect. Her marriage, her self esteem, her plans to go back to her art, all of it was so far past the point of no return that she wondered if the Road Runner had scooped it up and taken to the desert. Maybe it was all waiting for her in Vegas. She suspected anything she found there would be a mirage. At least she could take some comfort in the fact that Babette had stepped up for her with Lexi. It was a copout she would gladly take.

Besides, being away for a few days couldn't hurt. She'd never left the kids before. Maybe her absence would make them appreciate her more. "What time is my flight?"

"Six o'clock. Your limo will be here in twenty minutes to take you to O'Hare. I booked you a first class ticket, so don't buy any nasty airport food. When you arrive there will be another limo waiting to take you to the hotel..."

She looked down at her clothing. Her jeans were covered in dirt from crash landing on the showroom floor. Her shirt was stained and smelled of sweat. "What about my stuff? I don't have anything packed."

Suni walked to the closet and pulled out a rolling carryon bag with a freshly pressed blouse and slacks hanging from the handle. "I took the liberty of getting some things together for you."

Lanie eyed the bag with the outfit dangling off of it. The clothes were new. She could see the tags with the Chico's label blowing gently in the breeze from the palm frond blades of the ceiling fan. They were expensive. Probably another gift from one of Suni's protégés. "That's not my stuff."

Suni pushed the bag closer to the edge of the bed. "It is now."

"Where did it come from?"

"The store in town. Betts picked it up late last night. I put it in the closet while you were sleeping."

"Who paid for it?" She knew, even before she asked, that no one paid for it. Not with cash anyway.

Suni flared her nostrils and crossed her arms across her chest. "This is no time to develop a conscience. Put on the clean clothes, get into the limo, go to Vegas and enjoy yourself. When things settle down here, we will bring you back. Then you can slip back into your life, minus the slut your husband has been porking in his office."

The comment did what it was supposed to—hurt like hell. It was almost enough to smother her concerns about taking things that were obtained criminally. Still, her morals clamored to the forefront of her consciousness. "What if I don't go? What happens then?"

Suni's face went from warm and welcoming to ice. "You're going."

Lanie shuddered. She was used to Yvette's threats. She hadn't expected Suni to follow suit. It was as if her questions had flipped a switch and released a monster. She ran her hands over the gooseflesh on her arms. "You said no one would get hurt."

Suni's expression stayed the same. Cold. She lowered herself, lining her nose up with Lanie's. "I picked you for this group. I put my reputation on the line for you. I'd hate to have to have you eliminated. "

The word *eliminated* unraveled the last of her nerves. Her teeth began to chatter uncontrollably. Lanie knew she was in deep, deep shit. Anyone who could turn on and off their emotions so easily would have no trouble eliminating someone who crossed her. She'd probably follow it up with a black tie charity dinner. That way she could rake in millions from people who owed her favors. Keep her pristine public image while crushing people on her way to the top. It was insane.

And now she was one of them. She'd taken the clothes, the purse and the oath. If she backed out now, she might be next. Or worse, her children. Bob's death she could live with. If someone had to die, it should be him. But Lexi and Charlie? No, she would never let that happen. "I'll go."

Satisfied that Lanie was her puppet, Suni turned to leave. When she reached the door, she gave Lanie one final parting blow. "Don't worry. I'll take good care of Charlie until you get back."

The door closed and the key slid into the lock. Fifteen minutes until the limo arrived. With her bad ankle, it would take every second to roll herself into the new outfit Suni's minions had stolen for her. Suni had her kids, so for now she would play along. The minute she had a chance to make a break and go for help—she was out. Maybe that would be before Bob and Brittney were destroyed, maybe after. With a little luck it would be after.

* * *

The limo was a stretch, black with tinted windows. Lanie closed the panel between her and the driver and turned on the cell phone Suni had handed her after she hugged Charlie goodbye. It was probably bugged. A fact that she considered for a millisecond before dialing Bob's cell—no answer. Hanging up she dialed the house. The machine clicked on after the fourth ring, she hung up. Any message was sure to be intercepted by Yvette before Bob would get it. Lexi was her last try before the cops. Lanie was doubtful she'd answer. She had probably run off to a girlfriend's as soon as she heard that Lanie wasn't going to be home for a few days. Happy to be free from her grounding and her room cleaning. Free to engage in free love. Everything was free and easy for Lexi Marie Jackerson. She dialed the number and waited.

"Hello, Sugar—how's the limo?"

Shit. It was Babette. "Is Lexi there?" She asked trying to sound casual.

"Sorry, Sugar, I can't let you talk to her."

Double shit. Suni must have called to warn her about Lanie's new, sober conscience. "I didn't get to say goodbye to her...can't you just let me say goodbye? Come on, Babette, have some sympathy. I've never been away from the kids before."

Babette sighed into the mouthpiece. "If Suni finds out I let you talk to her she'll tan my hide."

"She won't find out. I promise."

"No funny business, you hear me? If you even breathe one word about needing help, or going to the police, or anything, I'll come get you myself."

Before she could promise, Lexi was on the other end of the line, as surly and irritating as ever. "What?"

She let out her breath. "Lexi." She was okay. One hundred and fifty percent annoying teen. Without bodily harm from the Mafia moms.

"I cleaned my room, you can even check—

"I'm not calling about that."

"Oh." She sounded deflated, like she wanted the fight.

"When was the last time you saw dad?"

"I dunno. This morning?"

"Early? Before he left for work?"

"Mom, I don't know—God. Why are you always so bitchy?"

Lanie wished she had spent more time washing out her daughter's mouth with soap when she was younger. "Damnit, Lexi, this is important!

When was that the last time you saw him?"

"I told you, I don't remember."

"When did you go to Sonja's?" If she could figure out what time Babette and her daughter had kidnapped Lexi, she could construct a timeline for the cops when they found Bob's lifeless body. *I spoke to my daughter on the way to the airport. She said she had lunch with her dad at noon...*

"I spent the night. Dad said I could go. He said you weren't coming home and it was okay."

Well that was no help to her alibi. "Did you talk to him on the phone today?"

"No. Mom—I gotta go. Sonja's mom is taking us shopping for homecoming dresses."

"When you see your dad, give him this number. Tell him to call me right away."

"It came up blocked."

Of course it did. Suni was one step ahead of her. "When I hang up, hit redial."

"That won't work."

"Don't argue with me. Just try. If it works, save the number."

Lanie could hear her eyeballs rolling as she sighed out her painful answer. "Fine."

"Check on your brother every day until I'm home. Promise me you'll do that."

"Can I take your car? Dad said you left it on the lot."

Brat. She was trying to use her car as a bargaining chip. Lanie had no choice. If she wanted Lexi's cooperation, she would have to give her what she wanted. "If you promise to check on Charlie and keep me updated."

"Sure, mom. Whatever. I really gotta go. Sonja's mom is waiting in the car."

"Lexi—one more thing—keep your mouth and legs closed around the boys. If I hear anymore trash talk about late night activities, there won't be a homecoming dance—got it?"

The silence on the other end of the phone was deafening. Lexi was probably considering her options. She had no idea where Lanie was, or when she'd be back for that matter. Was it worth the risk that she might swoop in and ruin her homecoming? Lanie decided to drive her advantage home. "I'm serious. No messing around. I told Sonja's mom to keep a very close eye on you."

"Fine. Bye."

There was a click and the line went dead. Pulling the phone away from her ear, she checked the display. Call ended. She won. She hadn't won an argument with Lexi—well ever. From the time her daughter learned how to speak around her golden spoon, she'd been taking Lanie to task. Talking at her. Around her. Down to her. In any other set of circumstances, she would have claimed this as a major victory. Now it just felt small.

She found the icon for the phone contacts and pushed it with her index finger. There were three numbers: Suni, Babette and Yvette. Her new best friends and captors. Who else could she reach? Bob's phone had rung endlessly. It was time for a test. She dialed 911 and hit the call button. Busy. She dialed zero and hit the call button. Busy. The person that rigged this phone must have owed Suni big time. At least she'd given her call privileges for Lexi and Bob. Fat lot of good it did her.

The wallpaper was interesting. It was a picture of Lexi and Charlie. An old one from a few summers back when they still liked each other and they still took family vacations. It was the year they went to Disney. Both kids had on their twin sets of ears. Bob was tucked in between, an arm around each kid. His smile looked genuine. A great fake. If Suni hadn't dumped the four plus years of cheating knowledge in her lap, she never would have known their marriage was a lie. If the dealership ever went under, he could always be an actor.

To get that picture on the phone Suni had gone through her personal belongings. The family photos weren't in books; she wasn't organized enough for that. But they were in boxes. She hid them on the highest shelf in the front hall closet. Out of sight out of mind. If she didn't see them, they couldn't haunt her. She loved her kids, she just wasn't a scrapbooking fiend like the other suburbanite moms. The last time she'd gone to the trouble of pulling them out was when Charlie put together his 'All About Me' page in Kindergarten. They'd been in her house. They'd been through her things. That picture was a warning. *Watch out, Lanie. We're everywhere. We have access to everything.*

Her finger hovered over the red power button. Lexi hadn't called back. More likely she had tried, but the call was unable to be completed due to the blocked number. Unless she wanted to try Bob again, it was best to turn it off to conserve battery power. Something white on the corner of the screen caught her attention. It was next to the picture. Lint? *What the hell?* She scrolled down and zoomed in. It was a torn piece of paper with writing on it.

If you want them to live call no one except me. 630. 555. 8269.

The picture on the wallpaper hadn't been uploaded to the phone. It was a picture of the picture, taken by the phone. She double checked the contact list. That wasn't Suni's number. It didn't match her henchmen either. Who the hell had posted a picture of her kids with an ominous message? She squinted at the screen looking for a hint of the perpetrator. She was about to give up when she saw something in the lower left corner of the paper. Small, red, out of focus and impossible to name. It reminded her of the micro photography contests they had in college. Lanie always lost. Her eyesight had been keen back then. Now she wore bifocals. No way she'd be able to identify the miniscule blob.

A throbbing headache was starting behind her eyes. Her ankle pulsated, keeping time with her heart. *Probably a test* she decided. Suni's way of seeing if she was going to try and escape or turn her in. She turned the phone off, threw it back into her purse and leaned back in the leather seats closing her eyes. She was screwed. Suni Calverson wanted her in the PTA Mafia. The destruction of her cheating husband and his girlfriend was the only acceptable means to ensure her loyalty. She just hoped that Suni would keep her promise not to commit any felonies that involved death and prison.

CHAPTER NINE

McCarran International Airport was a casino ghost town. Empty slot machines lined the walls. No amount of flashing lights or signs boasting of big winnings could entice fresh meat to the stools. Only a few hard core gamblers sat among the rows. Most appeared worn beyond reason. Losers that took solace in a last ditch effort to win back their money before the journey home. Lanie hadn't checked in any luggage. The bag from Suni was an exquisite Hartman that fit easily into the overhead bin. She skipped the baggage claim and headed straight to the tram that would deliver her to the main terminal.

The flight had been full and delayed by an hour, putting the time at half past eleven. Even though she'd slept until noon, she felt tired. Probably a side effect of all the stress and drama of the day. The rest of the passengers seemed to be familiar with the layout of the place and with the ins and outs of Vegas in general. Lanie overheard groups traveling together talking about their vacation plans; what shows they wanted to see, which casinos didn't water down their drinks, and where the best pools were located to sleep off their hangovers. She kept her ears open and her eyes on the ground. It was tough to keep up with her swollen ankle. The Ace bandage did little to stop the throbbing. She'd been tempted to get a wheelchair, but decided against it when she realized nobody under ninety used one. The doctor at the hospital had encouraged movement as tolerated. As long as she kept her weight leaning to the left, she could hobble. Ice would be the first thing she picked up when she reached her final destination.

The herd moved through the automatic doors, out of the climate controlled air conditioning and onto the street, splintering into small groups that disappeared into shuttles. The humidity, even at the edge of midnight, was intense. The change was too much for her lungs—they constricted forcing her to switch to shallow breathing. Alone, she scanned the street for the limo Suni promised. Once the shuttles cleared the street, it was easy enough to find. A white stretch with blue, fluorescent, running lights and a fine specimen of a man holding a sign with her name on it. From a distance, he was yummy. The black tuxedo style chauffeur's uniform skimmed the outline of muscles that flexed even at rest. If his close up was anywhere near as glorious as his panoramic, she was in for a very pleasant end to a really rotten day.

Dragging her bag across the street, she made her way closer to the prince leaning on the hood of the pimp mobile. As soon as he saw her limping in his direction he ran over and made a grab for her bag. "Let me help you with that."

Up close, he was even more amazing. Dark, wavy hair, olive skin, and perfect teeth that glowed in the street lamps. A Polynesian Adonis. She pulled her bag behind her. "No, thanks, I've got it."

He frowned. "You are Elaine Jackerson, guest of Mr. Ilg?"

She was Elaine Jackerson. She didn't remember if Suni had given her the name of her host, but logic led her to the conclusion that Mr. Ilg was the man that owned the suite at the Venetian. "I am, but I can carry my own bag."

He gently pried her fingers from the handle. "Mr. Ilg would never allow it. He wants all his guests to have complete comfort while they're here."

His hands were warm, his skin soft. She had the sudden urge to wrap her body inside his black tuxedo jacket and absorb his touch. Giving in to his insistence, she let go. "Thanks..." There was no name tag on the jacket. No way for her to identify him personally. No way to roll his name over her tongue like cream. Was it wrong to pick a name so she could call him something later in her dreams? Antonio or Cesar...or anything exotic and steamy would suit her just fine.

"My pleasure." His grin was perfect. It had warmth to it. Real warmth. Not the fake crap she'd seen so many times from Bob when he was trying to close a deal. She tried to guess his age. He looked young. Not as young as Lexi, definitely legal to drink, but under twenty five. His tapered waist was trim. He hadn't hit the age when men discover that fun, extra layer around the belly button. Bob called his 'the lovin' layer.' This one still had the muscle cuts above the hip bone that she only had the pleasure of seeing in Calvin Klein underwear billboards.

Her hot, mystery man had started back to the limo with her bag tucked under his arm. She was in Vegas. A hostage to Suni and her insane group of Midwestern moms. Her children had been kidnapped until further notice and her cheating husband was about to be castrated by a set of acrylic nails. This day should have put her in the ground. At the very least, she should be a basket case. But something about finding a piece of unexpected eye candy had saved her sanity. Either that or she had really gone round the bend and this was the eye of the storm. The false calm in the middle of massive turbulence. Tucking her hair behind her ears, she took a deep breath. If she lost her mind, her life, or anything in between, at least her last memory would be of a nicely toned tush leading her into a limo. Not a bad image. Not bad at all.

*   *   *

The room was a suite. All the rooms were suites, but this one was the size of three normal suites, over two thousand square feet. She knew the square footage because the mega chatty desk clerk had shared that with her. She had also shared all kinds of other useless random information about the hotel. Her rate of speech per cheery ratio made Lanie tune her out. She was too much like little, love bunny Brittney and looking at her made Lanie feel old and out of place. She put on her much practiced *I'm listening* face, the one that she perfected when her kids were small and needed her attention for the most tear your eyes out boring topics, and drifted off dreaming of a good night's sleep. By the time chatty Kathy had finished her monologue; Lanie had been awake too long and moved into her second wind. There was no way she'd get to bed before three.

She checked her watch; 1:30 Nevada time. That meant back in Illinois, it was only 11:30. By the time her nerves unwound and she hit the sack, the sun would be coming up. Not good.

A plain white envelope with her name on it sat on the living room table. Without hesitation she tore it open. Inside was a big, fat pile of cash—all in one hundred dollar bills. Picking through the stack she counted, being watchful for sticky bills. There were thirty in all. Three thousand dollars. That was more cash than she'd ever had at one time. Twice as much as their monthly mortgage. When she passed the last bill into her left palm she found a small, sticky note written in Suni's handwriting. *Have fun.*

The words were a mockery of her situation. How could she have fun? Sure, she was in Las Vegas, the birthplace of fun. But what kind of fun was there to be had when her children were possibly in danger? The urge to waltz out on to the balcony and throw the money over the rail and into the strip below was monstrous. The money had come from some illegal activity. Taking it made her an accessory to the crime after the fact. The sad reality of the situation was that she had to take it. She had no money of her own. Suni had emptied her wallet of everything except her driver's license and insurance card. She needed the illegal green to feed herself, maybe even to buy her ticket home once she figured out how to get herself out of this mess. Stuffing a few bills into her wallet, she made a silent promise to God to donate whatever was left to charity. If he got her home safe.

Her purse was a mess. Rummaging around to make room for the bulging envelope, her hand hit the cell phone. Bob, or someone with news about Bob, would have to call eventually. She pulled it out and hit the power button. It was dead. In her hurry to get Lanie out of town, Suni must have forgotten to give the battery a full charge. She unzipped the suitcase and rummaged through the contents. No charger. She would have to buy one in the gift shop if she wanted to use the phone again. Either that or make calls on the hotel landline. Remembering the ominous message on the wallpaper, she tried to piece together who would have put it on there. Suni was the one who gave her the phone, so her first thought was that it was a test. A way for Suni to determine if Lanie was for or against her. But why put something so tiny—something she could have easily missed? If she really wanted to test her, wouldn't she have made it something obvious?

It didn't matter. She couldn't take the chance that something would happen to her children. There had to be a next step. Something that would move her further from this nightmarish situation and closer to normalcy. Every minute that ticked by brought her a minute closer to jail for being an accessory to The PTA's criminal activity. But what could she do? Go to the Nevada police? It seemed that Suni had plenty of connections here as well. If they were under her control, then she was doubly screwed. The FBI? They were definitely out of Suni's grasp, but how the hell did you get somebody from the FBI to talk to you about a roving gang of PTA moms? They would probably laugh her out of the office. Plus, she had no way to look them up. Her cell phone only called five people and the suite's phone was most likely being monitored.

Bob's number had been one of her approved contacts. One last try from the hotel phone and she would call it a night. It rang three times before a voice came on the line.

"Hello, kitten." It was Yvette. They had him.

"Let me talk to Bob."

"I can't right now. I need to talk to you."

"Not until I know he's alive. Put him on or I'm hanging up." What the hell was she doing? Of all the Mafia mom's Yvette was the most dangerous and she liked Lanie the least.

"Sorry, Lanie, no can do. Now shut up and listen. You are in very deep trouble..."

She hung up. It was a childish automatic response. She knew she was in deep trouble. Having Yvette explain to her exactly how deep was something she didn't want to hear.

* * *

FRIDAY, SEPTEMBER 1ST

Thursday had been a blur. Sleep deprived and wired beyond all reason, Lanie found herself walking the Venetian's miles of the marbled flooring. Each time she rounded the corner and found herself in the front lobby, she had the same question. *How did I get here?* After two minutes of confused oblivion, she would turn in the direction of the casino floor and start the trek again. Retracing the path through instinct, she would try to find a piece, however small, of a solution. Daylight came and went without her knowledge. When the walking had stripped the anxiety from her brain, she slept. It was short and fitful, but it was sleep.

Friday morning, she shot out of bed. She wanted to get a jump on the day and get her thinking cap tied back under her exhausted chin. The solution to her problems had eluded her; but that didn't mean she'd given up. She'd fight to the death if necessary. The hotel was alive. It didn't matter what time of the day or night you walked through the lobby, it was always the same. People that were zoned into the machines of the casino with their blinking lights, the Grand Luxe Café full of diners, and the constant din of noise louder than the grade school Halloween carnival.

In an attempt at rejuvenation, Lanie treated herself to a large breakfast at the café. The buffet had exotic fruit, the orange juice was fresh squeezed, and the coffee was the good kind; the kind she could never replicate at home. She drank three cups loaded with cream and sugar while watching the crowd roll in and out. The all-night partiers opted for a cheeseburger to soak up the alcohol before bed, while the sightseers and convention goers munched on thick stacks of buttermilk pancakes. The waiters greeted them all like big-ticket lottery winners, hoping for the random hundred dollar big winner tip. Full and wired with caffeine, she paid the bill before heading back to her suite to plan her next move.

Scanning the panel of buttons in the elevator, she noticed that there were two pools. One was located on the same floor as the Canyon Ranch Spa, and the entire second floor was dedicated to something called 'the Canal Shoppes.' The opulence of the hotel with its marble floors, chandeliers, and rose scented air, was beginning to have a calming effect on her. As long as she stayed away from the hum of the casino, she could pretend she was a European artist on holiday. One of her many long-forgotten fantasies. She would make some time to go exploring. If a trip to the pokey was in her future, she wanted some good memories to take with her.

Back in the room, she caught sight of the red message button blinking on the phone. The only people who could reach her in the room were hotel staff and criminals. The voice of her enemies before she's digested breakfast was not what the doctor ordered. Still, they had her kids, both sour and sweet. Her timely response, if requested in the message, was insurance for their safety. She picked up the receiver and dialed nine. "Hope you're enjoying yourself, Sugar. Don't you worry about Lexi, she got the cutest darn homecoming dress you've ever seen. I'll have her call you later—so long as you're good. Bye."

"Hey, mom! I'm having such a great time. Did you know that Ajay has a movie theater in his basement? And they get the brand new movies that are in the theater! Tonight we are watching Avatar in three-D! Gotta go. Love you."

Day two of her kidnapping and her children were living better than they had in their entire lives. Maybe she was overreacting. If Suni had the capacity to murder, would she also possess the capacity to mother? And what about Babette with all her sugar and spice nonsense? Would she really go against her inbred southern hospitality and commit heinous crimes?

Lanie plopped down on the featherbed. Perhaps her apprehension was an overreaction? After all, which was a more likely scenario; a 'forced' vacation, by a group of friends or a mob of murderous suburban moms, kidnapping her children so they could terrorize her loser husband? The thought of trying to explain her predicament to the authorities, without being laughed out of the precinct, was enough to quell her distress; lowering her threat level from red to yellow.

This was a vacation. A much needed break from being everyone's go-to girl. Suni and the others were probably just forcing her to relax. What better way to get her to leave than to ramp up the PTA Mafia scenario? They were all probably sharing a good laugh about it over a pitcher of something strong and sweet. All the talk of destruction for Bob and Brittney was just their way of rallying around her. Making her feel better for being so totally humiliated.

It sounded good. She'd go with it until further notice.

* * *

MONDAY, SEPTEMBER 4TH

Lanie was on her fifth day of captivity in Vegas and had not left the hotel once. It wasn't hard to do. The Venetian was its own city, complete with dining, shopping, swimming, and culture. Instead of ending, it morphed into the Palazzo, which was a cultural Mecca of its own. From one end to the other, the two made a stretch of at least two miles per floor. Multiple levels brought multiple treasures, all for her exploration. She walked until exhaustion every day and had yet to see the same thing twice. Except the Grand Luxe. She saw the inside of it every day, sometimes twice a day. Red Velvet Cake with homemade cream cheese icing was her new best friend. It never disappointed her and it never talked back.

Charlie and Lexi called every night. Charlie made his calls willingly. His voice gushed over the line, his excitement over the day's events raw and fresh. Lexi spit out her words, as pissed as a cat thrown into a tub of cold water. Every moment on the line clearly more pain than her teenage brain could handle. The rug rats never once claimed to miss her. The question of her return to Glen Ellyn was buried under the enjoyment of mansion living and endless video game tournaments. Bob was the missing link in her daily digest. No one mentioned him or Brittney, and Lanie swallowed her questions about them. No news must be good news.

When guilt crept into the corners of her mind, she pushed it away with window shopping. Glittery eye candy was the best therapy. Nose prints on glass weren't just for children at Christmas. The high end shops inside the miles of Canal Shoppes sat empty, their employees dressed for the big sale that never came. The very fact that they stayed open hour after hour, day after day, was positive thinking at its best. Lanie imagined the orchestra in the Titanic, playing as the ship went down. The shops, void of rich purchasers, were sinking. The burden of cost far outweighing the meager sales. Plastered smiles and Coco Chanel suits could not save them. They just made the slow death more pleasant.

Her new digs were growing on her. Daily maid service, food brought to her piping hot at any hour, and sheer blissful quiet made the transition from underappreciated house slave to pampered, single lady easy. Her ankle had healed to the point that she was no longer hobbling. Only a few small bruises remained as a brutal reminder of that fateful fall in the dealership. She had settled into her own little routine; get up at nine, eat at the Grand Luxe, shower, hit the pool for a good chunk of the day, have an early evening cocktail, and meander around the second floor Canal Shoppes a bit before deciding on what to have for dinner. She'd taken her first gondola ride the other night and was thinking about getting a ticket to see *Phantom of the Opera* in the hotel's theater.

Oddly, all the luxury was free. She hadn't spent a dime of the money Suni had given her. Everywhere she went, people checked her room number and it was comped—compliments of her elusive host, Mr. Ilg. Lanie hadn't had the pleasure of meeting her financially well-endowed keeper. Her imagination ran wild. Each day, the scenario grew more vivid. Mr. Ilg, a gloriously muscled man, followed her in the shadows. His goal to meet her every desire from afar, while plotting the right moment to come into the light and sweep her off her feet. His love for her a flame ignited by the pure passion he saw in her soul. Or, at the very least, he'd keep her in the lifestyle she'd come to expect in the past week. His ideas about guest comfort and luxury were something Lanie appreciated beyond words. Her fantasy vision of herself had gone from poor European artist on vacation to royal princess. She now understood why the wealthy chose to jump off window ledges rather than face a life of poverty. Luxury was addictive, no different than cocaine or alcohol. Once it was in your blood, you couldn't live any other way without the constant thirst for it.

Fall had not hit the desert—not during the daylight hours at the rooftop pool. If the air temperature was a comfortable seventy-two, the concrete and reflection of the sun on the water made it sizzle like eighty. Tony, the pool boy, found Lanie a seat in the front row of chairs lining the empty aqua oasis. She held out a ten dollar bill for his service and he smiled. "No thanks, Ms. J. You know the rules about Mr. Ilg's guests—we can't take your money."

She ignored his refusal. One way or another, Suni's money would get spent. "Then how about a drink from the bar? I could use a good Long Island iced tea right about now."

"Sure thing, Ms. J."

"And keep the change, Tony, as a tip." He couldn't refuse a tip for bar service. That had to be allowed, no matter who the guest was.

"Sorry, Ms. J—no can do." He ran off to get her drink before she could argue, leaving her to stretch out on her plush, terry towel and nap in the sun.

She was starting to snooze when a shadow blocked the sun. The shift in temperature from lizard on a rock to bearable accompanied the darkness that moved over her body. She opened her eyes expecting to see Tony with her drink, instead her gaze landed on her tall drink of water limo driver. Mr. No Name. The God of high-end passenger transport. Wearing only red board shorts and tanning oil that highlighted the sharp edges and soft curves of his physique, he was a perfect desert mirage. His hair was longer than she remembered. A halo of soft black waves outlined strong angles. The perfect mixture of hard and soft. Mirrored aviator shades covered his eyes, but she remembered them clearly. Dark and intense, lined with thick lashes that any woman in her right mind would be jealous of—if it wasn't lust at first sight.

"Mind if I sit here?" He pointed to the empty chair next to her. How could she mind? A beautiful glossy skinned creature choosing a seat next to her unglossy wrinkled frame? Of course there were no other empty chairs in the vicinity, but he could have asked Tony the towel boy to chase someone away for him. "Not at all."

He plopped down next to her, stretching out his lanky frame. She admonished herself for lusting after him. Any boy that had that lean muscled look was still just a boy. The things he could learn from an experienced older woman...

"Elaine, right?"

He remembered her name. "Yes, you have a good memory."

"Mmmm. You're pretty easy to remember."

Oh, God, he was flirting with her. She felt herself start to flush.

"Not too many older ladies come here alone."

Shit. Little cretin. Where was Tony with her drink? She scanned the horizon of the deck, pretending that his words didn't smart. Older lady traveling alone, that's was how he classified her. Tony was on the other side of the pool, looking for side by side chairs for a pair of women. They were older, just like her, and they traveled in pairs. That was the norm. She was the exception that stuck out like a sore thumb. Tony caught her staring and put up his index finger to let her know he hadn't forgotten. In a fit, she threw herself back on the chair cushion and closed her eyes.

Her rotten companion chuckled. "I didn't mean to offend you. You're not old—just older than our typical girl flying solo."

She was transparent, always had been. Bob told her that if they'd bet the farm in a poker game, he'd have to lock her up before he played the hand. She pretended not to hear him. It galled her that he was laughing at her expense, what a typical, pompous, arrogant, little...

"Tell you what. Let me make it up to you. Have dinner with me."

Prick. First he insults her, and then he asks her to dinner. She wasn't a charity case. "I'm busy."

"No you're not. You do the same thing every day. You eat breakfast at the Grand Luxe, you lay in the sun, and you have a light dinner after walking through all the Canal Shoppes..."

Fear gripped her. He knew her daily schedule. That could only mean one of three things: he had fallen in love with her and couldn't stay away, he was some kind of pervert that derived pleasure from spying on women old enough to be his mother, or Suni was paying him to keep tabs on her. The first choice was appealing in a carnal, illicit, he-could-be-your-son, kind of way. The second was possible but not plausible. That only left one choice. "You've been spying on me!" Her accusatory finger came as close to his butter bronze skin as possible without touching it.

He wound his fingers around hers and moved it to a comfortable distance. "Guilty as charged. I live here and I work for Mr. Ilg. It's my job to keep an eye on his guests, make sure they have everything they need."

"Suni, too, I assume," she spat at him.

"Who?"

"Suni Calverson. Don't pretend you don't know her."

"Does she work for Mr. Ilg, too? I don't know *everyone* he employs, that would be impossible. Is she a maid?"

She ripped the aviators from his eyes and leaned in. Copying the cold stare of Yvette, she raised her brow in a direct challenge. The confrontation startled him. He pressed himself as far back into the chaise as he could without toppling into the row of gawkers behind them.

"Look, I don't want any trouble. I just thought maybe we could have dinner together. You seemed nice when I met you at the airport. That's it."

He was telling the truth. Damnit. In her rush to judgment she'd lost her composure. The group of onlookers had grown—she was surrounded. Heat crept through her skin. She began to sweat. Hottie limo guy was enjoying her embarrassment. He cocked his head and raised both brows, throwing her challenge right back at her. Tony and her Long Island Iced Tea had gone into hiding at the first sign of trouble. Defeated, she took a deep breath and handed him back his glasses. "I'm sorry. If you don't think I'm completely insane, I'd love to have dinner with you."

His fingers brushed hers as he took the glasses from her. The touch felt purposeful and sensual. Much too long and gentle to be an accident. Her heart jumped into her throat and she fought the urge to throw her body on top of his. Her judgment was poor. She was wrong about him working for Suni—she could be wrong about the caress as well. She swallowed, forcing the primal urge and the jackhammer beat back into her core.

"Alright, but you have to promise me no more insults and you can't rip things off my body—without my permission."

The innuendos were driving her mad. One minute she hated him, the next she wanted to do raucous things to him. "Promise."

"Good. I'll pick you up at seven." He stood, grabbing the cabana towel off his chair. "Dress casual and wear good walking shoes."

She didn't have good walking shoes. She'd have to ask the concierge where to buy some. He bowed in front of her, taking her hand and kissing her fingers. "Until we meet again, my love."

It was a line from something, she could tell by the way he deepened his voice, but she didn't care. It sent shivers up her spine. He turned to leave.

"Wait!" She cried out startling the fat, bald guy that had just fallen asleep in his chair next to her. Her bronze, curly-haired, love toy turned back. His eyebrows were drawn together in a question above his sunglasses. "I don't know your name."

He smiled. "Ben. Benjamin Oliana."

Hawaiian. That explained the beautiful skin, eyes and hair. "Nice to meet you, Benjamin Oliana."

He shook his head in disbelief. "You are an interesting woman, Elaine. See you at seven."

She watched him walk back to the towel hut. In his red board shorts, she got an even better view of his nicely toned tush.

CHAPTER TEN

Soon after Ben's exit, Tony materialized with her long awaited Long Island Iced Tea.

"Sorry, Mrs. J. I got busy for awhile there at the bar."

Little liar. He gave her the change and she stuffed it in the pocket of her terry cover up. He'd blown his chance at a tip. Even if she threw the money at him, he wouldn't take it. Why bother?

She inhaled. Rum, gin, tequila, and vodka, all blended so smoothly that all her nose could detect was sweet tea. Delicious and fake. Not a lick of sweet tea in the entire glass. At least there better not be. Slamming the drink down would do little for her composure, which she was sure to need at dinner. If the date turned sour, she could always hit the sauce hard. A drunken middle-aged woman would put a fast end to any event, date or otherwise. Plus, if his teasing touch was the real deal, she'd need all her strength to keep her from taking him to school. Just because Bob had bedded a baby didn't mean she had to follow suit. She took slow sips through the straw.

She had nothing to prove. She was happy the way she was. Having wild, crazy sex with a man who just passed the legal age to buy alcohol wasn't necessary.

But it sure would be fun.

* * *

Sipping the drink had been a waste of time. The pool bar wasn't known for strong concoctions, probably afraid of patronage dehydration and 911 emergency calls. Back in the suite, Lanie eyed the mini-bar. There were some nice, little bottles inside, but at sixteen to twenty dollars a pop, she couldn't bring herself to crack open the seal. Spending the cash Suni had left for her needed to be done carefully. She wanted every last dollar to feel sinful. Luxurious. Drinking alone from the mini-bar of her suite didn't qualify. She settled for some water she'd purchased at the sundries shop in the lobby outside the Grand Luxe that morning.

The dead cell phone sat taunting her from the coffee table. Putting off buying a charger didn't change the fact that she had to keep contact with Bob. With her dinner with Ben looming on the horizon, it hardly seemed fair—but she had to. Like it or not, they were still married. And, he was still potentially in danger. Until she heard his voice—got some reassurance that Yvette hadn't sliced and diced him—she had to keep trying. If he acted like an ass, she could hang up. Slamming the hotel phone would be so much more satisfying than pressing a red button on the cell. Resigned, she sat at the desk and dialed.

"Where have you been?" The voice on line snapped. "It's been days since you called..."

It was Yvette. Shaking, she hung up. What was it about that woman that put the fear of God in her? She could have stayed on the line—demanded to hear her husband's voice—but instead she sat in her suite, over a thousand miles away, quaking in her boots. It was ludicrous, the power she'd given Yvette, a complete stranger, over her emotions. But she was so cold. If the PTA Mafia ran about Glen Ellyn, Illinois committing heinous crimes, Yvette was a great hired gun. No compassion. No emotion. She possessed all the qualities of a killing machine.

But there was no proof. Not one single thing she could point to that proved these women were the real deal. They bribed a football coach, got free up do's, and loads of beautiful clothes, but that didn't make them murderers. She had been scanning the local news on the internet every day, searching for a story about a dismembered body in a dumpster or a burned down car dealership with two unidentified charred bodies in it, but so far there was nothing. The kids were living like movie stars in an episode of MTV Cribs. She was being paranoid. They'd made themselves sound serious to get her out of town, and she'd bought it. Enough was enough. Next time she'd tell Yvette she wanted to talk to Bob—no excuses.

Her phone call to the concierge had produced a new pair of Reebok running shoes at her door, paid for by the mysterious Mr. Ilg. They were a perfect fit and they matched her new sporty yoga pants and body hugging tee that she picked up at the Pink boutique earlier that afternoon. She'd finally outsmarted the staff by producing cash *before* they could ask for her room number. Dressed in dark glasses and a baseball cap, she was fully prepared to tell them she was staying at the Hard Rock. Once she flashed the dough, they never even asked. One small victory for Elaine Jackerson in the game of try-to-win-back-your-life. Plus, it was fun. Wondering if they'd catch her before the register could ring up the purchase—she was the naughty teen that shoplifted for a thrill—in reverse.

Turning, she checked herself out in the full-length bathroom mirror. The pants had just enough lycra to lift her sagging derriere without creating unsightly bulges in new places. Tight, lifted and round. Juicy. Flipping back, she sucked in her tummy. If only her breasts had held up half as nicely as her ass. Breastfeeding. That had been her mistake. Nature's way of providing the perfect nutrition for infants. Too bad nobody told women the casualties would be the one thing men treasured more than fifty-yard line seats at the Super Bowl. Lanie had never been well endowed. In her heyday, she topped out at an "almost" B cup. But, that was before kids. The aftermath from Charlie's cyclonic suction was beyond her body's healing capabilities. Once perky and round, the twins had turned into half deflated clown balloons. She was confident that her undergarment shopping kept the Wonder Bra Company in business. Less accident prone than the water bra craze, the padded wire traps kept her in the C cup range. Bigger knockers balanced out her Buddha belly and junk in the trunk, and nobody was the wiser.

Right about the time she was ready to panic over being a married middle-aged runaway who was going to dinner with a boy toy, Ben knocked. Shoving her conscious out of the way, she bolted for the door, stopping just short of yanking off the chain and throwing it open. *Elaine, you are a married woman. No matter how good the person on the other side looks, smells, or might even taste—you are not allowed to go there.* She wouldn't. She couldn't. It might feel right, but it was wrong. Taking her sweet time, she opened the door.

How could a person look so good? Each time she thought he'd reached the peak of hotness, he managed to climb one rung higher the next time she laid eyes on him. Tonight was no exception. The short amount of time he'd spent with her at the pool had deepened his glow. The flesh on his arms colored burnt umber. She realized she was comparing him to shades made by Crayola. How sad. He held out a single, pink carnation. "I call this a peace offering. Let's start over."

Faded and torn denim hugged him in all the right places. Topped off with a linen Hawaiian shirt in butter yellow, he had the corner on the market of hot without trying. Feeling self conscious, she slid half her body behind the door.

"Where are you going?" Catching her hand, he peeled it from the frame and wrapped her fingers around the green stem. "You look adorable."

He'd caught her in the act of trying to shrink and told her she was adorable. Suddenly he was the adult and she was the awkward wallflower. She blushed. "Thanks. Want to come in while I put it in some water?"

He smiled. The naughty school boy smile she'd seen a hundred times in her youth. He was, beyond a shadow of a doubt, flirting with her. This was a date. The real deal. Not just a pity dinner. Before she could admonish herself to behave again, he stepped over the threshold giving her a nose full of his scent. Clean, maybe a hint of cologne, but nothing that took away from his natural smell. Old spice and sandalwood. Her first date and a young version of her father rolled into one. Safety and sex, it disarmed and aroused at the same time. All young males came equipped with the same scent. Nature knew what it was doing. Her hormones started zipping around inside her involuntarily.

His close proximity sent her scurrying into the kitchenette to find a home for the carnation. Distance was going to play a large role in her maintaining her dignity. Pulling a champagne flute from the overhead cabinet, she filled it with water. "Hand me a butter knife, would you?"

Rummaging through the drawers, he found one and handed it to her, handle out. *Good manners*, she noted cutting off the bottom of the stem before crushing it with the handle.

He leaned on the counter of the island. "Why did you crush the bottom?"

She shrugged. "My mom always did it. She said it kept the bloom fresh longer."

"Does it work?"

"I'm not sure. It's just a habit, I guess." She walked over to the island and placed the glass on the counter next to him. "Now I'll be able to see it from every room in the suite."

"And think of me?"

She swallowed. It was the trick question. If she said yes, something would happen, right here, right now. If she said no, that closed the door. No. It was the right answer, both morally and politically, and yet she couldn't quite spit it out. She turned, pretending to look for her purse. "We should get going. I'm starved."

He stepped closer. Heat radiated off his skin enveloping her without actual contact. A heat bubble. Reaching for the flower, he gently traced the lace petals. "I like it when the bloom fades. I think flowers are at their peak of perfection when they are just past their prime."

She was melting. If she turned around, she would be a hair's breadth from his body. In the perfect spot to jump his just-past-puberty body, take apart his naive flesh and put him back together a man. She wanted to, and he wanted her to. His stillness, a predatory stalking pose waiting for her move.

The day in the dealership flashed through her mind. Brittney Baylor, the young woman Lanie had personally hired to take over for her so she could spend more time with her children, screaming and moaning out her husband's name. Bob demeaning her with his callousness. *Go home, Lanie. We'll talk about this later.* They had destroyed her world without a second glance. Then there was the note Suni had left her under the pile of cash. *Have Fun.* If anything was going to be fun for her in Las Vegas, this was it.

She was on him like a cougar taking down an antelope. The force of her body mashing into his threw him backwards, but only for a second. Then he had her up in the air, his arms easily lifting her onto the granite island. His arms swept sideways knocking the glass holding the carnation to the floor where it shattered.

"I should clean that up..."Her words were lame; a last ditch effort to keep her body out of the sin zone.

His voice, husky and low, was filled with desire. "Later."

"But, it's glass."

She was flat on her back, the cold of the stone seeping through her thin tee shirt. Before she could blink, he was on top of her. The roles switched, she was once again the prey. Pressing his body firmly on hers he began to devour her with his thick, soft lips. "No. I'll do it later."

She pushed him back just far enough to grab the bottom hem of her shirt. Pulling it over her head, she threw it in the direction of the broken glass. She had two last coherent thoughts as he pressed his lips into the curve of her neck, his hands seeking to undo the hooks between her shoulder blades. She could not forget to clean the glass fragments from the floor. One wrong step and she'd tear her foot to ribbons. But, more importantly, she hoped Ben wasn't too disappointed with the meager flesh resting under the cotton pillows of her Wonder Bra.

*   *   *

Lanie had overestimated her ability to rock hot Hawaiian Benjamin's world by a mile. He had the energy of an eighteen-year-old and the experience of someone who was a world-class lover. He'd done things to her that she hadn't even read about. Things that brought her to the edge of orgasm city, through the heart of it, and back around the other side. Repeat, repeat, repeat, until she was spent. Then, when she thought she would pass out from exhaustion, he had his grand finale. That thirty seconds made her feel like she'd accomplished what she set out to do—but she knew that it would have happened that way even if he were alone with a Kleenex and a bottle of Lubriderm. Men were men. They finished every time. Still, his final shudder made her happy.

For an encore, he dragged her out of bed and onto the strip. "I'm starving. You stole my Chi. I need to refill."

* * *

The strip was wall to wall people. Old couples, young couples, single ladies, single men and everyone in between pressed their way along the sidewalk. Lanie squeezed in behind Ben trying to keep up. Forcing her way through thick crowds was not high on her list of talents. Bob always got annoyed with her whenever they went to carnivals with the kids. "My God, Lanie—what are you waiting for—Christmas?" He'd snort, stepping in front of her, pushing people out of his way.

A break. That was what she was waiting for. Pushing and shoving was for bullies as far as she was concerned. Bob was just the bully for the job. He didn't care who was in front of him. Children, old ladies, pregnant ladies, they ranked the same as bikers and gang banger wannabe's. She always followed behind, mumbling apologies for his behavior. Ben had a natural ease in the crowd. He made his way through the throng and never once felt the need to lay a hand on a single person. Ben, the best looking, sinful creation in the desert, was also a young gentleman.

Reaching back, he made a grab for her hand. A harmless gesture meant to keep her close—prevent her from getting lost. Pretending not to see it, she stuffed her hands into her pockets. It was ridiculous. An hour ago she'd been completely naked in front of him, but put her in the general public and suddenly she found her missing marital morals. "Where do you want to eat?" She asked checking the street in both directions.

Ignoring her brush off, he placed the rejected hand on her shoulder and pushed her in the direction of Harrah's and The Imperial Palace. "I've got just the thing."

'Just the thing', was really lots of things. Mai Tai's that came in plastic glasses as tall as college beer bongs, shrimp on a skewer, a long piece of colorful cloth that could be worn fifty different ways. This qualified in Ben's world as 'just the thing'. Not a fancy steakhouse or front row seats at Cirque de Soleil. Walking the strip, gawking, laughing and pointing. Just the thing.

They stumbled across a street artist spitting out magic with cans of spray paint and cardboard. His hands flew, tossing cans into the air, mixing colors, moving blobs into shapes. Choreographed to loud music with a pumping beat, Lanie got lost watching him work. His art was good, commercial, but good. It was the show that held her attention. The practice and concentration that he had to maintain to keep up this little street stand was amazing. He tossed a can, sending it spinning into space. A flash of gold on his left caught her gaze. A wedding ring. This man found a way to make a living from his art. She had assumed that meant he was a young single guy. Closer inspection of his face turned up frown lines and grey hair at the temples. He was doing what she had passed up, all with a wife at home. Maybe even a child or two. A mentor for those that shriveled and died under the daily burden of married life, trudging along in suits to jobs they hated. Taking some cash from her pocket, she threw it in his tip cup.

"That's amazing, isn't it? The way he gets the aerosol spray to behave—I can't even spray paint the patio furniture."

"Oh, honey, don't I know it!"

The drawl was female, close to Babette, but not quite. Startled, she jumped. Where were Ben's hushed tones? Better yet, where was Ben?

The woman laughed. "I didn't mean to catch you off guard. You were looking for your tall drink of water, weren't you?"

Lanie nodded. "Did you see where he went?"

"Sorry, hon, I have no idea. He left awhile ago..."

She scanned the crowd trying to catch a glimpse of Ben. Had he left to get food? The small quadrant filled with street vendors was fourth row, center stage, Aerosmith loud. A bar in the back corner played music with heavy bass, strong enough to rattle her bones. Squeezing between the wall to wall people, she made her way to the nearest food stand selling elephant ears and corn dogs. There was no sign of Ben. He must have slipped back to the main strip. What direction would he travel? The strip only went in two directions, closer to the airport or back the way they'd come. Betting on the airport she turned in the direction of the Imperial. She was almost to the sidewalk when his scent hit her nose.

Sniffing the air like a cataract ridden bloodhound, she flipped in the direction of the sweetness. The street was filled with bodies. Lanie's height, even on ballerina tip toes, wasn't enough to see over the sea of heads. She'd just have to trust her nose and make her way toward the scent. "Excuse me..."

The distance she had to cover was short, but the trek wasn't easy. Taking a cue from Ben, she tried to guide herself through the throng without physical contact. The number of human sized squeezable gaps was few. After ten frustrating minutes, she let her inner Bob the Bulldog out. As much as she hated the idea of emulating Bob, she hated being stuck more. The compressed flesh created a cocoon of stagnant heat that wrapped around her, cutting off her air supply. If she didn't break into an open area soon, hyperventilation and panic were sure to set in. The last time she'd suffered a panic attack, she'd temporarily paralyzed her hands from lack of oxygen. It was not an experience she cared to repeat. "Excuse me!" The urgency of her voice and hands-on approach parted the masses as quickly as Moses parted the Red Sea.

She was free. Even better, in her state of near collapse, she'd held it together enough to keep tracking Ben's scent. After spending a few hours encapsulated by him, she was unlikely to forget or mistake that smell. If he were to go missing, and there was suspected foul play, the police could use her for search and rescue. Inhaling, she closed her eyes to help isolate the direction of her boy toy. It wasn't wafting from the crowd, but from a dark alley off to her right. Her mother had warned her about dark alleys—a warning so permanently ingrained that she almost gave up her hunt upon spotting the sliver of black between two corners of brick. Dark alleys were the location of rape and murder. Two more things Lanie hoped to avoid in her lifetime. *Go home. Wait for him there*, her inner voice begged.

She would not let her childhood fears keep her from finding Ben. She was a grown woman, standing on a street filled with people. If someone tried to grab her and drag her into the dark alley, she would scream and fight. Somebody was sure to see the commotion and come to her aide. Inching along the bricks, she reached the dreaded opening. Peeking around the corner she caught sight of two figures, highlighted by an overhead spotlight from one of the buildings, tete-a-tete. The tall, good looking one was Ben. The other, a short bulky man dressed in an overcoat, hat and sunglasses, was a mystery. Dressed like a villain in a James Bond spoof, he stuck out like a sore thumb. If he were a criminal suspect, he'd be the first man picked out of a lineup.

The noise of the crowd made it impossible to hear what they were saying. Ben shook his head in response to something the man said, which made him angry. A fat, stubby, index finger poked Ben's chest through the yellow print shirt. The display of aggression, played out by such a classic cliché, made her teeth chatter. If the exchange turned to violence, she was pretty sure Ben could take him. As long as he wasn't hiding a weapon inside the overcoat...

Ben broke into a smile and put his hands up in mock protest. The short man went into a fit—stamping his feet and shaking a fist inches from Ben's nose. Lanie backed away from the edge, searching for someone she could grab to break them up. Someone bigger and stronger than herself. There were plenty of folks to choose from. She would just grab someone— preferably tipsy enough to want the job—and drag them back into the alley. She glanced back to the dueling duo. Ben pointed in the direction of the Venetian. Overcoat ogre reached into his pocket, pulled out a wad of something she couldn't make out, and handed it to Ben. He smiled, shoved it in the front pocket of his Levi's, and shook the man's hand. That was it. The fight was over and no blows had been exchanged. Lanie breathed a sigh of relief.

Her relief was short lived. Now that the duo had no more business to attend to, they would be heading in her direction. Lanie made the quick decision to hightail it away from the exit of the alley before they came across her spying. Ducking into the Starbucks, she busied herself comparing gourmet coffees. What had Ben been doing with an alleyway criminal? He had pointed in the direction of the Venetian. Had he been giving him information about the hotel? And what had the man given him in exchange for the information? Money? Drugs? Her imagination was vivid. The man in the overcoat was probably a foreigner who was lost. A visitor from France or Germany who had too much to drink and lost their way. That would explain the odd clothing and the temper. Ben could very well have been a Good Samaritan that was giving him directions. If that were the case, then the wad he stuffed in his pocket was probably nothing more than a tip. A simple thank you for not taking advantage of him. That had to be the case.

She was deep in thought, a bag of unground French Roast in hand, when a white Styrofoam container held by the caramel-colored hand of her knight in Hawaiian armor appeared under her nose. The smell of Chinese food wafted up, mixing with the scent of hyper caffeinated beans. She pushed it away from her nose, but refused to turn and face him. Had he left to find food, or was the meeting with the man in the alley planned? She didn't trust her expression "You can't possibly be hungry? We spent the last hour eating our way down the strip."

His arm wrapped around her waist. Drawing her against his hips, he pressed his lips into the crook of her neck. "Once my Chi has been emptied, it takes a lot to refill."

He was sticking with food as the reason for his disappearance. Not that hard to accept as truth, if you considered the source. Ben clearly had the ability to eat constantly and never gain an ounce. Another gift of youth. All she had to do was smell the food and her hips spread. The aroma was enticing. Her stomach ignored the stern warning from her brain and growled under the ropy tendons of Ben's forearm. "What'd you get?"

"Sweetfire Chicken and Kung Pao Beef."

Panda Express. She'd had a teenager long enough to have memorized the menu. "This is Vegas dining at its finest?"

"It's not the food that matters it's the location that you eat in. I've had enough of the strip for one night. What do you say we head back to your suite and dine in?"

She turned and caught the glint in his eye. He was suggesting more sex. Good sex, no, great sex. It might justify the extra calories she was about to consume. "What are we waiting for?"

He threw a broad smile in her direction as she zipped past. "I was hoping you would say that."

* * *

Round two was far better than round one. All of Lanie's inhibitions from the first romp had evaporated, leaving a bundle of raw nerve endings dying to be teased. Ben had already seen her naked, with the lights on, and he'd come back for more. The very same night. She tried not to read anything into it—good or bad. Part of letting go and having fun was letting things ride without overanalyzing them. A skill that she never could have mastered in her twenties came so easily in her mid-forties. Then again, if she were to analyze one part of her fling with Ben, she'd be forced to analyze the entire thing. That was sure to drive her insane. How could she separate out what was rational, when ninety five percent of everything she'd done in the past week defied logic? Better to enjoy the sex and think about what it meant later. Much later.

They'd shared the Chinese, devouring each morsel as if it were the food of Gods. There was something about the anticipation of sex that made every bite better. Ben was right, refilling Chi was required. Nourishing the body in preparation of nourishing the soul. She savored the cheap take-out and dared her guilt to creep up. It was food and it was good.

She finished eating first and he'd begged her to allow him five extra minutes to finish refilling his Chi. Permission granted. Exactly five minutes later, she jumped him. Her Chi was in fine form and it refused to be wasted. This time, she rocked his world. Repeatedly.

The buzz-saw snoring that escaped through Ben's perfect lips made her giggle. The king of hot, when asleep, was as much of a goober as any man. His boyish features softened to the point that they became damn near angelic. Snuggled in as closely as she could manage without waking him, Lanie watched his eyes flutter under closed lids. *He's a baby, barely past adolescence. What on earth are you doing?*

Falling in love.

The thought was sudden—loud and clear in her head. It startled her out of her half sleep. Adrenaline coursed through her, making her sweat. She jumped out of bed and threw on her plush, white Venetian robe. She could not—would not—allow herself to have feelings for this man—no, boy—that she just met. They'd had sex. Granted it was the best sex of her life, but sex didn't equal love. Love was something that had to develop over time. This was just a casual fling. Something to help her rebound from Bob's massacre of their twenty-plus-year marriage. She did not love Benjamin Oliana, the swanky limo driver for the Venetian hotel. She lusted him. Lusting him was okay—loving him was a big fat no-no. Lust felt like love. It was an easy mistake. She'd been off the market for quite awhile. She was rusty, that's all there was to it.

She needed to do something to take her mind off the L word. Glittering bits of broken champagne glass caught her attention. She'd forgotten to clean it up, and Ben, being a man, had been more than happy to let it sit where anybody could step on it and slit open the bottom of their foot. The empty Styrofoam container would make a nice, safe home for the shards of death. Using her tee shirt like a broom, Lanie swept the glass into the sticky sauce, snapped the cover closed, and carried it to the kitchen garbage to be disposed of properly. She'd have to be careful until the maid came and gave the floor a thorough cleaning. Glass could be tricky. Invisible knives that could only be captured by the power of a Hoover were sure to be lurking, waiting for unsuspecting flesh to slice.

A hot shower. That was her ticket to dreamland, or at least deep relaxation. The Venetian bathroom was a spa in its own right. If she couldn't find her bliss in the gold lined marble and steam, she couldn't find it anywhere. Tiptoeing around the site of the glass explosion, she made her way to the double doors. Light from the vanity mirror slipped through the crack. Illuminating her path, it highlighted a pile of rumpled clothing. Ben's. He'd been in such a rush, heated beyond words, that he'd stripped before he made it past the entry hall.

The irate man in the vendor's quad popped into her head. They had argued, Ben had given the man something that made him happy, and in exchange, he had been given something. He'd stuffed it into the front pocket of his pants. The same pants that sat in front of her now, blocking the path to her heavenly shower.

Don't do it, Lanie. Whatever business Ben had with that man, it's none of yours.

Should she or shouldn't she? She'd waited too long to see Bob's true colors. If she had followed through on her suitcase instinct, she never would have embarrassed herself that dreadful day in the dealership. She also would not currently be enjoying the fruits of Benjamin. A quick peek around the corner. That's all it would take to ensure he was still sleeping soundly. Then a fast run through of the pockets. She'd done it plenty of times with Lexi, looking for drugs or notes that talked about drugs.

But Ben wasn't her child, and he certainly wasn't her husband.

He was...

Damnit! He was something, and she had a right to know if that something was into things that could take her already insanely twisted life and make it worse. In the next room, she heard Ben snore away, unaffected by her inner turmoil. Bastard. To hell with it. Before she could talk herself out of it, she thrust her hand deep into the pocket.

Money. Crumpled carelessly into a ball. Wrinkled and wadded. Stuffed and crushed, as if it had no value, no place in this world. Using the tips of her nails, she pulled it out by the corner and straightened the paper. It was worn thin, soft across the grain. It separated easily, not even a protest when she smoothed it flat with the palm of her hand on her thigh. One, two, three, four, five...hundreds. Not the drugs she'd feared she'd find; worse. Large amounts of money, transferred in back alleys by dark and mysterious strangers, never led to good things. They led to the kind of things you saw on the big screen in the dark. Drugs, stealing, lying, murder...

Suni.

The man was one of her dirty, rotten, back alley spies. But what kind of information was he paying Ben to get? Suni already knew where she was staying. She was the one that had set her up at the Venetian. Suni, Ben, the myserious Mr. Ilg and the man in the back alley, somehow all these people were connected. Their main goal was to keep her from becoming restless. Allow Suni to act out her evil plans, whatever they might be. But what role did Ben play in this mess?

He was her boy toy. Not just any boy toy, but one that was being paid for his time.

Her stomach churned, sending undigested orange chicken up her esophagus. It was one thing to be the pursuer of the boy toy, the one who went in eyes wide open to the crime, and completely another to realize the boy toy was a trap. A carefully spun web meant to entangle the unsuspecting, confused, dumped and left-in-the-dust mother of two.

The snoring in the next room cut off. The crisp, Egyptian cotton sheets rustled followed by the harmony of a few creaky springs. Ben was getting up. With the roll in the hay they'd had, there was a good chance he needed to pee. Any second now he'd come into view. Even half asleep, he was sure to notice that she was holding his pay off money. She stuffed the bills back into his pocket, tossed the pants in a heap where she'd found them, and slipped into the bathroom closing the door and pushing the lock button. Stepping back, she sat on the lid of the toilet. Watching the door anxiously, she felt like the victim in a grade B horror movie.

"Elaine, you in there? I really need to take a piss."

The handle rattled back and forth. "I'm..." she looked around the room hoping to catch sight of something to hit him with if he came in and tried to tie her up. She picked up the gold mirror on the marble vanity, "sick."

"Was it the food?" He sounded genuinely concerned. Probably worried that if she croaked he'd be out of his lucrative second income. She closed her eyes and his body, chiseled and gleaming came into view. He was so perfect in every other way, why did he have to be a Suni Spy?

Maybe she was being irrational. Men could fake attraction to a point. But to continually come back for seconds, thirds and beyond, it really wasn't necessary. Money aside, he had to know that. There had to be a piece of him that wanted to be with her. It might be a small piece—a pinky toe—but there was something. Setting the mirror back down, she made her way gingerly across the floor and opened the door a crack. "I don't know, but it's pretty bad. You better go. I don't want you to catch it."

"Is there anything I can get you? Tylenol, Gatorade?"

"No, I'll be fine. If I need anything I can call the concierge."

"Can I see you tomorrow?"

Another day of rock solid loving. It sounded heavenly. Impossible until she could eliminate him as a criminal mind, but heavenly to consider. "No, that's probably not a good idea." Closing the door she relocked it. Pressing her ear against the heavy wood she heard some scuffling. The moment of truth. When he threw on his pants would he notice his money had been messed with?

"Call me when you're better. I left my number on the table."

The sound of his voice, so close she could almost feel his breath on her ear, made her jump. He must have pressed his lips right up to the crack where the wood met the frame. Those luscious, ruby pillows begging to be kissed. She fought the urge to run out and say *just kidding let's go back to bed*. He had an unusual amount of money from an unscrupulous looking character on the street. It reeked of Suni and her henchmen.

The front door opened and closed. She waited another five minutes before exiting the bathroom. Partly because she wanted to be sure he'd really left, and partly because if he wasn't far enough away, she might run out the door after him for one more round of earth shattering coitus.

*   *   *

WEDNESDAY, SEPTEMBER 6TH

In her efforts to avoid Ben, Lanie discovered the much shadier and glorious tenth floor pool. The fourth floor pool was the hottie hangout, filled with tan toned bodies and loud, obnoxious music. The tenth floor pool was a landscaped garden complete with a French bistro, a waterfall, and a hot tub. Due to the lack of skin scorching sun, it was also empty. A private paradise. Inspired by the beautiful Wisteria and Bougainvillea draped over the wrought iron arches, she stopped in the sundries shop and picked up a sketch book. She took a seat near the fountain. The sound of the rushing water soothed her nerves and she tried for the millionth time to figure out what she should be doing. She'd been in Vegas for an entire week and every day her kids called and told her how fabulous they were doing without her, Yvette answered Bob's phone, and there was no news about anything tragic happening in or around her home. She wanted to go home the same way every mother did, to see her kids and kiss her little Poodle on the top of his copper curls before bed. Yet, she had no desire to go home, face Bob, or whatever was left of him, and her scattered life. She didn't even know if she could go home. For all she knew, Suni could have people ready to grab her the minute she tried to get on, or off, a plane.

Then there was the Ben incident. What the hell was she thinking bedding down a boy that she didn't know? Sure he was tasty and delicious, his skin was warm and his muscled were ripped, his lips unbearably soft anywhere and everywhere on her body...

Crushing the tip of the pencil into her palm she cursed. Maybe the pain could act as a brand and drive the desire out of her mind. If she didn't stop picturing him, picturing them together, she would never have the will to see him and stay out of bed. And she was bound to see him. He lived there and would turn up sooner or later.

The discovery of the money had muddled matters further. Now she had to stop herself from undoing his drawers and not raise suspicion that would get back to Suni and get her in deeper trouble. Assuming he was working for Suni; but what if he wasn't? What if the money exchange was innocent? Could she somehow assimilate him into her daily suburban existence?

Benjamin Oliana at the local Dominick's comparing laundry detergent sales, now that was something she'd like to see. Her heart might be tempting her to love him, but that could never come to pass. He was nothing more than a sexual toy. Too young to be a real relationship, too old to be one of her daughter's backseat blowjobs.

That's how Bob sees Brittney.

The thought came from nowhere and blew her out of her pornographic mind cocoon. Her relationship with Ben was exactly the same as Bob's relationship with Brittney. Never mind that he did it first, which totally exonerated her of any morality issues, it was still the same. They were old. Ben and Brittney were young. Seducing, or being seduced, by someone totally out of your league was enticing, exhilarating, and wrong. Even if Ben had thrown himself at her, she was the adult. It was her job to say, 'no thanks' and move on.

But, who made those rules? Ben was a legal adult. Her marriage was a sham. He wanted to have sex with her. Didn't that make it right? No, what made it wrong was the knowledge that she would never have a real lasting relationship with the beefy limo driver. It would just be sex, and for Lanie, that just wasn't enough. She wanted the whole enchilada. Everything that she thought she had with Bob and more if she could get it. Hot sex with someone who could afford a mortgage and wanted to share the house with her. That shouldn't be too much to ask.

Put the pencil to paper.

Her mind begged her to distract her heart from the pain of letting Ben go. She picked up her pencil and began to draw. Maybe if she put

114

some images down on paper a solution to her problems would materialize. Stranger things had happened, like living a new life in Las Vegas on someone else's dime.

* * *

Night of Wednesday, September 6th

Lanie wanted gelato. More specifically, she wanted Panna Cotta gelato from Cocolini. When the first bite of sweet cream melted on her tongue, it always brought her to unending bliss. Fear of running into Ben wasn't enough to keep her away. After all, if she couldn't get her bliss from bedding Ben or from gelato, where could she get it? Life without bliss wasn't life. That was one of the lessons time in Las Vegas taught. Swallowing the last bite of the Chicago style hotdog from Nathan's and a Budweiser from Sin City Brewery, she made a run for it.

There was a line. She scanned the halls nervously. The building was so full of shoppers and gawkers taking in the sights, there was no way to tell if he was there or not. *Relax. Get your dessert. You've made it through two days without him. You can get through one more. Even if he appears behind you, he doesn't bite. In through the nose and out through the mouth.* Nothing like some old fashioned Lamaze breathing to regulate the nerves.

The family in front of her was trying a taste of every flavor on the menu. They would probably get to the end and decide not to buy a scoop. She'd had gelato every day since her arrival and noticed that gelato tasting was a trend, similar to window shopping or just trying the Jimmy Choos on with no intention of buying. Only in Vegas. Just about the time she thought she'd explode, sending the preteen children running for cover, they settled on one single scoop of chocolate. Ten minutes of her life she'd never get back and they only bought one measly scoop of the most monotonous flavor for the entire family of five. Maddening.

Remy, the overworked and underpaid sales girl behind the counter seemed relieved to see her. She knew Lanie was an easy guaranteed double scoop sale.

"The usual?"

"Yeah. How about those tasters? I bet they drive you nuts."

"The theory is that they will come back and buy more later."

"Do they?"

"No. But my manager refuses to stop the free giveaways. That'll be seven-fifty."

Seven-fifty was a small price to pay for such sweet ambrosia. Pocket change really. Throwing a ten from the small fold of bills on the counter she smiled. "Keep the change."

"I can't do that. It'll throw my register off."

"Then stick the difference in the tip jar. At least you'll get a little something at the end of your shift to make up for annoying, cheap customers."

"I should'a thought of that." The young blond smiled sheepishly and Lanie noticed for the first time that she had a small gold hoop running through her bottom lip.

"Did that hurt?" She asked pointing her tiny green spatula at the shiny metal.

Remy stuck out her tongue and ran it over the loop. "Only for a minute or two. Why? You thinking of getting one?"

Lexi would die, both of embarrassment and jealousy, if she did. "Maybe."

"Really? God, you're way cooler than my mom."

Maybe not.

* * *

Lanie said goodbye to Remy, dug the miniscule spatula into the sweet cream and took her first bite. Heaven tickled her tongue and slid down her throat. It was just as tasty and indulgent as the day before, and every day before that. Somehow the experience seemed even more delectable now that sex with Ben was no longer an option. Kicks from sweets—how sad. Her sex faucet had been accidentally turned on full blast and was now being soldered shut with fat, sugar and cholesterol.

Ben's laugh reached out to Lanie's ears from somewhere in the main area of the canal. She recognized the sound, deep and throaty as it pushed out of his tempting mouth. The sound was a tractor beam seeking out her gaze, threatening to take her prisoner. Her will was melting faster than the gelato. She ducked, shrinking into the crowd and making her way toward the Trattoria Reggiano. Away from Ben. Away from Ben's laugh. Away from Ben's lips. Rounding the corner to safety she slowly peered around the bricks searching out the source of the sound.

Like a multi-million dollar playboy, he stood by the gondolier surrounded by three, young blondes. Each girl was trying to outdo the other for his undivided attention. Blond locks flew in every direction, along with the occasional rough elbow. Tube top covered boobs were perilously close to his face. The torrid affair she'd embarked on two days earlier seemed to have slipped his egotistical mind. Leaning down over the blond in the black sparkly spandex so she could whisper in his ear, he opened his mouth like a baby bird to allow another in electric blue to feed him gelato. White with dark specks, it was probably chocolate chip. Amateur. Only an unrefined palate would waste a gelato experience on chocolate chip. She could have gotten that at Haggen Daas.

He caught sight of her peeking at him from around the corner and raised his brows. *Shit. Caught in the act. Not cool.* Sensing a dip in Ben's attention, the trio of blondes turned sharply to take in the threat. Their gaze raked over Lanie, sizing up the competition. Their immediate dismissal told her she was less than impressive. The ball cap and yoga pants she was rocking left a lot to be desired. To the dismay of the frenzied pack of blonds, Ben didn't seem to be put off by her ragged soccer mom look. The intensity of his stare, the small smile that crept from the corners of his lips to the corners of his eyes, the way he pushed back from the tube boobs—all told a different story. If he was spending time with her because she was a paid job, then he was the greatest undiscovered talent east of Hollywood.

Don't buy the fantasy, Lanie. Get a grip before it's too late...

An exaggerated head shake and an open palm stopped him in his tracks. Was that hurt in his eyes? Couldn't be—not with the highlights that were in the process of swallowing him up. No man alive could resist that much Miss Clairol. He stood for a minute, his brows knitted, watching her for a change of heart. She had to cut him free.

He's all yours, ladies.

The gelato, her saving grace from moments before, burned in her throat. The sugar had gone from sweet to fire and back again causing her stomach to knot. Breaking Ben's hypnotic trance, she tossed the rest of the dessert into the trash and turned to leave. The holes being burned in her back from his stare stung; but it was better this way. There was no need to rehash every reason he felt like Mr. Right but was Mr. Absolutely Wrong. All she had to do was swallow her feelings and put one foot in front of the other. There had to be a place she could take refuge until the bevy of blondes cleared out leaving her an open path for the walk of shame back to her suite.

Serendipity art gallery was next to the Trattoria. People walked in and among the dark wood walls admiring the giant landscapes backlit and covered with some kind of glossy polymer. It was the perfect hiding spot. Ben was a lot of things, but cultured in the arts wasn't one of them. Of course that was an assumption based on an age related stereotype. She had no way of knowing whether or not it applied to Ben. Their conversations never made it much past what they were going to eat before they had sex. For all she knew, he could have taken art appreciation in college. Had he gone to college? It amazed her to realize how easily she'd jumped into the sack with someone she knew so little about.

She slipped in amongst the couples holding hands and headed for the nearest empty piece. It was a tree. A breathtaking visual cornucopia of gnarled branches that vaporized into a sea of orange fire and gold haze. The moment her eyes drank it in, all thoughts of Ben were lost. Too real to be a drawing, but too incredible to be a photograph, the nuances of the image were so perfect that they stunned her. How could something so impossibly glorious exist in nature? Photoshop could do amazing things, but this was beyond anything she'd ever encountered. If the piece were a hybrid—a drawing infused with a photo—then her absence from the art world had really left her in the Stone Age. With her index finger she traced the winding trunk from the emerald green of the grass, following one of the branches to the place where it disappeared in the blaze of leaves.

"Do you like it?"

The gravelly deep voice startled her out of her trance. She drew back her finger. *Shame on you, Lanie! You know better than to touch a gallery piece.* She turned to apologize for her error and was greeted by a man, both rugged and handsome. He had manicured scruff in shades of chestnut, red and silver on his face and matching hair that was rumpled but stylish. Black Sharon eyeglasses framed his eyes, which were olive green. Not Hazel, but pure intense olive. In a black fitted turtleneck and chinos, he was an attractive sight. *My God, is there anyone in this state who isn't a GQ model?*

"Is it real?" she asked.

He chuckled. "Of course it is real. What do you like about it?"

"It's inspiring. Look at how the tree bursts into flames jumping off the print. And the base, sitting on the grass, gives it tranquility. Everything is in perfect balance. I'm sorry I touched it. I'm sure the artist would be furious. I just couldn't help it. You won't tell on me, will you?"

He winked. "I know the artist. He wouldn't be mad. He makes all these pieces accessible to the people for their pleasure. Sometimes you need to touch something to really get to know it—to decide what meaning it has for you. The galleries that put everything on display surrounded by ropes and guards...how is that inspiring? Art is like fine wine. It needs to be sampled. Without connection there is no true appreciation, no true love."

Oh, my. He was handsome *and* French. He also knew the artist and was well cultured. These were all good things. "How did he do this? I've worked my whole life in some form of art—sketching, photography, you name it—but I've never been even close to what this man has achieved."

"What has he achieved? A studio in Las Vegas? A few more in some strategic locations? That's more about business than art. Advertising gets you these things. True art comes from inside the heart."

"I think he has both. Advertising did not produce this image, an artist did."

"I'm glad you think so..."

"Elaine."

He held out his hand. "Elaine! So finally we meet in person. I am the man who has been paying your bills this past week. Gerard Ilg."

She swallowed the lump that had popped up in her throat. Gerard

Ilg. Handsome, rich, and French. Friend of Suni Calverson, small town mafia mom. She took his outstretched hand. "Did you...I mean are you..." she pointed to the picture she had been putting her sticky gelato fingerprints on.

"Yes. I did and I am."

He did and he was. She was mortified not only by her middle-aged mom turned rap star wannabe outfit, but by her inability to conclude the obvious. This man was her host and an artist far superior to anyone she'd encountered in person before. "I'm so sorry," she mumbled covering her hand with the sleeve of her sweatshirt and wiping at the smudges she knew had to be there.

He pulled her hand down. "Elaine, please don't bother. These aren't the originals. Everything in this studio is made to be touched. It's so much more personal that way, don't you think?"

The way his hand felt when he rolled up the sleeve of her shirt, exposing her bare skin to his, that felt personal. "I do," she squeaked.

He pointed to the hand-carved wood settee directly across the room. "Come, sit for awhile, and tell me more about your work."

What work? All she'd done in the last seventeen years was reproductions of Ninja Turtles for Charlie and random landscapes when she had a free minute. "My work isn't very interesting."

"Nonsense." He placed his palm in the small of her back and gave her a gentle but firm push. "All artists undervalue themselves. It is as if we believe that uttering a good word for our own gain will leave us in poor graces with our muse."

They squeezed onto the seat, their thighs pressed together from kneecap to hip. He faced her, one arm thrown over the back of the dark tree trunk. The expectant look on his face told her that this was no joke. Gerard thought he'd found a kindred spirit. Someone to compare war wounds with. She would have to let him down easy. His dreams of talking shop with an equal were sure to be crushed when he heard her meager resume. "I haven't done much with my art since my kids were born."

"You have children? Marvelous! I love babies. How old are they?"

He thought she was young enough to have babies. That would be a good explanation for not working, but seventeen years was stretching it a bit. "Seven and nine." The lie slipped out before she could tuck it back in. "Ah. The perfect ages for you to come back to yourself. And your husband? He is thrilled to have beautiful babies and a beautiful wife who is an artist to boot?"

Her husband wasn't thrilled by babies or art. He loved the kids, just so long as the dividing line left the care in her territory. If he'd actually done any caretaking, he never would have been able to pursue his passion for copulation outside of marriage. "We are separated, most likely divorcing."

"I am so sorry. He sounds like a stupid man to let you go. But you have come to Vegas, so now you find yourself and your passion. That is why you are here, to work on your art, no?"

No. What was the hell was she going to tell him now? Suni must have told him *something* about his unknown guest. She didn't want to cross lies if she didn't have to.

"Excuse me for a moment, Elaine. I see someone needs my attention."

She was saved. Even if it was only for a moment, it would buy her a tad longer to come up with a semi-consistent story. Time for some more Lamaze breathing exercises and little, white lie practice. Gerard unglued his leg from hers, leaving her feeling slightly naked, and went to attend to a potential customer. She watched his swarthy form cut through the crowd and make his way toward the gallery entrance. Someone needed his attention and like the good shepherd, he would go to them. Squinting in the dark, she looked closely at the shape just outside the gallery door waving frantically for Gerard's attention. Whoever it was, they were clearly frantic. Lanie could swear she saw the person jumping up and down. It was hard to be sure. The gallery was dim, lit only by the lighting behind the images. There was something about the way the person moved... it seemed all too familiar to her.

Oh, no. No, no, no.

It was Ben, minus his pretty, blond posse. Gerard was with Ben. A very animated Ben. He pointed to her and she froze. Gerard turned in her direction and shook his head. From her position, Lanie couldn't tell if it was disbelief, shock or something else Gerard was protesting. Ben, the self assured son of a bitch, kept shaking his head, insisting yes.

For the love of all that's holy, go away Ben. Go back and find fifty more young girls just like the ones you ditched and sleep with them. Let me get over you without public humiliation. Let me wash my sorrow away in the company of a real adult.

He was relentless. She sat watching in horror as the two men went back and forth yes, no, yes, no. Finally, Gerard threw up his hands and walked back to her, leaving Ben to pace outside the gallery door. The jig was up. In a fit of testosterone fueled jealousy, Ben must have told Gerard about their fling. When he refused to believe a married artist with babies at home would be so ridiculous, Ben sent him back inside to get confirmation. She could make a run for it. Try to escape the humiliating questions in such a public place. Even if she tried, the only way out was past Ben, and he was twice as strong and fast as she was. He'd grab her up and God only knew what kind of scene that would cause.

On the other hand, the odds were good that Gerard wasn't working for Suni. It was comforting to know that there was one man in Vegas who wasn't on her payroll.

"I am so sorry to have to bother you with this, but my limousine driver insists that you have his sunglasses. He said you mixed them up today at the pool."

He lied. He might not have gone to college, taken art appreciation, or become cultured in any other fashion, but he'd been smart enough to save her butt from total humiliation. Now all she had to do was sink the final lie in the basket and she was home free. "Don't be sorry, it isn't a big deal. I can run up to my room and double check. It was so nice to meet you..." Regaining the feeling in her limbs, she slid off the bench seat.

His hand found her forearm. "Before you go, I have a favor to ask."

"Sure."

"I'm working on something new for the studio, and I could really use your opinion, one artist to another."

If she said yes, she was back to finding some plausible lie that didn't conflict with whatever garbage Suni made up about her and fed to him.

If she said no, she looked like an ungrateful guest and she risked another near miss with Ben. "I would love to help you, but I'm just not qualified enough for the job."

"Nonsense! You have real ideas, not like most of the people here— they just kiss my ass. Come by the studio tomorrow, before I open. Let's say eleven?"

His hand rested on her arm. The warmth of his palm threatened to melt the fleece of her sweatshirt and singe her skin. Behind them stood Ben, his palms pressed on the glass of the studio. His scowl could not be clearer if he were next to them. She needed to get out of the gallery before Ben came in and blew the beautiful lie he'd laid out for her escape. "I'd love to. I'll even bring coffee and croissants."

"Excellent. I look forward to working with you."

Ben would not approve of their meeting. Suni might own him, but that didn't mean that he in turn owned Lanie. In fact, she had set him free an hour ago when she saw him with the bevy of beauties feeding him gelato. As soon as she got out of earshot of Gerard, she would make sure they were clear on that issue. That would take one complication off her plate.

She had the growing suspicion that Mr. Gerard Ilg might be waiting to fill the same spot.

CHAPTER ELEVEN

Lanie stormed past him into the elevator. "I don't have your stupid sunglasses."

Ben stuck his arm in between the closing doors. "I know. I made that up to get you to talk to me."

He wedged in, pushed past the group of Chinese women dressed to the nines, and pressed himself up against her, pushing her body deep into the corner. "I saw you watching me by the Gondolier and I wanted to find out how you were feeling. The last time I saw you, you had your head resting on the rim of a toilet and I was thrown out, my offers to play nursemaid rejected."

He was so tall that his pubic bone was grinding against her belly button. Something she never would have thought of as a turn on, but it was. The brass button of his worn jeans rubbed against her midsection, between her erogenous zones, igniting a fire in her belly.

The elevator reached the lobby, the doors opened. Damnit. In her desire to get away from Gerard before he figured out that she bedded his limo driver, she forgot to check if the elevator was going up or down. The group of partying women departed for a night at the casino. A herd of young men, not much older than Ben, got on in their place. They took up more space than the petite Oriental women and she found her breasts crushed into the base of Ben's ribs. Her face pressed into the soft cotton of his orange Billabong tee shirt. She inhaled his scent and the fire in her belly shot up through her body exploding into her extremities. Her fingers tingled and the hair on her scalp rose with the gooseflesh. This did not bode well for making him go away. *Repeat after me...it's an illusion. He is paid to make you feel this way.*

Resting her cheek on his rock hard upper belly, she called out to the man closest to the buttons. "Can you please push twenty-eight?" It irritated her to hear the slow rhythmic beat of his heart just above her ear. Her heart was slamming against her ribs hard enough to crack them. Once again, she was the oversexed maniac and he was in total control.

One of the herd tipped his open Corona in their direction and smiled a 'congrats dude' grin at Ben before pushing the button to her floor. She kept her cheek pressed against his shirt, figuring it had to be less enticing than breathing in his scent. With any luck, his cargo train heartbeat might have a calming effect on her nerves.

The elevator stopped a few floors up, the doors chimed open and the herd got off leaving her alone with Ben. The two-handed shove to the navel didn't move his frame far enough for her to catch a full breath. Ducking under his arm, she moved to the front of the elevator jamming the button forcefully with her thumb. "Come on. Give me a break..."

His hot breath on her neck gave him away. "Why are you so mad at me?" He whispered poutily.

"The last time I saw you, everything was great. Then you got sick and disappeared. Next time I see you, you are in the arms of another man. If anyone should be mad, it's me."

He sounded so damn convincing. How did men lie so easily? His voice was laced with want and need, heightening her wants and needs tenfold. Lanie tried to block the smell of his baby soft skin out of her nose. "I saw you with that man by the vendor's quad. I know what you were doing." She was half bluffing. She had seen him with the man. She watched as they exchanged conversation and money. The rest all came from her awesome powers of deduction. Considering the gigantic elephant she'd missed in the living room back at home, her powers probably left something to be desired. Depending on how much information Suni had shared, Ben might or might not be aware of that tiny tidbit.

"Is that why you went to Gerard? To tell him about me?"

Holy crap, she was on to something. Ben's body heat, which had been burning into her backside a few seconds before, was gone. She hit a nerve. A big one. If she could draw him out all the way she could get confirmation on whether or not her suspicions were in the ball park. "Why would I do that?"

He sounded panicked. "Because I drive for him? Because he holds my life in his hands? I don't know. You tell me."

The old question with a question game. Too bad she couldn't channel Lexi's teenage mind. She was an expert when it came to that charade. It sounded so serious. Gerard was famous. Gerard was rich. Gerard knew Suni. Did Gerard really hold Ben's life in his hands, or was that just serious drama being created by a limo driver who really liked his job? "I met him by accident. I wandered into his gallery looking for a place to hide from you and your girlfriends. I had no idea he was the Mr. Ilg everybody talks about all the time."

His voice softened. "So you didn't tell him about the man and the money?"

"No." So much for her master detective skills. In trying to be sneaky she had managed to give up her entire losing hand and learn nothing new.

"Those girls aren't my girlfriends. The only girlfriend I want is you."

Except that. The word girlfriend in relation to whatever was going on between her and Ben was definitely new.

The heat was back—scalding this time. He wrapped his arms around her waist and kissed the nape of her neck. "Thank you, Elaine. I'll make it up to you. I promise."

*   *   *

Possible criminal activities and the new girlfriend terminology aside, it took all Lanie's strength to keep him out of her suite. The neck nibbling and heavy petting that started inside the elevator intensified to the point that he had her up on the railing when the doors opened. An older British couple she'd seen on the floor brought her back to reality with a rather loud 'tut tut' from the husband and a sharp inhale from his wife. Ben smiled lazily at the pair, completely unashamed, and sauntered out of the elevator pausing long enough to raise his brow at her and ask, "Coming, darling?" in a terrible British accent.

Humiliated at being caught in the act, she ran out of the doors, carefully keeping her eyes glued to the patterned wool carpet as if memorizing the details of the designs woven into the fabric would wash her free of her sins. The doors closed behind her, and Ben broke out into a hearty laugh.

"It isn't funny!" She hissed.

"Oh, yes, it is," he replied. "It is very, very, funny."

"That's because you don't have to see them every day in the hall. I do."

"Why do you care so much about what other people think?" He asked tracing the outline of her nipple through her shirt.

Stop responding! She screamed at her body. *Think about your children, think about his criminal ties to Suni, think about...*

He swept her up in his arms and carried her down the hall to her door. "Open it."

"Put me down and I will."

"I don't trust you. If I put you down you might run inside and lock me out."

"I won't," she lied.

He set her on her feet. She fumbled around inside her pocket and pulled out the plastic key card. Before she could swipe it he took hold of her wrist and spun her body around to face him. The force moved her just far enough away from the door to allow him to press her flat against the satin wallpaper. Holding her arms over her head, he lowered himself to line up for a liplock.

"I won't force you to sleep with me, Elaine. I know you want to, but the choice is yours. The game stops here. When I let go, you have to be a big girl and make a choice. Are you a willing participant or not?"

He was so close, she could taste him. If she moved even a fraction of an inch, he would scoop her up and it would be a done deal. She wanted him in the most primal way.

So would your daughter.

Damnit. Why did she have to be the one with the conscience? Good, old, Bob the Bulldog never seemed to have that problem.

He let go and took a step back opening a clear path to the door. "Well, what's it gonna be?"

This was agony. She rubbed the plastic key between her index finger and thumb, wishing the skin would rub off and give her another type of pain to deal with. The lusty heart trials were beginning to wear her thin around the edges. "Goodnight, Ben."

He shook his head in disbelief. "Alright, I'm backing off—for now." Stuffing his hands back into his pockets he shrugged his shoulders and walked off down the hall to the elevators.

She went in alone.

*   *   *

A cold shower and a call to her children helped to reinforce Lanie's decision. Charlie was already asleep by the time she called, but Lexi was awake and as surly as ever. Lanie had become more and more grateful for her teenage butthead mood swings. They gave her a sense of security when it came to her kid's safety, however false. If Lexi was still acting like the world owed her, and her mother was an idiot, she couldn't be in too much trouble. If she started asking for Lanie to come home, then she'd worry.

She tried Bob, and this time there was no answer. Not good. She'd grown used to Yvette's voice saying 'Lanie—don't hang up,' right before she hung up on her. It had become their ritual over the last week. The thing that told her Bob was probably okay, and made her feel somewhat justified in her ridiculous behavior. If Bob was still alive, then she wasn't an accomplice to murder. Since he cheated on her and made their marriage a huge pile of lies, his safety wasn't a concern as much as skipping a trip to the penitentiary. Even memories of sleeping with someone as hunky as Ben wouldn't be enough to sustain her through becoming Big Bertha's jailhouse bunkmate.

Flipping on the computer, she scanned her local news section for the Glen Ellyn police blotter. Since learning the truth about the PTA

Mafia, the weekly crime reports took on a whole new meaning. A slashed set of tires at the home of the mayor's election rival looked a whole lot less like teen pranks and a whole lot more like a paid warning before a big hit. Earlier in the week she'd seen an article about Lexi's arch nemesis, Ms. Sigmund. According to the press, Ms. Sigmund had been relieved of her duties as head of the cheer squad and was under investigation for taking bribes to put certain girls on the team. More likely, she *wasn't* taking bribes and Suni's crew had somebody lob some false allegations at her. Combine that with the crooked police force and some carefully placed evidence against the one girl who made it on her merit and it made a pretty juicy story. For now, there was nothing about Bob, Brittney, or any unidentified remains.

No one was dead. If Ben was being paid by Suni to keep her from making waves, he probably wouldn't report their latest spat that ended with her alone in her suite with time to kill and money to burn. The casino didn't tempt her and it was too late to get show tickets. She'd have to settle on surfing the web for entertainment. Googling Suni proved to be useless. All the pages that popped up about Suni Calverson were carefully orchestrated to show her as a model wife and citizen. Babette had a short blip about her on the Herschel Grammar School page for single handedly raising the cash needed to repave all the staff and parent parking lots. Every member she could remember the name of had something about them that was traceable, with one exception. Yvette was oddly absent from the fray. She didn't even appear in the group photo for the annual PTA roster. Her name was there, but where she should have been in the shot was just an open space.

Satisfied that she'd searched every nook and cranny for evidence, Lanie turned her attention to searching out something fun: Gerard Ilg. Twenty-six pages highlighting the fanciful Frenchman popped up. Out of curiosity she Googled herself. Nothing. Gerard Ilg had twenty-six pages of pictures and writing dedicated to him. Elaine Jackerson didn't even exist. She hit the back button and clicked on the first link.

His face downloaded, taking up the entire fifteen inch screen. His charming smile and beautiful eyes, framed out by his trademark dark Shuron Ronsir frames, warmed her heart. Even in two-dimensional black and white, he was a sight to behold. His smile came across as personal. Like he was sharing a private joke with the lucky person who came to visit him in cyberspace. Across the bottom of the page ran a rolling photo gallery. Sliding the cursor to the first one, she held her breath and opened it.

Just as she suspected, it was an exercise in perfection. *Every* picture was an exercise in perfection. A sand dune that became a stairway to heaven, disappearing into clouds of cotton candy. Mangroves reflected in the mirror of an empty lake surrounded by an army of fireflies twinkling like the Christmas tree in the tea room at Marshall Fields. Nature on steroids. He had good instincts, a great camera and a flawless eye for detail. How could one person see such incredible things when others only saw trees and dirt, sand and water? His work spoke of pure joy. An artist who loved his subject. Now, under some delusion that she was an artist in the same playing field, he wanted her to comment on his latest project. Not only was she not in the same field, she wasn't in the same solar system.

What a loser I am. Holed up at a hotel in Vegas, hiding from the woman who runs the PTA and pretending like I'm a grownup who can hold a conversation with this man. He was an artist that made a living from his work. The landscape spray painter she'd encountered in the artist's quad was the guppy who darted around in the waves to avoid becoming dinner for men like Gerard. She was unworthy of his attention or respect in any form. Feeling thoroughly depressed, she shut off the computer and crawled into bed, hoping for a glimmer of inspiration that would put her on some kind of level footing with the artistic genius of Gerard Ilg. Short of a miracle, she would at least like to keep herself from tripping over her own predictable, boring self in front of him.

*   *   *

THURSDAY, SEPTEMBER 7TH

Lanie was late. The depression that sent her scurrying for the covers the night before also prevented her from setting an alarm. A quick glance at the clock on the nightstand told her the bad news. It was ten-thirty. Step one of making a good impression officially ruined. Her sleep had been peppered with nightmares. The hot, sex crazed Ben, the smooth as silk Gerard, and asshole Bob took turns tormenting her. Today was a day she'd have to rely on coffee and spackle to hold it together. Good thing Suni had stocked her makeup bag with primer, illuminator and various highlighters. All things that Lanie had only used on canvas now made available for her sagging skin and plum-colored eye bags.

She'd promised him breakfast. By the time she was dressed and ready to go, she'd be lucky if she could find any breakfast to bring. Somehow lunch didn't have the same professional business appeal. Artists' chain smoked and drank coffee by the pot. At least that's what they did in college. Now, who knew? Coffee, bagels and art felt more appropriate than a hotdog, a diet Sprite and art. If Vegas operated under the universal law of the McDonald's Corporation, eleven was the magic no more serving breakfast hour. She'd have to forgo being put together. Trading it in for the too cool to care artistic look could be a good thing. She threw on her new, gauzy blue dress from the Camille Flawless boutique, raked a brush through her knotted hair, swished some Listerine, grabbed her sketchbook and made a run for the elevator.

The snotty, older British couple who had mocked her out of the elevator the night before were back. Dressed in their stuffy Sunday best, they stood in silence, waiting for the doors to open. A trip to the ice closet would be preferable to another round of insults from those two. The precious few minutes she'd have to wait for the next elevator wouldn't be a big deal on any other day. Today, she had no choice but to bite the bullet and face the drier-than-Gin ridicule of the Queen's loyal subjects. The down arrow lit up and she quickened her pace. "Good morning." She chirped out the greeting. Better to face them head on and get the snide comments out of the way.

The pair turned in unison. The wife raised her brow, the British version of bitch slapping, and flared her nostrils. "Good morning." Her words were as clipped as Lanie's were chirpy.

"Ah, yes," the husband added running his hands over the brim of his white Bailey Billy Fedora. "Good to see you, back on your feet, that is."

Lanie nodded. Keeping her gaze straight ahead, she threw back her shoulders and marched through the open doors. They followed directly behind her, whispering up a storm. The Phantom of the Opera, being the current venue at the Venetian, had the sound track piped into the elevators twenty-four-seven. The sound covered their words but the conspiratorial glances they were throwing in her direction gave her a good idea that she was still their main topic of conversation. Her live make out show with Ben was probably the raciest thing they'd seen since arriving in Sin City. Doubtful they'd be the types to hit the Playboy Club at the Palms. She busied herself reading the poster advertising Wolfgang Puck's newest concept restaurant, the Postrio Bar & Grill and absorbing the lyrics of *Think of Me*. The duet played so frequently she was surprised it didn't invade her sleep.

They reached the second floor Grand Canal Shoppes and Lanie made haste. The heat in her cheeks could only mean that she'd turned a nice shade of beet red. Giving the dynamic British duo more fodder at her expense was something she'd like to avoid. The quick exit might not hide her embarrassment from them, but the faster she moved, the farther away she'd be if they laughed. Perhaps far enough that she wouldn't even hear it.

The Coffee Bean & Tea Leaf had a line a mile long. Waiting for bagels and joe a deux was out of the question. She would have to fake amnesia on her breakfast offer. Better yet, she could establish her presence and take his custom order. Maybe she'd earn a few points for being thoughtful. Undo some of the insanity of her barely out of bed appearance.

Rounding the corner to the gallery, she stopped short. Aluminum garage style doors covered the entry and exit. She'd rushed for nothing. Her Frenchman hadn't even arrived.

Or maybe he thought you stood him up.

It wasn't like he didn't know where to find her. If he'd already made the trip and classified her as a no show, wouldn't he have called to find out what happened? She was staying in the man's personal suite. If he forgot the direct number he could just access it through the main switchboard at the front desk. Easy peasy. Odds were on her side that he had yet to show up. Plenty of time for an about face to the line around the corner for her caffeine fix.

Something red caught her eye. Leaning in, she examined the small circle. A doorbell set in the dead center of the door, just waiting to be pushed. Before she could decide whether or not to give it a ring, the door began to move. Slowly, it lifted from the ground, exposing her to the dark interior of the gallery.

"Come in. Follow the sound of my voice to the back."

Not only had he been waiting for her, he could see her. Good thing she didn't indulge in any particularly nasty habits like secret nose picking. If something like that fell into the hands of a minimum wage security guard, it would surely end up on YouTube. Scanning the walls, she checked for a hidden camera. She couldn't find a thing. No wires. No lenses. Not even a pinhole. Nothing that would lead someone to the conclusion that they were being watched. Vegas security; technology that could rival the CIA, paid for by dollars of dreamers.

Lanie stepped over the threshold. "Sorry I'm late. I was sketching and I lost track of time." The lie slipped past her lips with zero effort. Not even a hint of guilt or a blip of a stutter; just pure, smooth falseness. Lexi would have been proud.

The response was the heavy door sliding closed, engulfing her in darkness. Following voices in the dark brought back painful memories of the day she caught Bob with Brittney at the dealership. *There is no other woman here, Lanie. If you end up in a state of ridiculousness today, it will be all on you.* Slow steps were safe. Gerard was safe. She was safe. She would move through this dark gallery unafraid, one baby step at a time.

A slice of light along the floor caught her attention. Where there was light, she was sure to find Gerard. Her eyes refused to adjust to the new shades of night, forcing her to slide her feet along the floor like the undead in the classic Son of Svengooli Saturday horrorthon. If the security cameras had night vision capabilities, they were sure to capture some excellent footage of her half blind trudge. If it weren't for the sketchbook clutched tightly against her chest, her arms would be thrust out changing her demeanor from zombie to mummy. Not very chic, unless you happened to be a monsterphilliac. If such a disorder existed, Lanie's current strut would put her in the running for the group's top sex symbol. She could make millions off the merchandising rights.

The slice of light was close enough to touch with her toe. Time to release one hand of her death grip and find the knob of what she assumed was the door to Gerard's office. Before her fingers found the wood, it moved. Light, blinding and unexpected, filled the room. Forgetting the sketchbook, Lanie blocked the shock with her open palms. Taking a step back, she felt the floor sliding away from her. Before she could reach in the direction of the open door, presumably where she could fall into the arms of Gerard, her front leg kicked up high enough to pull the rear one off the ground by the hem of her skirt. Flying through the air took a mere second. Her padded rump smacked the wood floor, her legs askew. Her vanity was crushed but her bones were intact.

He laughed, adding to her misery. Bastard. Frenchmen were supposed to make women feel sexy, not clumsy. She kept her eyes squeezed shut. Effective in sealing out the light that sent her sailing, it did little in the way of protection from humiliation.

"I'm sorry." He chuckled. "I didn't mean to scare you! Come, open your eyes! See why I brought you here today."

Slowly, Lanie opened one eye. The dropped sketchbook, the culprit of her blundering ballerina fall, sat at the tip of Gerard's caramel colored huaraches. The cover was torn at the edge, exposing her drawing of the garden pool. Afraid to look up, she opened the other eye and made herself busy brushing imaginary lint and dirt off her stinging palms. Smoothing the front of her dress, she hit an extra sensitive spot and stopped.

Oh, God. Tell me that isn't what I think it is.

Trying to appear casual, she cast a quick glance down her front. A perfect pink crescent gave her an upside down smile. It was exactly what she thought it was—nipple slippage. The front of the wrap dress had come loose during the fall, giving Gerard a nice peek at her goods. Combine that with her sprawled open leg crash landing, and she was only one pair of aqua blue panties away from being naked. Trying not to be obvious, she jerked the dress across her exposed flesh and crossed her arms, tucking her fingers deep in the pockets of her armpits.

If he noticed, or got a cheap thrill from her flashing, he didn't show it. His smile was warm and genuine. He reached for her hand. "Come! I insist that you see this before it goes out into the world."

Without looking down to see if it worked, she reached out and let him pull her to her feet. Guiding her into the back room, he closed the door behind them. "What do you think?"

Lanie took in the scene. "I...." She was at a loss for words. The work propped along the walls could not be that of the famous landscape photographer. She wanted to like them, she really did, but they were atrocious. Absolutely horrible. Gone were the scenes snapped from nature, so beautiful and serene that they brought tears to her eyes. What replaced it was disastrous. Each piece was a mutant mix of animals dressed in clothing, the lights of the strip, and death. And they were big, at least four by six feet each. The one closest to the door contained the fountain in front of the Bellagio, a greyhound in a suit sitting on a bench, and a dead Flamingo hanging by its legs from the streetlight.

"It's..." He was watching her closely. He wanted the truth; she could see it in his eyes. "Awful. Really, truly horrible. Is that Flamingo hanging by a streetlight really dead?"

He shook his head, his hand cupping his chin, his index finger stroking his facial hair. "The bird is not real. Does that change your opinion?"

She wished she could spare his feelings. "No."

He continued to dissect the piece with his stare. "You do not find this appealing, on any level? This is not what you would call, pop art?"

"I'm sorry. I told you, I'm not any good at this. It's probably great pop art—I'm just not qualified to make that determination. The last piece of work I sold was a sketch of a rose garden. My mother bought it for her garden club."

She watched as he walked over to the piece, picked it up, and threw it into the giant green trash can by the back door. Turning back he looked around the office, taking in each piece.

"You are right. This is terrible. They are all terrible. I knew it when I shot them. It's not natural to put animals in clothing and take pictures of things that are dead."

"Then why did you do it?"

He ran his hands through his silver streaked mane. "I'm old, too old for this place. Nobody here wants nature. They want sound, light—

shock value." He moved to the next picture, an African parrot in a pirate costume, sitting on a short palm, with a man on the sidewalk with a knife in his back. "Help me throw these out." Lifting the pirate murder menagerie he made his way back to the trash.

She eyed the picture closest to her. A scary clown, with an even scarier dog on its shoulder, snarling through vampire teeth at a bleeding white Siberian tiger dared her to come closer. "Are you sure?"

He crossed the room and came to rest with his hand on her shoulder. "Please, Elaine, you see them for what they are—garbage. Now help me take out the trash."

She hoisted the picture up. It was surprisingly light for such a large piece. Covering the distance to the trashcan, now overflowing with obnoxious pictures, she crumpled the horrid picture down into a ball and threw it in with the others. From across the room Gerard watched her, smiling.

"That felt good, no? Now, let's go share a meal and dissect the tragedy that is my life."

It was exhilarating. Destroying art, even bad art, felt naughty. The newest creations of the famous Gerard Ilg were potentially worth millions. Throwing them away was as reckless as burning a big fat pile of Ben Franklins. And who would be to blame if the pieces were deemed genius by the artistic community? Elaine Elizabeth Jackerson, that's who. Oh God, what had she done? Why did he listen to her? Reaching into the trash she pulled a balled up picture off the top. "I really think you need to talk to someone in the industry before you throw these out."

He took her arm. "You might not trust your instincts, but I trust mine. Right now they are telling me that we need to get some food. Forget the photos."

"But—"

"I have the originals saved on a flash drive. Does that make you fret less?"

They were saved! Oh miracle of miracles, she was saved from making a make it or break it career decision for the famous Gerard Ilg. "Yes."

"Now we can eat?"

Stress always made her hungry. This event left her ravenous. "Yes."

*   *   *

Dos Caminos, the Mexican Mecca inside the Palazzo, lived up to the hype. It was swanky, empty, and fairly expensive for a get-to-know-you meal. Amber lighting gave the late night hot date feel. Sun outside be damned. Human skulls lined the back wall and a strong Latin beat drummed in the background. Lanie was impressed.

The perfect gentleman, Gerard pulled out her chair. "Don't let the skeletons scare you. They are cast resin."

"I know."

He pushed her chair in. Leaning down he whispered in her ear. "Sometimes symbols of death can be sexy, no?"

Normally she would say no. Death was not something she found sexy. But the way he said it, whispered as a private message for her ears only, heightened her senses in what could only be classified as sex ready. "It's intriguing."

He settled into the seat across from her. In a flash, their waiter appeared. A metrosexual dressed in black with thick framed wayfarer eyeglasses, he greeted them with two blue drinks in martini glasses. "Good day, Mr. Ilg. I've taken the liberty of bringing you your usual beverage. I've brought one for your friend as well. Our special for today is the Lamb Barbacoa. That comes with rice, beans, seared fresh corn and soft corn tortillas."

"Thank you, Bradley. We need a minute. This is Elaine's first visit."

"Ah," Bradley replied shaking his head in a sympathetic manner. "I will return shortly to take your order."

Lanie picked up the deep blue mystery drink in front of her and sipped. Alcohol, fruity, sweet and strong, slid down her throat. "Mmmm. What is it?"

"A blueberry pomegranate margarita. I prefer them over the prickly pear house specialty. Do those sounds mean you approve?"

"I approve. More than I should for a morning."

He waved his hand dismissively. "Who sets these rules for you? If you ask me, Americans are repressed in all the wrong areas. They think nothing of eating swine for breakfast, but reserve a good drink for after five. You are in Vegas. There is no such thing as the proper time to have a drink."

She tipped the glass and finished the drink. "Okay boss, now what?"

He smiled approvingly. "Now," he said raising his hand to call Bradley back to the table, "we eat."

* * *

Lanie was stuffed. So stuffed that the walk back to the elevator was painful. She had eaten every bite of her meal. The seared steak tacos, marinated in lime and chilies and grilled to perfection, the roasted corn, beans, and two more margaritas had made it down her gullet. Gerard talked quietly throughout the meal, taking a bite from time to time with a sip of his drink. Her plate was licked clean while his looked like a toddler had stolen a few bites on the way to catch Sesame Street. She stopped her inhalation long enough to wonder if her piggy eating habits were a turn off. Setting down her fork, she turned her full attention on her host.

"Why did you stop?"

She swallowed the lump of meat she'd been working on. "I wanted to give you my full attention."

"You cannot do this when you are chewing?" He asked puzzled.

"I can, I just thought it might be rude."

"Nonsense. You are enjoying your food. Listen with your ears and keep eating."

That was all the encouragement Lanie needed. She ate and he talked. Most of his monologue was about himself, but not in a way that seemed narcissistic, more of just a rambling biography. He'd been everywhere, done everything, made a mint of money following his passions, and never compromised his ideals. It was great entertainment, plus the longer he rambled, the more she could follow the curve of his lips without looking like a love struck teenager.

The meal lasted over two hours, and now as she walked to the elevator that would take her back to her suite, she wished it had been at least double that. They reached the split in the Canal Shoppes, the point where she would go right and he would go left. She slowed down trying to savor her last precious moments of their date.

"Thank you again for helping me today. If it weren't for you, I'd be hanging those horrible pictures right now."

"It was my pleasure, Gerard. Thank you for the wonderful lunch."

He rubbed his chin scruff. He looked like he was in turmoil. "I feel so bad."

"You can sneak the trash out and burn it in the desert, and then no one will ever know it existed."

He laughed. "Not that—you. I feel so bad that I didn't get to hear more about you. I want to know all about the mysterious Elaine who showed up as my guest to find herself." His voice dropped midway through speaking, dipping into a sexy baritone whisper and he stepped forward to brush a lock of hair that had fallen into her face behind her ear. "I want to hear about the man who left a beautiful woman with two babies and such passion. I want to know what could possess someone to be so, very stupid."

His fingers had barely touched her, and yet she felt like he had caressed her soul. There was a heat there, but unlike the hormonal force she felt with Ben. This was a different sensation. A volcano that had lain undisturbed for years coming to life under the shifting of the tectonic plates that were her life. "We could talk more in your office. I left my sketch book there."

What was she doing? Propositioning Gerard, hoping that he would take her into his office and ravage her right there in the floor among the littered portraits, maybe even on them? Yes, she decided. That was exactly what she was doing. Gerard said she should find her passion, and right now, her passion was a distinct French landscape photographer who found her beautiful and passionate.

"Elaine...I..." he looked surprised, shocked even.

This was a precipice. Bigger and scarier than joining the PTA

Mafia. Worse than discovering her husband's philandering and her daughter's loose morals (which, she was realizing, probably came from her oversexed mother). More difficult to navigate than sleeping with Ben Oliana, the sexy limo driver. This could be the real deal. He was a grown up. A famous grown up who could have his pick of any woman on the planet. Would he take the bait? Even if it was a quick affair, how many women could say they'd slept with someone of his notoriety? A romp with Gerard would make her time with Ben easier to forget.

Taking a deep breath, she gave him what she hoped was a sexy smile. Without ten minutes in front of a mirror to practice, her confidence in the move was low. It was hard to feel good about something you hadn't used since Madonna's release of the Material Girl album in 1985. But, at the moment it was all she had. "I'm going to get it." Tightening her butt cheeks, she sauntered into the now open studio. If he wanted her, he'd follow. If he didn't, she would save face with the sketchbook—a legitimate reason for going back—and spend the rest of her Vegas days in hiding. She had just reached the office door when she felt a hand on her shoulder. *It worked!* She thought triumphantly.

"Excuse me, ma'am, you can't go in there. That room is for employees only."

Shit. It hadn't worked at all. Taking her hand off the knob she mumbled a quick apology. Ducking her head, she made her way to the safety of the exit. She was about to cross the threshold when she felt a familiar hand on her shoulder again. "What now? I said I was sorry..."

"Did you think I would let you leave so easily?" It was Gerard. Flushed and discombobulated, he took her by the hand. With a firm grasp, he led her back the way she'd fled. Back into the studio, past the gawkers and the lovers on the loveseats, past the spot where the irritated male employee had shooed her away, and into the office where they could be alone. She held her breath, afraid of what was coming next and wanting it all the same. Without a word, he pulled her to him, gathering her body up in his arms.

"Why do you tempt me like this?" His nose pressed against her neck, breathing in her scent. "I can't do what you ask, not like this."

She had been expecting him to ravish her. He had made all the perfunctory moves, but now he was backing off. She pushed him away, peeling herself from his warm embrace. "Why not?"

He sighed. The sound came from the deep well inside his soul. He looked to be in mourning. He walked to his desk and picked up her sketch book. Opening it to the first page he admired her drawings of the gardens surrounding the tenth floor pool. "You do underestimate your talent. These are magnificent." Closing the cover, he held it out to her.

She took it from him, her ego bruised beyond words. How could she have misjudged his feelings about her so drastically? "I don't understand. I thought—"

"I am not able to love you, Elaine, not in flesh or in spirit. Part of you belongs with someone else, I can feel it."

He knew about Bob, or Ben, or both. Suni must have told him something. Or maybe he was on closer terms with his limo driver than he let on. Or maybe he'd reviewed her elevator antics with the security crew. Every scenario was painfully embarrassing. Clutching the sketchbook to her chest, she bolted out the door.

CHAPTER TWELVE

Back in the safety of her room, Lanie cursed her stupidity. Why had she made such a blatant pass at a man like Gerard? He was brilliant, talented, and well aware of her relationships back home. His comments back in the studio about belonging to another were an obvious reference to her failed, but still legal, marriage to Bob. She slammed the sketchbook on the desk. Why had she buried her head in the sand for so many years? If she had only been true to herself, then she'd be free and clear to follow her passion and bed her sultry Frenchman, or any man of her choosing. She'd blown it in so many ways. Her life was just one failure after another. This one, being the most current, stung the most.

The buzz of the lunchtime margaritas had worn off. Lanie desperately needed another drink to act as a salve on her burning humiliation. Red wine would do the trick. It had a high enough alcohol content to ease her pain in a single glass and held the honor of being a heart saver. At the moment, her heart needed all the help it could get. Before she could get to the mini bar, the blinking red light on the desk phone stopped her in her tracks. Could it be Gerard calling to tell her he regretted letting her go? Holding her breath, she picked up the headset and dialed nine.

"I know I told you that'd I'd wait for you to contact me, but I miss you. I scored some tickets to Cirque tonight. Good seats. What do you say? Can we give this another chance?"

Ben. He'd given her less than a day to get over him. It wasn't enough. He was wrong in all the right ways. His voice on the line sent her into involuntary sexual flashbacks. If he was being paid to keep her content he had earned every penny. He'd even gone the extra step and claimed her as his girlfriend—a term that hadn't applied to her since college. Now that her plans to bed Gerard had failed she'd have to find another way to forget his sweet warmth.

Replacing the headset on the cradle she plopped onto the velour sectional. This was insanity. All of it. She'd left her children with an insane suburban mafia mom, who was getting some cheap thrill out of kidnapping Bob, the slime ball, and Brittney, the slutty secretary. She'd attempted two Judy Blume worthy affairs only to fall for the boy and be rejected by the man. It was time to face facts. Her life, as screwed up as it had recently become, was still back in Glen Ellyn where she'd left it. There was no way out by digging deeper into the fantasy. She'd have to make a deal with Suni and her crew. If they refused to listen to reason she would have no choice but to go to the police. Resigned to her fate, she dialed.

"Lanie...don't hang up."

Yvette. Waiting for the dial tone and hoping for something different. "I won't."

There was a brief silence on the other end followed by a click. *Christ I hope she doesn't shoot him while I'm on the line.*

"You got my message?"

What message? Her gaze went back to the desk phone. The red button was off. "Did you call the hotel? The cell has been dead since I landed."

"Never mind. Where are you?"

What kind of game was Yvette playing? She knew where Lanie was, she had to. "Suni didn't tell you?"

"You are in big trouble. Bigger than you realize. Now please, tell me where you are."

Suni hadn't told Yvette where she was hiding Lanie. A secret kept from the inner ring implied trust issues. She must have been worried that Yvette would go rogue on the group. "Not until I talk to Bob." Bob's state of existence would help determine her next move. If he was breathing she could attempt some kind of negotiation. Dead bodies didn't make good leverage. She really hoped he was still alive.

There was some shuffling on the other end of the line, followed by a whimper.

"Bob, is that you?"

"Lanie, please, tell them where you are."

Bob. He was crying; but he was alive. Blubbering his plea for her location into the mouthpiece of the phone he'd used the word *them*. *Them* meant that there was more than one person with dragon lady Yvette. Who had she dragged into her sordid circle?

"Who else is with you? Are they other PTA mom's?"

"There's no time for guessing games. For the love of God, you have to tell them where you are! Think about Charlie and Lexi."

She was thinking about Charlie and Lexi. If Yvette found her she'd kill them both leaving her children orphans. Making a deal with blood thirsty Yvette was out of the question. She'd have to bypass her and go straight to Suni. If she was as mistrusting of Yvette as it appeared, she might be willing to let Lanie go to the police. It wasn't a great plan, but it was something.

"Lanie, are you there? Please, just tell me where you are."

"I'm sorry, Bob. Tell Yvette I said no deal."

Before he could protest, she depressed the button on the base and cut him off.

* * *

Lanie's call to Suni went unanswered. Lexi didn't pick up, and neither did Charlie. Now she was in a full blown panic. Her plans of using their mutual dislike of Yvette to bond and make the horrors of the past few weeks disappear only worked if she could get Suni on the phone and convince her to give it a go. Running through her conversation with Bob, she tried to pick out any clues that would give her an idea of where her children were. Bob's pleas to reveal her location to Yvette confused her. He had insisted that she give herself up to ensure Charlie and Lexi's safety, but how could that be? What was she missing?

She could sit tight and wait, giving Lexi, Charlie, Suni and Babette more time to contact her, or she could call Yvette back and wing it. Trying to sort out her choices was like trying to decide if she wanted to dance with the devil or swim with the sharks. Pacing the hotel suite, she tried to find a good solution, but all she could come up with was one morbid scenario after another. What if she never saw Lexi or Charlie again? What if her little Poodle became a corrupted criminal like Suni and her little thug in training, Ajay? The boy couldn't lie to save his life. Suni was sure to tear him to bits the minute he told the wrong person the truth. And then there was Bob.

What were her feelings about Bob? After coming close to breaking her neck in the dark car dealership she had been so full of venom that she'd given the command to have him taken out. Sure, she'd retracted the wish, but where did that deep anger come from? They'd built a life together, but somewhere between the hot blooded passion of young love and drowning herself in a bottle of red, they'd lost each other. She knew it was happening, the distance that crept in and left her cold most nights in spite of the fact that his heat was only an arm's reach away, but the reaching seemed so hard. A light touch that could have brought them together was a task so insurmountable that she gave up. The question was—who gave up first? Did it even matter? Suni and her crew had broken the remaining illusion that it had been just one girl. There had been many. The indiscretions frequent enough that they were obvious to anyone who looked beyond the concrete drive lined with hedge roses. She might have grown cold, but she'd never launched herself into the arms of another. Ben didn't count. Retaliation sex couldn't be held against her, not after boffing Brittney in the back office.

Home. Her little corner of the universe, both stifling and safe. She had to go back. She would save her children and her husband. Even if they'd mucked it all up beyond repair, this last journey together would be seen through until the very end. Then Bob could go off and sleep with every blond from Illinois to Texas, Lexi could go off to college, and Charlie would be safe in her arms.

Could she make it out of Vegas without getting caught? She'd have to try. Even if Suni's spies grabbed her, they'd probably take her to wherever Lexi and Charlie were being held. At least then they'd be together to face whatever was waiting for them.

The polka dot Hartman bag sat in the closet next to her new wardrobe. Tearing the clothes off the rack, she stuffed them in, trying to make everything fit. The cash that had mysteriously fallen into her possession upon arrival remained bundled in the envelope on the table. She counted the bills. Only fifteen hundred remained. How could that be? Other than her splurge at Pink, some drinks and gelato, she hadn't spent a dime. Everything she'd thrown a glance at had ended up in her room at no charge, thanks to Gerard's well trained staff. One of the maids must have been lining their pockets during the morning clean up. It would be enough to get home so long as she didn't have to grease any palms.

Gerard's face popped into her mind. His voice, husky and rough when he'd turned her down, echoed in her mind. He would never know what happened to her. Would he wrongly assume that she fled because of embarrassment over his rejection? Or worse; would he believe she was too spineless to reach for her passion? Ben, her favorite mistake, would find another sexual outlet lickety split. Being replaced, even if it was with an imaginary woman, stung. Hot tears sprang from behind her lids and ran down her cheeks. Wiping them away, she tossed the envelope into the bag and zipped it shut.

She was debating the best way to sneak out of the hotel undetected when a knock rattled the door.

"Elaine?"

Speak of the French devil. She stuffed the bulging bag under the bed and crossed the room. Muffled male voices just outside the door gave her pause. One was definitely Gerard. The anger in his voice was clearly audible through the heavy wood. Pressing her ear against the locked barrier she tried to identify the other voice. It didn't sound like Ben, but if it was she could forget making a graceful exit. Once they compared notes she would be labeled a washed up pathetic cougar *and* a two timer. Given her choice, she'd scratch out pathetic and take the standard cougar label. It implied that, on some level, she was sexy enough to catch a stud. Nobody had to know he'd been paid.

Gerard growled. Straining to make out words she picked up a few things—*give me a minute, I don't care who you are*—but nothing that made sense. The other man growled back. It couldn't be Ben. The voice was too deep. Ben maintained a just past puberty huskiness. So who the hell was it? Tired of playing the guessing game she twisted the handle and threw open the door.

Her gusto to discover the mysterious man was a mistake. The stranger dressed in blue made a grab for her, but Gerard wedged himself between them ushering her back into the suite.

"Don't worry, Elaine. This is just some kind of misunderstanding." Gerard had her by the elbow and was gently leading her in the direction of the living room. Numbness spread through her body. The tingle of shock that struck prior to passing out ran along her nerves and she stumbled. "Do you see what you've done?" Gerard shouted over his shoulder to the predator trailing a half step behind. "She is in shock."

"Sir, I'm going to have to ask you to step away from Mrs. Jackerson."

"She needs to sit down." He stopped in front of the gold sectional. "Elaine, sit. Let me get you a glass of water."

Shaking from head to toe, she grabbed his hand and pulled him down next to her. Water would have to wait. The velour couch was no comfort. Even Gerard's strong body next to her couldn't stop the chattering of her teeth. There was no port for the shit storm that was about to strike. No Frenchman saucy enough to save her. No hot Hawaiian to lay her on his surfboard and catch a wave out. She was sunk. Swallowing, she took in the imposing figure. One hand on his shiny black belt, the other rested casually on the leather holster.

"Elaine Jackerson, I'm Sergeant Joe Peterson, Las Vegas Police. You are under arrest."

CHAPTER THIRTEEN

The next six hours were a blur. The cuffs went on smoothly, she was too numb to protest, or even ask why she was being taken in. Sergeant Joe read her rights after informing her that she was being charged with obstruction of justice. Gerard had exploded, jumping to his feet and demanding more information, but after several threats to take him in right along with her, he watched as she was led away promising to send his attorney down to set things straight.

So far, the attorney hadn't shown up. The concrete room she'd been thrown into didn't have cell bars. Just a regular steel door with a small window up high enough that she couldn't catch a glance at what was on the other side from the chair she was chained to. High in the corner where the wall met the ceiling an indiscreet video camera peered at her, the small red light blinking. Every so often Sergeant Joe would pop his head in and ask her if she wanted anything. What she wanted was to go back in time and get a do-over. Coke, Pepsi, even Starbucks, could not provide her with a time machine. She passed on the offer of a sugar and caffeine laden beverage.

When Sergeant Joe had materialized at her door, she assumed the worst. Straining to stay focused, she watched his lips, waiting for the M word to announce Bob's demise. Obstruction of justice sounded ominous. Bad, but not nearly as bad as being charged with multiple murders. If Bob was alive, what justice had she obstructed? The ice pick between her brows chipped at her brain while she ran through the events of her life looking for something that fit those terms. If the charge was attempted murder for unleashing the mafia on Bob, she would have confessed to the corner camera and signed the written statement hours ago. Any way she sliced it, obstruction threw her for a loop.

Her bladder throbbed. Where was Sergeant Joe when she needed him? In desperation, she pleaded with the camera. "Please, I really need to use the bathroom."

On cue, the door flew open. The person who breezed in, casually taking the seat across the table from Lanie, wasn't Sergeant Joe.

It was none other than psychotic kidnapper and potential killer, Yvette.

* * *

"You are one tough cookie, Lanie. Ever think about working for the CIA as a spy?"

Lanie forced her mouth closed and resisted the almost involuntary need to crawl under the table. She shook her head.

Yvette stuck out her hand. "Special Agent Cheryl Black, FBI."

Lanie shrank away from her outstretched palm. How on earth did Yvette pull off impersonating an FBI agent well enough to infiltrate the Las Vegas Police Department? She eyed the corner camera. If Yvette made a grab for her and tried to drag her out, she would scream holy hell. Maybe there were a few good cops left on the force. Maybe they would find the video and realize what had happened. Maybe...

The manila folder that had been tucked safely under the arm of Yvette's blue blazer hit the table with an impatient smack. "Snap out of it!" Yvette's fingernails, the red dragon talons, were clipped short and were bare of any polish. They snapped in front of Lanie's eyes, drawing her attention back to Yvette's face. "Stay with me. I need you to focus on what I'm saying."

"How did you do it?" Lanie whispered. "You won't get away with this. They can't all be bad. Somebody will hear my screams—"

"What on earth?" Yvette frowned. A look of confusion clouded her face followed by amusement. "You don't get it do you? You still think I'm one of them." She leaned across the table closing the gap between herself and Lanie. "I'm an FBI agent, you idiot, not one of your flunky, wannabe mobsters." She opened her blazer exposing a bronze star. "I've been an agent with the Federal Bureau of Investigations for the past thirteen years."

No. There was no way Yvette was an agent for the government. Yvette was an extremely threatening mafia mom who had kidnapped her lousy excuse of a husband. She had red talons that could kill with dagger precision and probably ate girls like Brittney Baylor for breakfast.

Yvette raked her naked, clipped nails through her shoulder-length blond hair. "I tried like hell to keep you out of this, but you just kept showing up. Suni had you pegged as a target from the beginning. I knew you had no idea what you were in for."

Lanie eyed her suspiciously. This woman sitting in front of her was Yvette, but she wasn't. Yvette screamed tacky rich woman not to be fucked with. This woman was different. She was all business, but not over-the-top-look-at-me glam. Her hair was still platinum, but it was sleek and straight. Her face had been scrubbed clean of all the layers of makeup, her suit said business professional and her nails—well they looked downright normal.

Nails. The picture with the ominous message on the cell phone popped into her head. The red blip in the corner of the message had been painted acrylic. It was Yvette, or rather Special Agent Black, holding the sign. She must have put it on the screen hoping that Lanie would call her. "You put the message on my phone?"

"Yes. When I picked up Bob at your house, I put the picture message on the screen. I thought you might realize it was taken in your own house, take a chance, and call the number on the screen. Boy, was I wrong on that one. Thank God you finally stayed on the line long enough for us to trace the call to your location. I was beginning to worry we wouldn't get you in time."

"In time for what?"

"We think Suni's on to us. She and Babette went dark. We have no idea where they went, or what they have planned."

* * *

Lanie felt weak. The strong coffee that Sergeant Joe kept trying to make her swallow did nothing to ease her nerves. Suni had taken her children to an undisclosed location and the entire FBI had been unable to find them. Yvette's disclosure that she was really Cheryl Black, an agent for the FBI, had left her mind reeling. The questions continued to bubble up, and Special Agent Black, as far as Lanie could tell, was doing her best not to lose her cool.

"Remember in Suni's kitchen, when they asked if anyone protested to you becoming a member?"

She remembered. Yvette had been the only protestor. She had openly challenged Suni.

"That was an attempt on my part to keep you out of trouble. Suni had it in for you. She wanted you to go down in the worst way."

"Why?" Lanie didn't even know Suni before the day she got railroaded into signing up for the PTA at the back to school coffee.

"Jealousy. Raw hatred over your simple, suburban life. I hate to be the one to tell you this, but Suni was Bob's first affair."

On a one to ten pain scale, finding out that Bob had bedded Suni ranked a high nine. It would have been off the charts if she weren't terrified for her children's safety. "When?" She asked weakly.

"Around the time Bob opened the dealership. She went in for a Mercedes and came out with a special bonus. See, Suni's husband, Michael, had left for New York. His job as the head of finance required that he be away from her for weeks at a time. They both agreed it was best for her to stay behind—Glen Ellyn being an ideal place to raise children—but Suni was bored and needy."

Apparently, Bob had been bored and needy as well. "But why go after me? I never even knew the affair happened."

"Michael found out and left her cold. She thought Bob would step up and take Michael's place. In her mind, the two of them had a nice, little future all carved out. Between her big, fat divorce settlement and Bob's money from the dealership, they would have been set. Bob had other plans. For him, it was just a nice break from the hum drum."

Bastard. She was not hum drum. "How did you get involved in this?"

"Michael noticed things when he would come to see the kids. If he ate or drank anything at the house, he'd get sick. One morning, he got in his rental car to head back to the airport and his brakes failed. That's when he came to us."

"She tried to kill him."

"Maybe. That hasn't been proven yet. It was my job to get close to her and try to find out what she was really up to. Most of her dealings were petty. Typical small town scams—you scratch my back and I'll scratch yours. Illegal, but not murder for hire."

"Something changed?" It was a big leap from con artist to murderer.

"Suni's world revolved around being the top dog, even if it was just the top dog of the Herschel Grammar School PTA. Some of the ladies in the group were beginning to question her authority. They thought she was all big talk. Some were considering voting her out at the next election. When Suni got wind of that, she panicked. If she lost her spot as President of the PTA, then she really was a loser. She'd lost her husband, her plans with yours, and now this? It was too much."

"I still don't understand why she wanted me?"

"You were the perfect patsy. Telling you about your husband's affairs tore apart the perfect, little life you had that she wanted. If you agreed to have Bob taken out, then she really could become the big, bad mafia mom. Maybe even land you a spot in jail for murder. You could have taken a crime of passion charge if you were willing to kill him yourself."

It still didn't make any sense. Suni hadn't told Lanie about Bob and Brittney, she'd stumbled on that all on her own. "She didn't tell me about the affairs, I heard them on the phone. Bob tried to tell me I was crazy, but I caught them red handed."

Special Agent Black flipped open the manila folder and pulled out an 8x10 glossy photo of Brittney and Suni having drinks at the Cosmos Martini and Manicure Spa. "You weren't the only one handpicked for Suni's games. The phone call that tipped you off to the affair was no accident."

Brittney was a kid, barely out of high school. "I didn't think she was old enough to drink."

"She's older than she looks." She replied thumbing casually through the other items in the folder.

"How much older?"

"Thirty-four."

Great. Brittney was still super hot at thirty-four. Didn't look a day over twenty-one. She glanced across the table and caught a smirk on the detective's bare lips. Without the lacquered red pout, she looked to be about thirty-four herself.

"Don't tell me that it bothers you that she looks good at thirty-four?"

Yes. It bothered the hell out of her. "No. I'm just surprised."

"Ah. Well, if it's any consolation we have Ms. Baylor in custody. She confessed to working with Suni right away. Now she sits in the Metropolitan Correction Center in Downtown Chicago awaiting her status hearing. She doesn't look so great behind bars."

"Is that where I'm going?" The thought of jail made her queasy.

"Right now, the only thing we can charge you with is obstruction of justice, and that only works if you refuse to cooperate. Then again, if you were to refuse, not only would you land in jail, your children would be left at the mercy of an insane woman. "

"How can you charge me with obstruction of justice? I haven't destroyed any evidence."

"True. Obstruction extends to interfering with a criminal investigation. While it might seem a stretch, I would argue that refusing to cooperate in our attempt to find and arrest Suni and Babette could be viewed as obstruction. I know a few judges who would agree with my argument. In fact, I was able to have you arrested because a judge agreed with my arguments and signed off on a warrant. Will the charges stick, after your attorney pokes holes in my case?" She shrugged. "I can't answer that. But, really, Lanie, do you want to go that route? Wouldn't it be better for everyone if you cooperate like a good girl?"

Jail was a daunting prospect. Losing her children was a nightmare beyond what she could handle. "What do I need to do?"

"As I said before, we have no idea where Babette and Suni are right now—they disappeared off our radar three days ago. That's when we grabbed Brittney. Her confession made it easy for us to obtain search warrants for their property. The houses were empty. Babette's husband is in Germany on business. We are fairly certain she has her daughter with her."

A small wave of relief washed over Lanie. If Babette had Sonja with her, then Lexi had a better chance of being safe. "What about Ajay? Do you think Suni has him with her?"

"He's with his father in New York."

Lanie swallowed the bile that crept up her throat. Her poor, sweet, little Poodle. He was in really deep trouble and she'd been so wrapped up in her daydreams with Gerard and her lust-filled nights with Ben that she'd allowed it to happen. "Oh, God." She groaned doubling over in her chair.

Special Agent Black came around the table. Lanie's wrists twisted slightly and then were free from the restraints. "Deep breaths."

"What do I do? How do I fix this?" She gasped for air. Tears splashed on the tile floor between her feet.

"There's a good chance that Suni is on her way here right now to try and get to you before we do. This is a woman on the edge. She has lost everything dear to her. Her plans to secure her future as top dog in the PTA, her marriage, her back up guy, have all vanished before her eyes. I'm afraid if we don't find her soon, she will do something more horrific than anyone ever imagined possible."

All of the vacillating she'd done during her stay in Vegas—she'd toyed with the idea of Suni being a monster; a real honest to goodness boogey man—but she'd pushed it away. Who would hurt children? Surely, not the neighbor down the street who had chastised Lanie for dressing like a slob. It just wasn't possible. But here she sat, in front of Special Agent Black, taking in the insufferable news. "You believe she'd hurt Charlie?"

"Yes, I do. Suni is backed into a corner. She won't go down without a fight."

"And Babette?"

"Babette is a follower. I don't know how far she'll go. But, if Suni suspects she is wavering, she won't hesitate to eliminate her as well."

Bile crept up her throat, burning her tongue. "You have to stop them. Please, I'll do anything…"

Work with us, Lanie. Help us put Suni behind bars where she belongs. I promise you, I will do everything in my power to bring your children home safe and sound."

Lanie nodded. Who could have predicted that the safety of her children would rest in the hands of a detective that had posed as a rich mafia mom? The sheer terror she had felt when Yvette pressed her fingernail knife into her throat in Suni's bedroom was a memory she wouldn't forget anytime soon. If the detective had half the venom that pulsed inside of Yvette, Suni would soon find herself on the receiving end of a serious butt kicking. "Are you sure she's on to you?"

"Hard to know beyond a shadow of a doubt—but it appears that way."

Lanie knew the deck was stacked against Ben being a good guy; but she couldn't help wishing for a miracle. "Who was the tipster?"

Special Agent Black frowned. "We don't know. Suni and Gerard are old friends. That makes him a suspect. However, friendships that are born of business don't normally turn into partnerships of murder, but you never know. We are looking for someone who had constant access to you. Someone who would know if you were considering going to the cops. This person would also think nothing of being unscrupulous for money."

Lanie thought she knew who had that kind of access and would do anything for money. Her wish for a Hail Mary miracle was shattered. The tipster had to be none other than the hunky, hot, Hawaiian—Ben Oliana.

CHAPTER FOURTEEN

Physically, the car ride back to the Venetian was far less painful than the trip in the back of the squad car to the police station. Lanie rubbed the red rings on her wrists, trying to make the flesh blend with her Indian summer tan. The black undercover squad car, complete with tinted windows, would have been obvious in most little towns. But on the strip, it drew no attention—people probably assumed it was a small airport limo.

Special Agent Black, or Cheryl, as she had instructed Lanie to call her, sat alone in the backseat. Lanie was positioned in front in case Suni had somehow slipped past the guard who had set up shop at the hotel. If Suni or Babette saw Cheryl, or Yvette, or whoever they thought she was, get out first, they'd make a run for it. God only knew what they would do to Lexi and Poodle then. Detective Black had spelled out an ending that Lanie couldn't accept. Looking out the window, she forced the heinous images out of her mind.

Night-time traffic on the strip was a nightmare that rivaled the I-290 at rush hour. People milled along the sidewalks trying to catch a glimpse of the flaming volcano at the Mirage, the fountain display at the Bellagio, or anything that spoke of free entertainment. Spilling out into the streets with no regard for the color of the traffic lights, they made the already jammed lanes of cars a solid wall of honking metal. Sergeant Joe, dressed in plain clothes, cursed under his breath. "Sit tight, ladies. It's going to be the longest five mile trip you've ever had. If Ms. Jackerson wasn't considered a flight risk, I'd suggest a nice, evening walk."

Lanie caught the snicker from the backset. "Don't worry, Joe, she won't run. Not while they have her kids." According to Cheryl, her jaunt to Vegas had given the judge even greater cause to sign off on what might otherwise be considered a questionable warrant. Another reason to throttle Suni if—no, *when*—they found her. If was a word she had to strike from her vocabulary, for sanity.

A strong hand grabbed her shoulder from behind, causing Lanie to wince and sink deeper into the leather seat. "Since we have some time on our hands, let's go over the plans. I think you'd better start by telling me about your relationships, especially the one with the Mr. Ilg's nephew."

Lanie hadn't met any of Gerard's family. She'd barely gotten her foot in the door with him. "I never met his nephew."

Next to her, Sergeant Joe let out a low whistle. "Oh boy, this is going to be a bumpy ride."

Lanie scanned the traffic. Nothing looked bumpy about it. Slow maybe, but not bumpy.

Cheryl squeezed her shoulder again before letting go. "Benjamin Oliana? He was your limo driver from the airport. Back at the station you said that you thought he might be working for Suni. I ran a quick background check based on his employment records. Turns out he's been in trouble plenty—petty theft, selling marijuana—even tried his hand at running a prostitution ring in the city limits. Sounds like your hunch might be right on the money."

Lanie's memory flashed back to Ben's extreme reaction when he thought she had told Gerard about the money she saw him take from the strange man in the artist's quad. He had completely freaked out. He even went so far as to say that Gerard held his life in his hands. At the time, she thought Gerard might be a criminal, like Suni. How wrong she'd been.

It seemed like she was always wrong. Wrong about her marriage to Bob. Wrong about Yvette. Wrong about Ben. Her complete lack of intuition *had* led her to Gerard, in a twisted, round about fashion, and he was one of the most interesting men she'd ever known. Her chances of getting to know him after the drama of today were probably a big fat zero.

If seeing her dragged off in handcuffs wasn't the flaming red flag that told him to run, finding out she'd shagged his next of kin would do it for sure.

Cheryl's disclosure that Brittney had duped Bob as harshly as she'd been duped by Ben gave her a miniscule amount of comfort. He looked like just as much of a boob as she did. When you took into account the fact his cheating had pushed her to where she sat now—some would say he was an even bigger boob. But nobody wanted to win the big, fat loser of the century contest, not when it hit the press. There wasn't much to write about in the police blotter back in Glen Ellyn, Illinois. This was going to be really big news. She could see the headlines now, *Middle-Aged Couple Beds Hot Young Criminals. Children Kidnapped as a Result.*

Taking a deep breath and smoothing her face into what she could only hope looked like composure, she twisted in her seat to face Cheryl. "We were, well, it was sort of intimate."

Next to her, Sergeant Joe laughed. "Told you. You owe me lunch."

Cheryl shot him her Yvette look of death, boring into the back of his skull. He must have felt its penetration, because he stopped mid laugh, cleared his throat, and kept driving. Lanie needed to learn how to do that. The power to scare people without even making eye contact was like Jedi magic. Satisfied, Cheryl turned her attention back to Lanie. "Were you intimate with Mr. Ilg as well?"

"No. We were…" She struggled to find the right way to describe what had been budding before the world crashed in around her. "Considering our options."

"I take it he has no idea that you slept with his nephew?"

"No. But Ben knew that we'd been spending time together. He cornered me outside my hotel room door and told me that if I wanted him, I knew where to find him. After that, he left me alone."

Cheryl chewed her bottom lip. "This complicates things a bit."

Sergeant Joe snorted and Lanie tried her best to give him the look of death. He turned his head, caught her giving him the evil eye and raised a brow at her. "What's your problem? Got something in your eye?"

Embarrassed, she rubbed at an imaginary piece of lint in her eyeball and turned to face the road. The look of death needed some work.

Behind her, Cheryl sighed and tapped her fingernails impatiently on her laptop. Sergeant Joe was right. This was going to be a very bumpy ride.

*   *   *

FRIDAY, SEPTEMBER 8TH

The sun streamed into the posh suite, pulling Lanie from her restless slumber. Her entry back into the hotel had occurred under great stress, and only after every security angle had been covered. Cheryl had purchased a charger for Lanie's cell phone. So far, no calls from Suni or Babette. Lanie hadn't given Bob's circumstance much thought. When she finally asked about him, Cheryl told her that he was in protective custody and there was nothing to worry about. There was a small part of her that wished his bodyguards might fall asleep on the job, just once or twice. Bob had always been, until very recently, one of those lucky bastards that got out of scrapes without a single scar. She doubted that this would be any different. After the shockwaves died down, he'd be right back to business as usual. Assuming the kids came out okay.

Her room had been wired for sound and Cheryl had spent the night on the couch to make sure nothing went awry before they were ready to start the official Suni stakeout. "How are you feeling?" Cheryl asked handing her a fresh coffee from the Coffee Bean. She looked well rested and almost unrecognizable in her denim capris and fitted tee shirt. Her blond hair was pulled back in a pony tail, still damp from her shower.

"Like I've been hit by a truck." The coffee smelled delicious. She took a sip and prayed the caffeine would hit her system quickly. "Did I sleep through you showering?" She had lain awake a good chunk of the night, tossing and turning in the plush, feather bed.

"Sure did. I've been up for hours. Got a good look at the hotel. Nice digs if you have to be a fugitive. Bob is in a room at the Days Inn off North Avenue. His room is the size of your bathroom."

Lanie smiled. The fresh coffee combined with news of Bob's unfortunate circumstances was clearing her head and making her day brighter by the minute.

"I poked around the Canal Shoppes. Ran right into your friend, Mr. Ilg, coming out of his studio. He looked like he'd been up all night. I think he's worried about you. His lack of sleep should make your job easier."

Her happiness over Bob being stuffed in a hotel room the size of a postage stamp was quickly replaced with angst. Cheryl's comment about Gerard sat like a rock in her stomach. "Do you really think it's a good idea for me to be taking on the role of undercover agent? My instincts are terrible."

The truth was she didn't want to face Gerard, not yet. More than that, she didn't want to lie to him. When he found out about her and Ben, he was going to write her off. No need to make the situation worse by using him as a pawn in the bringing down of the PTA Mafia.

"We've been over this a hundred times. We need to know how close Mr. Ilg is with his nephew Ben. You are the only person who can get that information without blowing the case. If Ben knows we brought you into the station, then we can assume that Suni knows. We can't afford to waste time. Every minute that she has your children, they are in danger."

On the other side of the suite, her cell phone started to ring.

"You can do this, Lanie. Just think about your kids."

Lanie swallowed the lump in her throat and jumped out of bed. No matter who was on the other end—it was show time.

* * *

"Mom, I'm bored. Ajay's gone and Mrs. Calverson won't let me talk to Lexi. When are you coming to pick me up?"

"Poodle!" He was alive. Lanie collapsed on the sectional. "Baby, where are you?"

"I don't know. I woke up one morning and I was in this really strange place. It's dark and..."

Static rang in her ears. "I can't hear you, Charlie. There's a lot of static. Can you move to a spot where there are more bars on the phone?"

"There's no sun here, mom. I can't find any doors."

Shit. Her pulse quickened. She turned to Cheryl who was

listening in at the desk.

"Keep him talking. If he shuts the power button off we are screwed."

"Keep your phone on Charlie. Even if you hang up—keep it on. That way I can come get you—"

"You bitch. Are you trying to double cross me?"

Lanie heard Suni's voice where Charlie's should have been and felt weak. "I got worried. I kept trying to call Lexi and Charlie, but nobody answered." She held her breath waiting to see if Suni would buy her lie.

There was a pause. "Yvette killed Bob. It had to be done. You are going to have to stay put until things cool down."

She bought it. "Oh my God...how could you let that happen? You promised me that no one would be killed."

"Calm down. Right now the police think it was an accident. The last thing we need is for you to show back up in town in hysterics."

Now to lay it on extra thick and bring her Poodle home safe. "You're right. I need to come back and take care of my children. I'll be calm."

"No. Not yet. Stay put and I'll contact you as soon as things settle down."

Lanie heard the click of the phone and the line went dead. She threw a glance at Cheryl who gave her a big grin and thumbs up. "We got her. Pack your bags Lanie. We are heading back to Chicago."

CHAPTER FIFTEEN

Lanie was in the middle putting the finishing touches on her hurricane packing when there was a knock at the door. Cheryl caught her attention and gave her a silent signal that she was going to hide in the bedroom. Lanie crossed into the kitchen and waited for the click of the bedroom door before walking to the door and checking the peephole.

A disheveled Gerard drooped on the other side. His hair stood on end and his glasses were slightly askew on his nose. Cheryl had been right. He looked like a man on the edge. Lanie's heart skipped a beat. If her arrest had left him in such a state of chaos, then perhaps he cared more than she knew. More than Ben had. She pushed the thought out of her mind. She knew he was a lying thief, but her heart hadn't gotten the message and ached from the sound of his name running through her head. It was something she'd have to process later, once her children were home safe.

She took a deep breath and forced herself to turn the knob casually. He must have expected her to be there, but she would have sworn he was shocked to see her standing on the threshold.

"You're here."

Now that he was right there, close enough to touch, she found herself at a loss for words. Ben made her heart ache and Gerard, even in a state of chaotic drama, made her heart throb. When things settled back into normalcy she would have to schedule her follow up with Dr. Woo and have her hormone levels checked. This much yo-yo lust wasn't normal at her age. Not trusting herself to say the practiced script, she nodded.

He grabbed her, crushing her into his chest. He smelled like sweat and spice—delicious and manly. His lips brushed her hair. "I tried to get you out. My attorney said they flew you home to face a judge. I thought I'd lost you."

He thought he'd lost her, which meant he wanted her. Good news if she were a normal person pursuing a normal relationship. "No. It was a mistake. Someone stole my identity and had been passing bad checks. They thought she was me. They realized their mistake and let me go with a nice apology." God she hoped she sounded convincing.

His grasp around her tightened, taking her breath away. "That's awful. How can I help you? My attorney is very good. I can send him to Chicago to help you straighten out this mess."

The weight of lying to him crushed her more than the strength of his embrace. She pulled away and took two steps back. "I have an attorney working on it."

He stepped inside without her invitation. This was the hard part. She had to approach the subject of Ben without raising suspicion or letting on that they'd been inappropriately close. She found her way out of the entryway through her blinding guilt. His footsteps echoed on the terrazzo floor close behind her.

The kitchen seemed like a safe space, not too formal and not too intimate. "Can I get you a drink?" She asked pulling the door of the stainless steel refrigerator open. A can of Diet Coke sat in the middle of the shelf. She grabbed it before he could answer. If he didn't want it, she would gulp it down herself.

He took a seat at the barstool on the granite counter. Lanie stifled the urge to shout *No! Not there!* She forced the memory of Ben's body seducing her on the cool rock to the back of her brain and focused on pulling the tab on the can. "Sorry, no ice, but it's cold."

"No, thanks. You enjoy it."

She took a short swallow and set the can on the counter deciding to jump into her questioning before she lost her nerve completely. "How well do you know Ben?"

His expression clouded over. "Why? What has he done now?"

"I think he stole some money from me. I don't know for sure—"

"How much?"

"Fifteen hundred dollars."

He reached into his back pocket and pulled out a brown leather wallet. Removing a wad of bills he began to count.

"I can't take your money." The money was raised through illegal activity anyway. Better that it went back to a criminal.

He finished counting and held out his hand. "I only have five hundred on me. Take this now and I'll see that you get the rest later today."

"I can't." She repeated. "I'm not a hundred percent sure it was him. It could have been anyone. I could have dropped it on the floor of the casino."

He set the bills on the counter. "Ben is my nephew. He gets into trouble like this from time to time. Believe me, if there is money missing and Ben was anywhere nearby, he took it. Please, take the money."

He looked so tragically sad. "I won't take your money. I just want to know why. You obviously care about your nephew very much. You've given him a good job and a place to live—why would he do things that come back to haunt you?"

He raked his fingers through his chaotic spikes. "No one is more haunted than my nephew, Ben. No one."

* * *

If Ben was Suni's hotel spy, they were still safe. After stealing Lanie's cash he'd disappeared. According to Gerard, stealing and running were patterns he repeated from time to time. Each trip followed less than angelic behavior; but he came home at some point more or less unscathed. At least he always had in the past.

After she finished her Diet Coke, Gerard had insisted they order room service and move to the couch. If Lanie wanted to learn the gritty details of Ben's past, it would be over an intimate, late lunch. Cheryl hiding in the bedroom did hamper the romantic possibilities a bit, but not enough to completely ruin what might be her last meal with the man.

Baked French onion soup and Turkey with Prosciutto and melted Fontina cheese seemed the perfect accompaniment to the sordid tale she was about to hear. After taking a sip of the soup, she leaned across his lap to retrieve a linen napkin, allowing her hand to casually brush his thigh. Thick, strong muscle under denim sent her mind reeling. Pulling herself back to the task, she dove into her predetermined line of questioning. "Why do you think Ben gets in and out of trouble so often? He's really just a kid. He can't possibly be a hardened criminal yet?"

"Ben's a womanizer. He falls in and out of love with women all the time. Sometimes I think his criminal activities are his way of trying to amass a fortune. If he's rich, maybe one of the women will stay and he can live happily ever after."

Interesting. According to Gerard's theory, Ben stole from her in order to gain a fortune and keep her. Impossible and juvenile, but interesting just the same. "That sounds a little farfetched, don't you think?"

"Which part?"

"All of it."

"Trust me, Elaine, he is a womanizer. Look how quickly he seduced you."

Now that was a slap out of left field that she hadn't seen coming. It answered the question of whether or not he knew about their relationship. He sipped his espresso, watching her face. She could only imagine how transparent she looked to him. Her cheeks grew hot. "I don't...I'm not sure what you're referring to?"

"Don't feel bad. He does it to every woman he can, especially those with money. Why should you be any different?"

Every woman with money. She wasn't any different, on any level, than any of the others. Unless you counted the fact that the money wasn't hers. "I'm so ashamed." She blurted it out before she could stop herself. "I don't know what happened. I came here to escape the humiliation of my husband's affair with his secretary and wound up in bed your nephew. I'm just as bad as he is. In fact, I'm worse!"

"Don't be so hard on yourself. You were a victim." He took her hand. "I knew when he came by the studio asking about the sunglasses that you'd been involved with him. You were mad as a hornet that he showed up and interrupted our conversation. It made me think that whatever happened between you two was over."

Close enough. "I had *no idea* he was your nephew."

"My nephew and my charge. My sister, Myrna, asked me to look after him when she died. If she saw how he turned out, she'd shake the life out of me for doing such a poor job."

"How did she die?"

"She had ovarian cancer. She found it fairly early, but that type of cancer is almost always terminal. As soon as she was diagnosed, I contacted Michael Calverson to move my studio to the United States. I gave up everything I had in Europe and relocated here. It wasn't enough to save Myrna. The cancer spread to her organs and six months later she was gone. It was a terrible time for Ben. He was so young then, not even out of grade school."

She couldn't imagine how a young child could thrive after watching their mother die from such a horrible disease. If she had cancer and Charlie had to go through something like that, who knew how he'd turn out? "That's awful. I'm so sorry for both of you. Losing your sister had to be devastating."

"Ben was the only reason I got up many mornings. He never got over losing his mother. I was a poor substitute. I never married. There was no mother to nurture him and no siblings to play with. I tried to keep him out of trouble. He rejected me. All my efforts were wasted."

The hurt, both of losing his sister and the disaster that was Ben, were still etched on Gerard's face. The deep crags between his eyes and above his brow took on new meaning. Distinction was worry. Permanent reminders of sleepless nights and inner turmoil. The next time she saw that little shit she was going to give him a piece of her mind. Ben was a grown adult, acting like an ungrateful spoiled brat. Running amok in the streets, taking money from his uncle and anyone else he could filch it from. Sleeping with scores of women sounded like a punishment meant to hurt his mother for dying and his uncle for not being able to prevent it. Gerard was being too kind. "You did the best you could. He's a grown man. You have to stop taking the blame for his mistakes."

He shrugged. "It's easier to say such things than do them."

Lanie bit the inside of her cheek and threw a glance at the closed bedroom door. There was something she needed to do, and she would have to be quick about it. Once Cheryl caught on to her, she would rush out and start screaming. She might even put Lanie back under arrest. The thought of jail scared her, but Gerard's reaction to what she was about to do scared her even more. "I admire your honesty, Gerard. Telling me about Ben, forgiving me for my indiscretions with Ben, you are such a special man." She caressed his cheek with the back of her hand. "Thank you so much for taking such good care of me over the last few weeks, and for having so much faith in me."

His eyes widened. "That sounds like a goodbye speech."

She wasn't going to be the one to say goodbye. She was just going to lay out all the cards and let him see her for who she really was. Leave him free to make the choice. "I hope not. But, the choice will be yours, after you know the truth."

"What truth?"

Lanie tried to think of how to spill her criminal involvement to Gerard. Cheryl hadn't burst through the door, which would have given her a dramatic edge that might tug at his protective heart strings. She would just have to wing it. "I know Michael Calverson helped you get your financial affairs lined up. I'm just curious, how well do you know his ex-wife, Suni?"

"She and Michael were my guests here before they decided to divorce. We had dinner together once or twice. She seemed nice enough. On the surface she was attractive. Underneath...well, I got the feeling she was very headstrong. I could tell Michael was unhappy. I wasn't surprised to hear that they decided to split up. I was surprised that she called and asked if she could send a friend here. Of course I said yes, there was no reason to say no, but I was still surprised."

"Did she go into any details about me or the trip?"

"No, and I didn't ask. The suite wasn't in use. No reason for it to sit empty when someone wanted it."

He wasn't making this any easier. She was going to have to spit out as much of the story as she could before Cheryl figured out what she was doing. "Suni is a wanted criminal. She tried to kill her ex-husband

Michael, had an affair with my husband, Bob, tried to get me to put a hit on him, and kidnapped my kids—"

"Slow down. You aren't making any sense."

Wow. Cheryl had let her spit out all the nuts and bolts of the story without a peep. Maybe she'd fallen asleep. No time to waste. The longer she dallied, the more likely she was to be interrupted by a scary, screaming blond. "She is running a criminal circle made up of PTA moms. These women get roped into her insanity because they have too much money and time on their hands. They're bored and the power to get a Gucci bag or free highlights in exchange for a primo spot on the basketball team for their kid is a cheap thrill they can't pass up. Suni takes it very seriously. She had an affair with my husband, and when he refused to leave me, she plotted this elaborate revenge scheme. When I refused to have him killed, or do it myself, she took my kids, had my husband kidnapped, and stuck me on a plane to come here. She told me if I told anyone, she'd kill my children. I know it sounds crazy—but you have to believe me."

He rubbed his chin. "So you lied to me about the police? There is no case of mistaken identity?"

"No."

"Where are the police now? Surely, they didn't leave you in a vulnerable position when this mafia mom could come and get you?"

He was angry. She could hear it in his voice. The simmering rage scared her. It seemed misplaced. "They are waiting for me downstairs. They want to move me to a new hotel." The lie slipped out like a protective overcoat.

Gerard seemed doubtful. "That doesn't sound like something the police would do. If they thought you were in real danger, they'd be crawling all over this place. Now," he leaned in, leering an inch in front of her nose. "Let's be honest. The police are gone, aren't they? They've left you here alone to defend yourself against the wolves..."

Lanie's mind raced. Was he commenting on the Las Vegas Police Department's lack of professionalism, or was his disdain directed at her? "They've arranged for me to move to a new hotel on the strip. They're expecting a phone call to let them know I've arrived safe and sound before dinner." That should cover both angles.

He leaned in running his fingers over her bare calf. "It will be such a shame to disappoint them."

* * *

Lanie's brain stopped processing when Gerard wrapped his hands around her ankles. This was Gerard, her hunky, French photographer. He was the man who she was going to ride off into the sunset with and live happily ever after. He forgave her for sleeping with his nephew and she trusted him with her less than perfect truth.

But he had her by the legs and was leering at her like a choice steak.

"You were having such a nice time here. Such a shame that you went to the cops." Keeping one hand around her ankles, he reached into his front shirt pocket and pulled out a cell phone. "Sorry about your kids. If you'd just followed Suni's instructions, no one would have to be hurt."

Her heart stopped beating and sank to her ankles, which were turning a shade of purplish red from the death grip Gerard had on them. From the tangled mess in her head, two thoughts slipped past the confusion guard and screamed at her.

Gerard was Suni's spy and today would be the day that she, her children, or possibly both, would die.

She had to try to stall him from making that call to Suni. The longer he talked to her, the better her chances were that Cheryl might spring from the bedroom and pull some of her scary, blond killing machine moves on him. "No, Gerard, you...I..."

"*No, Gerard, you,*" He whined with mock horror. "Oh, Elaine, don't tell me you thought I cared about you? Back in the studio, when you tried to kiss me? I rejected you. You are a fat, lazy, slob of a woman who allowed herself go down the tubes. I would never be even the tiniest bit attracted to someone like you."

Being called a fat, lazy, slob would have hurt a lot more if she wasn't afraid that her next breath might be her last. "I'm not fat and I'm not lazy." It came out in an unconvincing whimper.

He laughed. "Have you checked a mirror lately? I cannot imagine how Ben got through it. Tell me, did he keep his eyes closed and the lights off every time? Or did he get used to your saggy, old lady skin?"

Who you calling old, buddy? He was from the early end of her decade. Besides, Ben had left the lights on every time. She'd been the one that had shied away from the exposure. "He liked my body."

"No, Elaine, he liked your money. Which I find quite humorous, because we both know that not a penny of it was yours. I couldn't share that with him, of course, it would have jeopardized Suni's plan. You could ask him yourself—but by the time he shows his face here again, you'll be long gone." Flipping open the phone, he began to dial.

It was time to fight. Since Gerard brought up her excess girth, she might as well use the extra ounces to help defeat the French bastard. A few swift kicks in the direction of his precious manhood and he just might let go. Drawing her knee up in the direction of her saggy chest flesh, she prepared to donkey kick him square in the nuts.

Before she could administer the blow, Cheryl's service revolver, held by none other than the blond ambition herself, appeared at the base of Gerard's cocky skull. "Drop the phone and get your ass down on the ground."

Damn she was good. Lanie hadn't even heard her enter the room. He released her legs and dropped the phone, but made no move to get his ass on the ground, as requested. By her estimation, refusal to cooperate when a gun was involved was usually a mistake or a brazen attempt to defy the most basic laws of the universe—like death.

"I'm not fucking with you, Frenchie. Get your sorry ass on the ground before I put a bullet in your head!"

The ferocity of the threat sent her to the ground, hands covering the back of her skull, right along with him. Getting taken out by a stray bullet from a struggle between Cheryl and Gerard was not going on her obituary. The safest place was in a submissive, grade school tornado drill position on the floor. Casting a side glance in Gerard's direction, she caught the defiant challenge on his face. Squeezing her eyes shut, she fought the urge to vomit and tried to pray. *Please, God, I cannot handle pieces of skull and brains being sprayed around the room. Just let this thing end peacefully so I can go get my children and avoid a lifetime of night terrors.*

The front door of the suite flew open and the room filled with the sound of men repeating Cheryl's threat to blow Gerard's head clean off his shoulders. Behind closed lids, visions of blood spatter caused her to break out in a cold, clammy sweat. She was fading. The voices, so loud that her eardrums pounded with their reverberations, began to soften and swim away from her.

Then she passed out.

*   *   *

Lanie was having the most wonderful dream.

A tuxedo clad Ben had her in his arms and they were swaying to the beat of "Mack the Knife." It wasn't her first choice for a romantic dance. Her pick would have been "Can't Help Falling in Love," by Elvis. But, low and behold, Bobby Darin himself was there snapping and crooning it out just for the two of them.

She was so happy to see him. Wrapping her arms around his neck, she entwined her fingers in his thick, dark hair. "Where did you run off to?"

A small smile crossed his lips. He remained silent.

"I was afraid you weren't coming back. Gerard told me about your mother. Did you really steal my money and run off to find someone else?"

He kissed her once, gently, and spun her across the floor, letting go just as she reached the edge of the glossy parquet. "What I felt for you was genuine, Lanie. I'm just sorry you couldn't see that." Turning, he moved in the direction of the door.

He loved her, and he was leaving. "Ben...stop! I'm sorry. I believe you. Please don't go!" She reached for his tuxedo jacket, but he was just out of reach. Her fingers closed around thin air.

Before she could raise the hem of her satin ball gown to chase him down, Bobby Darin stepped in front of her and began to snap. She tried to maneuver around him, but it was no use. He matched her move for move, snapping all around her face. "Get away from me!" She cried, swatting at his arms. "Can't you see he's leaving?"

CONFESSIONS OF A PTA MAFIA MOM

Bobby just kept right on singing and snapping while Ben disappeared through the ballroom door.

"Wake up. Lanie. We don't have time for hysterics."

Bobby Darin, who sounded rather feminine himself, was accusing her of being a hysterical female. Bobby Darin was also dead, thereby unable to croon out a song or trap her with his fancy footwork and finger beat. And yet, those damn manicured fingers kept right on snapping in her face.

"If you don't snap out of it, I'll be forced to slap you back to reality."

Now she recognized the voice and remembered where she was. Lanie didn't want to come back to reality. Reality was bad. Bad things happened. She made bad decisions and people got hurt. She tried to crawl back into her mental black hole. Maybe she could manipulate her dreams and bring Ben back through the ballroom door. This time, she would do everything right. Her real life might be a total disaster, but her dream life could be picture perfect.

A sharp sting blasted across her cheek and forced her eyes open. So much for perfect dreams. "That hurt!"

Cheryl lowered her open palm. "Sorry about that. It was either a good, hard slap, or a trip to the hospital. We don't have time for the hospital."

Lanie forced herself to a sitting position. "Did you shoot him?"

Cheryl laughed. "Oh, God, no. The minute the backup cavalry arrived, he cried like a baby. He begged us to take him out through the employee stairwell. The man does have a reputation to protect."

Slimeball. Too bad she'd missed him in a cowering fool state. After his angst producing body comments, she would have enjoyed his discomfort. "You knew he was the one and you let me go on like a lovesick fool."

"Not exactly. I knew it was *one* of them, but I didn't know which one. Ben had the criminal record, but Gerard had a bigger motive. His studio appeal had taken a big nosedive. If he didn't come up with some capital fast, he would have to file bankruptcy or close his doors."

The sorry excuse for art he'd shown her back in the studio had been a real attempt to grow his craft. She should have kept her big mouth shut and let him run the exhibit. Watching him bomb on such a grand level would have been amusing. "But Ben was the one who stole my money and ran."

"Maybe. Or maybe Gerard sent him away because he was afraid Ben would catch on to him. Or, maybe the two of them were in cahoots but Ben got cold feet. Or maybe—"

She didn't need to hear fifty different ways they might have conspired to humiliate her. "I get your point. Did he tell you where my kids are?"

"He lawyered up before we could interview him. The only thing he told us was that he didn't call Suni when we picked you up the first time because he was afraid of her. He wanted to wait and see if he could resolve it with his attorney first. No need to upset the mafia mom unless it was unavoidable."

She rubbed the sore spot on her cheek. "Couldn't you have slapped it out of him?"

"Police brutality doesn't go over well in court. We triangulated the cell signal back to the water tower on Cottage Avenue."

The Cottage Avenue water tower was in her subdivision. "If the signal is from that tower they might still be in the neighborhood."

"She turned the phone off as soon as the call ended, cutting off our ability to track her. But, let's assume she stays in one place. She's a smart lady, I'm sure she's aware that cell phones can be tracked any time they are on. So, she turns it off to avoid changing hideouts. Then, question is, where could they hide that is right under everyone's nose?"

Charlie had described his surroundings as dark. No windows or doors to let in light. "Underground?"

"It couldn't be. It has to be a location that allows the cell signal to go in and out."

Now that Gerard's cover was blown, they were under the gun like never before. They had to figure out where the kids were before Suni realized they were coming for her. Gerard's attorney had enough clout to really raise a stink. Once leaked, the case would produce immediate media mayhem. All Suni would have to do is turn on the news or check the internet and she'd know what happened.

Lanie closed her eyes and tried to conjure up the image of Suni's hideout. Dark. Dreadful. Above ground. Out in plain sight. Commonplace—so much so that nobody would ever think of it.

She was stumped. "I have no idea."

Cheryl stood and brushed off her pants. "There's a plane waiting for us at McCarran. The flight will give us more time to brainstorm. By the time we hit the tarmac at Midway, we'll have some ideas—you'll see." She grabbed her briefcase and computer. "You ready?"

Lanie followed suit. The slap, followed by desperation to find her children, had cleared her head. Her senses were on high alert. She took one last, long look around the opulent suite. What had once felt like a retreat now reeked of a deathtrap. She grabbed her rolling suitcase and marched toward the door.

She was ready.

CHAPTER SIXTEEN

The early evening flight out of McCarran International Airport was close to empty. Most Vegas partiers preferred the red eye. Stretching out the potential to strike it rich at the casino until the very last minute, followed by total collapse on a cramped flight seemed like a punishment to Lanie. Vegas junkies were a hard core variety.

The beauty of a brilliant desert sunset was lost on her. The seed of worry that she'd pushed out of her mind during her stay had sprouted, taking root deep in her belly and blooming into full blown agony. By the time the plane touched down in Chicago, it would be close to midnight. Hunting Suni down during the witching hour only added to the drama. Cheryl had promised they'd have some good ideas before the landing gear came down. Lanie knew it was a police tactic. She was just pretending. The illusion of control was for her benefit. A key witness going off the deep end on a four hour commercial flight was the last thing Special Agent Cheryl Black wanted to deal with at the moment.

Then there was the Bob factor. Cheryl had waited until she was buckled into her seat and taxiing down the runway to inform her that they would be staying together at the fleabag hotel he'd been living in. Her time at the Venetian had ended badly; but going from the lap of luxury to the Days Inn was going to be a painful adjustment. Lanie hadn't been close enough to the Bulldog to get personal since the fateful night of their sexcapade. After the PTA makeover, he had practically swallowed her whole. The look he'd given her that night in the kitchen contained levels of lust she hadn't seen since their dating years. The lingering involuntary sexual response to the cheating louse she'd been married to for the last twenty years needed to be completely extinguished before they were holed up together for an indefinite period of time. She flipped through her rolodex of imaginary images until she found one of Bob peeing down his leg in fear when Cheryl showed up to arrest him. That would do the trick nicely.

The dreadful dealership disaster seemed a lifetime ago. Her ankle, which had been in perfect condition for weeks, shot a painful reminder up her calf. If she could go back to that day, she would stand her ground and make her half naked husband squirm. Her nosedive to the floor had injured more than her ankle. It had taken her already low self esteem and crushed it. Now Bob would be walking the humiliation plank and she would get to be the one sticking the tip of the sword in his back. It was sweet revenge a long time coming.

Across the aisle, Cheryl squinted at the screen on her laptop. Her ability to concentrate in chaos was commendable. If there was a clue in the files that had been missed, no matter how small, she'd be the one to find it. "Find anything?"

"Not yet. Try to get some sleep."

Sleep was out of the question. On a good night, she required a nightcap to unwind. The events of the day and lack of alcohol was an insomnia cocktail that could have a week's worth of aftershocks. "I know you said we have to share a room, but do Bob and I have to share a bed?" Cheryl threw her a look that oozed irritation. "Is that really a concern right now?"

One bed. "Is there any way we can get two rooms? I'll pay for one." She fingered the envelope with the fifteen hundred dollars in it. Cheryl hadn't asked for it, so she took the liberty of stuffing it in her pocket on the way out the door.

"I'll see what I can do when we get there."

"I'd even settle for twin beds as a last resort."

Cheryl snorted and slammed her laptop shut. "I will see what I can do."

Lanie was getting the distinct impression that the Days Inn might not have suitable sleeping arrangements for her situation. "Can I get a drink?"

"You have to wait for the cabin service. A stewardess will be around soon."

"I'm really thirsty. Can't I just go to the back and ask for something now?"

"I'll do it," she snapped. "I'm not giving you alcohol, so don't ask."

Well, that was a bummer. Cheryl disappeared down the aisle. A moment later, she returned handing Lanie a warm, diet Sprite. "No Diet Coke, or, at least some ice and a glass?"

"My God, you're a pain in the ass. No, you cannot have a Diet Coke. The caffeine will keep you wired and then you'll be yammering in my ear all night."

"They probably have caffeine free..." The expression on Cheryl's face told her to zip it. "Never mind, Sprite is fine." The constant pampering of the Venetian was several hundred miles and thirty-five thousand feet away from her. Pulling the metal tab, she sipped the warm, fruity fizz. "What happens when we land?"

"You go to the Days Inn, where you will stay until we find Suni and the kids."

"Where will you go?" Cheryl had been her shadow for the past forty-eight hours. Lanie didn't think she'd feel safe without the blond mercenary standing ready to swoop in and save her in an emergency.

"To work." Cheryl reclined her chair and closed her eyes, effectively ending their conversation.

Lanie sipped the warm pop and tried to clear her mind. With Cheryl refusing to listen to her incessant babble, the four hour flight was going to feel like an eternity.

* * *

Lanie was still wiping the drool from the corners of her mouth when the undercover car met them outside the airport. Anyone paying attention would know it was a squad car. Only the police were allowed to park and wait at arrivals without being screamed at and threatened with tow trucks. Cheryl walked briskly in front of her. Her nap on the plane must have left her batteries fully recharged. Lanie wasn't as perky. In fact, she was downright groggy. Falling asleep with thirty minutes left of flight time had left her with smeared kohl halfway down her cheeks and a case of serious cotton mouth. The backseat of the Crown Vic police cruiser seemed fitting for the hot mess she'd transformed into.

The man sitting behind the wheel struck a chord in her memory. His dark, squared off haircut and matching jaw line were familiar. A little too familiar. Where had she seen him before?

"Honey, I'm home." Cheryl announced climbing into the front seat.

He chuckled. "I was wondering when my lovely wife would make it back."

"Elaine Jackerson, meet Special Agent Matt Kellerman. You might recognize him as my undercover husband."

Lanie met his stare in the rearview mirror. His dark brown eyes sucked her in. He was handsome. Cheryl was lucky to have a good looking work husband. He raised his brow and gave her a broad smile. Perfect teeth to match a perfect face. "Welcome home. Rough flight?"

The smug comment was a reference to her unkempt appearance, no doubt. The last of her surly, sleep deprived crankiness reared its ugly head. She bit her cheek to keep from spitting something rotten at his Adonis reflection.

Cheryl pulled the shoulder strap on her seatbelt as the car started moving. "Anything new turn up?"

"You didn't check your messages?"

"If I checked, would I be asking?" She barked.

He ignored her tone. "I think you should check your messages."

Lanie suspected Special Agent Kellerman's avoidance of anything resembling a direct answer was his way of saying there was some information that she was not meant to hear. She busied herself, pretending to look for something buried in her purse. If they thought she wasn't paying attention, they might slip and say something to clue her in.

The beeping of the keypad followed by a deafening silence left Lanie hanging like a spider on silk. She was afraid to exhale. If she did— she could miss something.

Cheryl snapped her phone shut. "When did this happen?"

"About an hour after your flight took off from McCarran. Interesting, huh? Never saw that one coming."

Lanie couldn't stand it any longer. "What happened?"

Cheryl twisted in her seat. "Babette turned herself in. She wants to make a deal."

Her daughter's captor was in custody. Her request to make a deal gave Lanie hope that her next question would have a response that answered her prayers. "Lexi?"

"Safe and sound." Special Agent Kellerman interjected. "She came in having a fit. I guess this kidnapping really put a damper on her social life. The school had the nerve to hold homecoming without her. Can you imagine?"

Relief washed over her. Lexi Marie was safe. Now there was just one more chick to bring home to roost. "What about Charlie? Did Babette have any information on where Suni is hiding him?"

Cheryl set her jaw. "She says she doesn't know." She turned her gaze back to the street.

Cheryl had her doubts about bringing Charlie home. Lanie could hear the distress in her voice and it made her want to toss her Sprite all over the back seat. Instead, she bit her knuckle to keep from screaming and said a prayer.

* * *

By the time the Crown Vic rolled into the Days Inn Parking lot, Lanie had managed to stop crying. A quick check in the lighted lipstick compact revealed her swollen eyes, lips, and nose. Her lips looked good. The crying fit left them rosy and plump. They hadn't looked that good without an emotional breakdown since her mid thirties. Her nose, stuffed in addition to the red swelling, looked ridiculous. The fact that her tears had washed away the streaks of Kohl that had adorned her cheeks after her in flight nap was only redeeming if she really stretched her imagination to its maximum.

Bob was still a complete jackass. His obnoxious behavior was painful to watch. Lanie couldn't tell if he was laying it on extra thick for her benefit, or if he'd been torturing the undercover agents for the entire length of his stay. The terrible jokes and back slapping were in full swing before she'd crossed the threshold. If facial expressions were considered a good indication of feelings, Bob's police protectors cared for him the way people enjoying a spring picnic cared for a hill of fire ants. If they thought they could get away with it, they'd probably smear him on the bottom of their shoes. Bob appeared oblivious to their disdain. Nothing new there. He assumed everyone found him as wonderful as he found himself.

She was scanning the room for Lexi when he launched himself in her direction. Before she could sidestep him, he threw his arms around her in an overblown act of affection. "Lanie! Thank God you're all right."

He smelled rank. She breathed through her mouth to avoid gagging and wiggled out of his arms. His hair had gone gray. The greasy strands hung past his eyebrows. "Where's Lexi?"

Ignoring her question, he continued on the Bob show warpath. "Everyone here doubted you, but not me. I told them you were one tough cookie."

Lanie looked past him and spied Lexi sitting at a table near the window. She looked so small surrounded by the black bullet proof vests and guns. Ignoring Bob's continuing soapbox speech, she went to her daughter. "Hey baby—you okay?"

Lexi turned and Lanie saw the streaks on her cheeks. She hadn't seen her daughter cry in twelve years. The last time had been when Lexi was five and their dog, Lamb Chop, had died. After that, she'd developed a force field around her soul. Her hard edge came out and softness stayed locked inside. "What kind of trouble are we in, mom? Sonja's mom came back because she was afraid. She made them put her under guard to keep them safe. Charlie is still missing. What if Mrs. Calverson hurts him?"

Lanie wrapped her daughter in the folds of her embrace. From her seated position, Lexi's head came to rest just under Lanie's breasts. It brought out her momma bear instinct and she smoothed her daughter's hair protectively. "Don't worry, baby. Mrs. Calverson won't hurt Charlie. I won't let her."

"How will you stop her? Nobody knows where she took him."

Lanie kissed the top of Lexi's head. Crouching down, she swiped away the tear stains on her swollen cheeks with the pads of her thumbs. "Stay with your dad and the detectives. You're safe here. I'll be back soon. I promise."

Lexi's eyes widened. "Love you, mom. Be careful."

Lanie gave her one more hug and a quick kiss. "You too, baby. Don't worry about me. I'm one tough cookie. Just ask your dad."

She brushed past Bob, still blathering on about some damn thing, and faced off against Cheryl who was blocking the door. "Babette is here in the hotel. I want to talk to her."

Cheryl took one look at her face and skipped the denial. "Sorry, Lanie, no can do. All I need to round out this night is to have the two of you get into a physical altercation."

"I think she knows more than she's saying."

"Of course she is! She's trying to play her cards right so she can stay out of jail. If she gives us everything upfront, she has nothing to bargain with."

"What about the mother card?"

"I'm not following you."

"We both have girls the same age. Don't you think it will be hard for Babette to look me in the eye and lie when she knows my son's life is in danger?"

Cheryl crossed her arms. Underneath the skepticism, Lanie thought she saw a hint of wavering. "You would need permission from her attorney and someone to sit in on your conversation to make sure you ladies play nice."

Babette's attorney would never allow it. Even if he had a momentary lapse in judgment and decided to let them talk, she'd never get the information she was looking for. It had to be off the record. "Sure, if you *ask permission* first. What if I overheard you telling someone what room she's in? Maybe I'm really crafty and I slip past my guard. Maybe the security outside her room falls asleep and I sneak past. Maybe—"

Cheryl threw her hands up in protest. "I get your point. It's just too risky."

Lanie channeled the patented Special Agent look of death and stared her down. "Five minutes, that's all I'm asking for. He's my son. If anything happens to him I'll never forgive myself."

Cheryl turned on her radio and stepped out of the way. "I could lose my job for this. She's in room two-twenty. The Special Agent in front of her door is an old friend—Stanley Marcusek. I'm going to give him explicit instructions to drag you out of there five minutes after you go in. He's a big guy. You don't want to tangle with him. Go before I come to my senses."

Lanie shot her a look of gratitude and raced out the door.

*   *   *

Cheryl wasn't joking about the size of Special Agent Marcusek. He had to be at least six foot four. The top of his head stopped an inch below the door frame. Lanie begged her nerves to stop rattling and made her approach. "Special Agent Black sent me."

Even though he was baby faced, Lanie could tell he was close to her in age. The streaks of gray and deep mouth wrinkles gave him away. He gave her a curt nod. "Go on in. I expect to see you back in the hall in five."

"Is it locked?" She wanted the element of surprise. If Babette peered through the peep hole and saw Lanie staring back, she might refuse to let her in.

"After Agent Black radioed that you were coming, I told them room service had been ordered."

Nice touch. She squelched her desire to throw the door open and run inside screaming like a banshee. Better to cast an illusion of control. It didn't matter if she was quivering with fear on the inside or filled with desperation. If Babette didn't see her insecurities written on her face, the chance of uncovering Suni's lair went up. Three deep breaths later, she squared her shoulders and marched in.

Sonja was sprawled on the bed watching an episode of *Sixteen and Pregnant* on MTV. Babette sat at the table by the window painting her nails. "Hello, ladies. I trust you're less than pleased with your accommodations?"

Babette snorted. "You got that right, Sugar. I've been in gas station bathrooms that had more class than this dive."

Not the response she'd expected. Sonja was so wrapped up in her show that she hadn't even bothered to peel herself from the T.V. to see who was addressing her. So much for the element of surprise. She'd have to play on their discontent of the digs provided at the Days Inn. "Unless you want to make this your winter retreat, you'd better tell me where Suni went with my son."

Babette patted the seat next to her. "No need to make threats, Sugar. Come on over and take a seat. We do have some things to discuss."

Now she was getting somewhere! Time to pull out all the stops and let her inner bitch loose. "You bet your sweet ass we do. Where the hell is my son?"

Babette cringed. "Please, watch your mouth in front of my daughter. There's no need to shout. Come on over here and we'll talk this out like ladies."

Damnit. She'd played the bitch card and came out looking like a fool. She should have known Babette wouldn't bite. Time to throw in a bold-faced lie. "You have five minutes to give me something good or you and Sonja are being moved to the Metropolitan Correction Center downtown. You can share a cell with Brittney."

That peaked Sonja's attention. "Mom, they can't do that, can they? I don't want to go to jail!"

Babette rolled her eyes and blew on her wet polish. "Don't be so dramatic, Sugar. They can't put children in jail."

Buckets. She'd forgotten that minor detail. Babette raised an eyebrow. "Come on over. I won't bite."

Lanie checked the room for a clock. She probably only had three more minutes until Special Agent Marcusek came in and pulled her out by her hair. She sulked over to the chair.

"That's right, Sugar. Now, let's see, where do I begin?"

"Charlie." Lanie begged. "Tell me where he is before Suni does something terrible to him."

Babette leaned across the table. "I want immunity," she hissed. "I'm talking no jail time. Not even one day."

Cheryl's instincts were right on target. Babette knew exactly where Charlie was. She'd been holding out to make sure she saved her own skin. The mother card made no difference in a game with such high stakes. "I can't promise you that."

"I know *you* can't—but she can." She pointed her shiny pink nail in the direction of the door.

Before Lanie could follow the direction of the nail, Cheryl's voice cut across the room "If we find him alive I could pull a few strings. The longer you play this guessing game, the less likely it is that we'll find him alive. I sure hope I don't have to slap an accessory to murder charge on you."

The words *accessory to murder* rang in Lanie's ears. If Babette didn't start talking soon, she would be the one charged with murder.

Babette shuddered. Her jaw dropped and clamped shut again faster than a bear trap. She flared her nostrils. "Sonja, put your headphones on, baby."

"I'm watching TV."

"Put them on before I come over there and slap you into next week for sassin' me."

Sonja stuck out her bottom lip in a huff. Without another word, the headphones went on. A moment later, heavy bass vibrated from her ear buds. No worries about teenage eavesdropping. Given her choice of music and eardrum shattering volume, Sonja's days of gathering information on her mother's crimes and spreading them on the small town adolescent rumor mill were severely numbered. The low tones of whispers were the first to go.

Babette waited until she was satisfied that Sonja was out of the listening loop before continuing. "I didn't know Suni was serious about killing people. I thought the kidnapping was her way of flexing her muscles to keep people in line. But, murder? That's serious stuff."

Cheryl approached the table, coming to rest directly in front of Babette. "Are you telling me that when she asked you to kidnap Lexi Marie

Jackerson you thought it was a joke? Some sort of game? Kidnapping is a felony. And, since the FBI is involved, it's a *federal* felony. That means, if I want to screw you to the wall, I can ask for life in prison without parole. How's that for flexing some muscle?"

"You'd never get it."

"Not only will I do everything in my power to make sure the book is thrown at you, I will make it my life mission to make sure that every media outlet hears about it. I will plaster your picture in every news source from here to Timbuktu. When I'm finished, there won't be a rock left for you to crawl under. Your life, your dignity—all of it will be gone. How will the combustion of your entire existence affect the future of your precious Sonja?"

Babette grew pale. "I'm sorry. I got caught up in the game. Suni is very persuasive."

Cheryl softened her tone. "I know she is. She is a master manipulator. You were just one of her many pawns."

"I really believed that this was just one of her usual stunts. Once she'd succeeded in making Bob's life miserable, I thought everyone would be free to go. When she started talking about killing people, I panicked. I packed up Sonja and Lexi and ran home to my momma in Texas for a few days."

Lexi in Texas. Now that was a sight Lanie would have liked to see. Her bet was that the southern boys who crossed her daughter's path were still rubbing their heads wondering what had hit them.

"As soon as I got there I confessed everything to my momma and she did just what I knew she'd do—she sat me down and talked some sense into me." Turning to Lanie, she added, "I know what I did was wrong. If somebody took my Sonja, I'd be sick with worry. It probably doesn't mean much now, but I swear, Lexi was never in any danger with me."

Lanie believed her. Lexi hadn't been in any danger, but Charlie sure was. "Do you know where she took Charlie?"

Babette nodded. "He's been right under your noses all along."

CHAPTER SEVENTEEN
SATURDAY, SEPTEMBER 9TH

The line of undercover and marked squads zipped silently through the suburban streets of Glen Ellyn. Red and blue flashing lights were the only identifiers that whatever was happening was serious business. A few predawn joggers and people walking their dogs stopped to gawk as they passed. From the back seat of Special Agent Kellerman's Crown Vic, Lanie watched and prayed that they would ignore them and go back to business as usual. She didn't recognize anyone on the street. That didn't mean that they didn't know or work for Suni Calverson, so there wasn't any comfort in her anonymity. All it would take was one person to make one call to tip her off that they were on their way to come and get her, and it was all over.

Cheryl had tried like hell to keep her at the Days Inn with Bob and Lexi. Lanie stood her ground, refusing every argument, no matter how logical. When Poodle's rescue team arrived, she needed to be there. It didn't matter that it violated every policy and procedure. Codes of conduct and law were not her concern. Bringing Charlie home, that was her only concern. Finally, she'd threatened to sneak out and follow them in a taxi if they left her behind. Cheryl knew she only had two choices: cuff her to the bed or let her come along. She gave in after Lanie promised to wait in the car until Suni was in the back of a marked squad and on her way downtown.

From her shotgun position, Cheryl gave her a stern warning.

"Remember, you stay in the car until I come out and give you the all clear."

Lanie nodded obediently. The Kevlar vest they'd made her wear was cumbersome. She checked the velcro straps. "Did I do this right?"

"Looks good. I know it's heavy, but keep it on until I tell you it's safe to take it off."

The cars turned down Cottage Avenue and came to a stop outside the water tower. Men and women covered in black Kevlar and carrying rifles sprang from their cars waiting for further orders. A truck pulled up with the Tactical team and bodies climbed out in such a large number that they looked like ninja's that had been packed into a clown car. Their big, black shields and covered helmets reminded her of the characters in Halo. Charlie had been begging for her to buy it for him. She'd resisted. The violence had been a major turn off. Now he was living in the very thing she'd tried to protect him from.

Nobody made a sound.

The early morning light was just beginning to change the sky from black to gray. The light from the cell antenna on top of the balloon-shaped cement tower blinked a red warning. Lanie shivered. Her son was in there with a maniac. If Babette hadn't turned herself in, they never would have known where to look. The signal came back to the tower—but everyone assumed it was off by a few feet. Who would think to look inside the base of the tower? With so many houses surrounding it, by the time they realized she wasn't hiding with a neighbor, she would have slipped out, taking Charlie away forever.

Cheryl squeezed her shoulder. "Once we open that door, there's no going back. It's the only way in and out."

"Do you think she'll climb the pipes? What if she forces him up there and pushes him off?"

"It's still very early. She's probably sleeping at the base."

God she hoped so.

Cheryl handed her the cell phone she'd confiscated from Gerard. "Don't make the call until I give you the signal. Got it?"

"Got it." The phone call was a long shot. A last ditch effort to throw Suni off balance so the tactical team could bust in and grab her before she could do anything stupid. The odds that she'd turned the phone back on were slim. She watched from the backseat as Cheryl jumped out and ran toward the crew. The entry team took their place by the door with a battering ram and a hydraulic spread cutter for backup. Once everyone settled in their defensive positions, Cheryl gave her a wave.

Scrolling through the contact list, she found Suni's name and hit the green call button. One, two, three rings…

"Where the hell have you been, Gerard? I called your room and your studio, so don't give me any crap about being immersed in your art."

She picked up! Lanie waved frantically out the window. "It's not Gerard. It's me, Lanie." She just needed to stall her a little bit longer. "How's Charlie?"

"I'll tell you how Charlie is—he's a brat that's going to get what's coming to him if he isn't careful!" Her scream echoed off the walls of the tower.

"Don't hurt him, Suni. I'll do whatever you want, just don't hurt my son."

She chuckled. "At the rate he's going, I won't have to hurt him. He'll take care of that all by himself."

Lanie didn't like the sound of that. "What's that supposed to mean?"

"Never mind," Suni snapped. "Where've you been these last few days? Gambling away my money? Plotting your new life with a handsome, French photographer?"

Lanie watched as the battering ram swung back. "I think you are asking the wrong questions, Suni. You really shouldn't be worried about where I've been. Your real concern is, where am I now?"

* * *

Charlie, her baby, was asleep in her arms.

Lanie had never been one for miracles, but the events of the day made her a convert. Her son had been saved by the heroes of the FBI. As far as she was concerned, the Kevlar covered men with pistols, rifles, tasers, and other assorted weapons, were angels straight from heaven. Special

Agent Cheryl Black was the Archangel Michael, happy to open a serious can of whoop-ass on the devil herself.

Waiting in the back of the unmarked squad, listening to screaming and gunfire was the hardest thing she'd ever endured. Every time a bullet fired she closed her eyes and said a silent prayer her baby wasn't in the trajectory. The flash bang explosives the team used when they gained entry made her teeth rattle.

He's alive. He's safe. Nothing will touch him.

The entire incident lasted twenty minutes.

Suni was on the ground, proving once again that Cheryl had instincts that bordered on being psychic. She was still on the phone with Lanie when the entry team slammed through the door of the water tower. After that, it was all downhill for the head of the PTA Mafia. She pulled a gun and pointed it at Cheryl. Big mistake. Before she could fire, Cheryl unloaded an entire clip into her tiny frame. Just like that, Suni Calverson was dead. Cheryl felt it was suicide by cop. Lanie suspected it was her severe egomaniacal behavior that left her no choice but death in a blazing gun battle with the law.

Charlie had waited for her to fall asleep the night before and climbed to the top of the water pipes. When Suni woke up, she was furious. The general assumption was that Suni was afraid of heights, because she didn't even attempt to come after him. She just stood at the bottom screaming about how she was going to kill him and his entire family if he didn't come down. Lanie was thankful that her children were resourceful and stubborn. Those qualities were irritating to deal with as a parent, but boy, oh, boy, they sure came in handy in a pinch.

The smoke from the flash bang was still lingering across the ground like a thick fog when Cheryl appeared with Charlie in her arms. Relief flooded Lanie's body the minute she realized he was exhausted and in shock—not wounded or dead as she had feared.

She took him from Cheryl's arms. "Poodle. Oh my little guy, I'm so glad you're alright."

He opened his eyes. "Mom, is that you?"

"It's me, baby. Lexi and dad are at a hotel waiting for us. They are going to be so glad to see you."

"What hotel?"

"It's called the Days Inn. It's close to home."

"Does it have a pool?"

She brushed a dirty, copper curl from his forehead. "It does have a pool. A nice, heated pool."

"Tomorrow, can I go swimming?"

She smiled. "Tomorrow you can have anything you want."

* * *

WEDNESDAY, DECEMBER 1ST

The first snow of the season fell softly blanketing the world in a hushed white. Lanie sipped her coffee from her perch on the bare wood floor in front of the bay window. The packing boxes had all been loaded on the truck and she was glad she decided to send Lexi and Charlie to spend the weekend with their father in his newly rented condo. She hadn't realized how emotional she was going to feel leaving the brick building she'd called home for the past fifteen years. It was the threshold she'd crossed when she brought her babies home from the hospital and the hearth she'd tended to make others feel welcome.

Lexi took the news about the move harder than Charlie. She didn't want to have to change schools in the middle of the year. Bob got busy and found a place in the district to keep her happy. Charlie didn't care where they went. The further from Glen Ellyn and the Cottage Avenue water tower, the better. He still had nightmares and ended up in bed with Lanie twice a week. With the help of a counselor from the Children's Center, they were making progress. It was slow, but it was something.

The divorce papers gobsmacked Bob, knocking him down long enough that he almost had to sell the dealership due to debilitating depression. Lanie felt sorry for him. Not sorry enough that she would consider taking him back—just sorry enough that she went over and rousted him out of bed and forced him to get some help. She'd sunk a lot of time and energy into growing that business when they were young.

She'd be damned if she sat idly by and let him run it into the ground.

A car pulled in the drive. Cheryl's blond hair peeked out from under her knit, wool cap. She jumped out and waved to Lanie through the window before tromping to the door and letting herself in. "How you doing, stranger? Ready for a change of scenery?"

"It's silly, but I'm sad. When I moved here, I thought I'd be here forever. Bob and I were young and in love. We had the whole world at our feet."

Cheryl put her arm around Lanie's shoulders. "It isn't silly. You tried your best to build something lasting."

"I failed."

Cheryl laughed. "Hardly. You have two great kids. You are heading out into the world to start a new adventure *and* you put an end to the corruption of the Herschel Grammar School PTA. I'd say you are a huge success. "

She shrugged. "Sure. I guess."

"Did you take the book deal?"

She snorted. "Confessions of a PTA Mafia Mom? I passed."

"It could have been your ticket to fame and fortune."

The amount of the advance was a staggering sum. Enough to leave the country and never work again. As tempting as it was, she couldn't put her children through rehashing the nightmare every time someone recognized her from a book signing or newspaper article. "I wasn't cut out for the notoriety that comes with fame and fortune."

"I had court yesterday. Looks like your Frenchman might go free."

Lanie wasn't surprised. The case wouldn't go to trial for years. By then, who would care about a group of women in a tiny little town ripping people off for free Fendi? Babette had a well-respected defense attorney working on a nice, easy plea deal to save her from jail. If she could pull it off, Gerard was sure to go free. He had money, and the court case actually helped renew interest in his photography. By the time his attorney ripped apart the case, they'd be lucky to slap him with conspiracy to commit a crime. A jury of his peers was sure to be wooed by his charm and good looks. "Figures. Did you ever find Ben?"

"I wish we had. I bet he could have told us some really interesting things about Gerard."

"You think he's alive?"

"I find it hard to believe he grabbed fifteen hundred dollars and disappeared for good. If he's alive, he is smarter than I gave him credit for. If not, I would bet Gerard knows how he died."

Lanie absentmindedly put her fingers to her lips remembering his hot kisses. "I hope he's alive. I really do."

"Nobody wants to find a body in the desert."

"No, they do not." Especially not a body that was fine enough to steal the sanity of young and old women alike. "I can't believe I thought he was Suni's drone."

"You took a chance, kid—you just bet on the wrong horse. In your defense, I think most people would have bet the same way. Even now with all the evidence I lined up, women everywhere are throwing themselves at him. Personally, I don't get it. That foofy French accent is a major turn off, if you ask me." Cheryl liked her men rugged and real.

"How's Matt?"

"Well, now that you ask..." She pulled her hand out of her black driving glove and flashed a petite, Princess cut diamond in a gold basket setting in front of Lanie's eyes. "He's good."

"Congratulations. I bet when you started this detail you never thought your work husband would end up being your real husband."

"I guess when you spend that much time playing house, it sinks in."

"I hope you have a lifetime of happiness."

Cheryl linked her arm in Lanie's. "Me too. Enough of this sappy talk. Let's get you out of here and on the road to your new life."

EPILOGUE

The change of scenery had done wonders for Charlie's nightmares and Lanie's overall well being. The media feeding frenzy had been worse than she'd anticipated. After turning down numerous offers for book deals and talk shows, she bought two tickets and flew Charlie and herself down to spend the winter in a small cottage on the tip of Estero Island near Fort Meyers Beach. It was a fixer upper, but the location was superb. Every morning she slathered Charlie up with sunscreen and dragged him out to walk on the sand. After breakfast, he would nap or bury himself in a book while she sat at her easel and sketched. When the elderly woman who owned the place listed it for sale in March, she sold her interest in the dealership and made it their permanent home. Charlie was happy until he realized he'd have to go back to school in the fall. Then he was a little pouty—but it passed as quickly as a summer storm, giving her hope that he was healing.

Even Lexi liked it. She promised Lanie over Christmas break that she'd be back to stay for the summer. Lanie wasn't stupid. She knew it was the thought of being savagely tan and surrounded by hot bodied man boys that was the real draw. She started college in the fall at the University of Illinois with a nice, large track scholarship, so the summer would fly by and then she'd be gone. It was a scary prospect sending her only daughter to a huge school, but she'd manage. As long as she had some peace and quiet to create some art that would buy groceries, everything else was gravy.

By the time spring rolled into summer Lanie had turned her postcard sketches into a business that made her an island celebrity. She got the city to let her cross zone her property and open a gallery named *Island's End*. The official opening was set for June fifteenth so Lexi could attend and she was ready. Everyone and everything was humming along smoothly.

It was early, too early, when she got out of bed and threw on her running gear. The excitement over the opening day of *Island's End* had left her with a bad case of insomnia. The minute she saw a sliver of light peek through her shades, Lanie was out of bed like a shot. If she moved quickly, she could run, shower, and read the paper before the doors opened at nine.

She locked the door behind her. Halfway down the front stairs she saw a shape lurking next to her car. At first she thought it was a large dog. Then it moved, standing from where it had been crouched, and she realized it was a man. Panic flooded her veins, sending her heart into hammering spasms inside her ribs. Like an actress in a bad horror movie, she fumbled with the keys cursing under her breath.

"Elaine, it's me."

She'd know that voice anywhere. The mellow tone that whispered to her in her dreams.

It was Ben.

It couldn't be. Ben was dead. She looked to the shadows, expecting to see a ghost. "You can't be here. Your uncle Gerard killed you."

He stepped out from the shadow and stood in the light from the porch bulb. "I ran. I wanted to tell you what Gerard was up to, but I knew you wouldn't believe me. When I uncovered his plan and confronted him, he threatened to have me locked up. I did some stupid things when I was young—things that are still on my record. I panicked and I blew it."

"You sold drugs, stole things, dabbled in running a prostitution ring..."

He cringed. "So you heard about my idiocy. I have no defense, Elaine. I was a really angry, messed up kid. I spent two years in therapy after my last arrest. I worked through the issues I buried after my mom died."

"Prostitution?"

"You do know that prostitution is legalized in Nevada? My crime was bringing it into the city. Small potatoes compared to some of the other things I've done."

He had a point. She had to touch him and make sure she wasn't dreaming. Her legs felt like rubber bands, but they got her where she wanted to be. The heat from his body radiated through her palm before she could make contact. He was alive. Overcome with anger, she gave him a hard shove. "You lied to me. You stole half my money and left. I thought you were dead!"

He grabbed her wrists in one hand. "Let's be honest. You lied to me too. I knew that money wasn't yours. I never would have stolen from you."

"You knew it was Suni's when you took it?"

"Gerard and Suni cooked the whole thing up before you got there. I knew all about you before your plane landed and you limped into my limo. There was just one thing they didn't prepare me for."

She eyed him warily. She thought she saw a hint of mischief in his eyes. In the light of early dawn it was impossible to be sure. "What was that?"

The hand on her wrists tugged her to him. Her belly met the waist of his red board shorts, her face a hairsbreadth from his chiseled, bronze chest muscles. She inhaled. The memory of his scent did not do him justice. She felt the heat spread between her legs. His free hand went under her chin and he pulled her face up to meet his lips. "How hard I would fall for you." He whispered. "From the moment of our first date, I knew you were the one. Think about what I was up against. Gerard and Suni were too much for you. Can you imagine what they would have done to me?"

"You knew they were planning to kill my family...and you left?"

"I was never away. I paid a private investigator to keep watch over you while I was hiding. He told me about the FBI. As soon as I heard that, I knew you would be safe."

The man in the alley? "But he gave you money. I found it in your pocket."

"So you spied on me as well! That money was mine. I caught him sleeping on the job and forced him to refund the money for those lost hours. He wasn't happy, but he stayed awake after that."

That explained the fight and the cash.

His finger traced the outline of her lips. "Can you forgive me?"

Her will was melting under his touch. She threw out the only rational argument she could come up with. "I just finalized my divorce. My children will never accept this...I..."

He kissed her. His tongue teased the outside of her mouth until she gave up and let him in. It was soft and hot sending her hibernating hormones into a feeding frenzy. After a few minutes he pulled back. "I'm not asking you to give me forever, Elaine. I'm just asking you to give me a chance to prove myself. I told you back in Vegas, I'll never force anything on you."

Ben was here. Her hot Hawaiian had followed her. She didn't have piles of cash. She wasn't a young peacock anymore. She was Elaine Elizabeth Jackerson, a middle-aged woman with a lot to offer and a young hunk smart enough to take her up on it. "I want it."

"You're sure? I know you're pretty worked up right now—"

"I missed you, Ben. I know this might not last forever, but you are the best thing that happened to me in a long time. I'd be a fool to pass this up. But you have to promise me that as long as we're together, it will be just me. No other women waiting in the wings."

"Done."

"And you have to be productive. None of this sponging off your insane relatives. You need a job, a place to live..."

"Of course. I already have both."

Incredible. He'd been there under her radar long enough to become a productive member of society. God, he was good.

"Anything else we need to clear up?"

She could read the mischief in his eyes. "There might be later. For now, we've covered the basics."

He scooped her up and sat her on the hood of the car. "I was hoping you'd say that."

"So, we'll just enjoy this day by day and see where it goes?"

"Until I can convince you to make me a permanent fixture."

A permanent fixture. She liked the way that sounded. It was definitely a deal worth sealing with a kiss.

~*~

Acknowledgements:

I owe a heartfelt thank you to my wonderful editor, Ms. Salina Jivani. A good editor fleshes out your best story; a great editor teaches without condescension. Ms. Jivani did both for me. Without her endless patience, this book would never have gone to print. And last, but certainly not least, thank you to Justin James and Dare Empire for an outstanding opportunity.

MORE PAGE-TURNERS FROM

Elsie Love

COMING SOON

HEAD OVER TO OUR STORE
AND SEE WHAT GRABS YOU

empirebookstore

REPO CHICK BLUES

Reformed car thief Leah Ryan is trouble. But she is keeping her nose clean when her Jeep is repossessed. Unfortunately, most of her money is going toward past due attorney fees for her younger brother Jesse; a mischievous hacker serving his last few weeks in prison. Without a way to get to her construction job, she is fired. Leah needs a job fast. She's a natural at stealing cars, and decides to ask Callahan Parker, the man who repossessed her Jeep, to hire her. This decision marks the beginning of a nightmare for Leah Ryan.

During her first night of work, Leah makes an enemy of a twisted drug lord, Brent Woodard, who targets her for revenge. Things go from bad to worse when Leah discovers that Woodard is smuggling Asian women into the United States and forcing them into prostitution. She is determined to stop him, by any means necessary. But Woodard has friends. Among these is a crooked, sadistic cop who makes her plan more dangerous than she could have ever imagined. Soon it's not only her life at stake, but that of her brother Jesse, who disappears within a day of his release from prison. Leah enlists the help of Callahan and a few friends from her shady past; a past she promised herself she'd never return to, to enter into a dark underworld of sex, drugs and death.

UNWRAP ME

Makayla has the perfect boyfriend and a fulfilling job. A hot, sinful threesome would make things perfect for this prim and proper librarian. An upcoming anniversary provides the ideal opportunity, if only she can gather the nerves to ask. Confessing could bring her ultimate pleasure, or end her relationship forever.

Is the risk of losing one man really worth a forbidden fantasy?

TASTE OF PASSION

"SMOLDERINGLY SEXY..."

Bakery owner Valentine Benington's day just went from the best of her life to the worst. Toronto Tribune reviewer, David Fraser, shows up for a review just after a fire comes close to destroying her kitchen.

After David's last assignment, which ended with food poisoning, it's not the best of starts, especially since the job is a last-minute thing. He doesn't expect to run into a woman from his past. First looks can be deceiving. The food isn't the only thing on the menu he'd like to taste.

When these two get baking, the flames from the oven aren't the only thing setting the kitchen on fire.

Made in the USA
Lexington, KY
22 September 2011